DEATH'S HELPING HAND

Sergeant Greeley waved Officer Shay toward the car. "Tell them to send out the medical examiner. But tell them they don't need to hurry—it's a simple case of death caused by falling off a horse."

Miss Withers looked at her fingers where she had brushed them against the big thoroughbred.

"Go on, Shay," urged the sergeant. "Get to the phone and make a report so we can get home. That is"—he turned to Miss Withers—"that is, if it's okay with you, lady. No objections?"

"My only objection," Miss Withers announced calmly, "is to this." She displayed her fingers daubed with carmine. "If that young woman died from her fall I don't quite see why there should be a splotch of blood on the thigh of this animal."

Sergeant Greeley swore mightily. "Blood on the horse—then it doesn't make sense. What does it mean?"

"It means," Miss Hildegard Withers told them, "that this dead girl was *assisted* into the next world. . . ."

Bantam Books offers the finest in classic and modern American murder mysteries. Ask your bookseller for the books you have missed.

Stuart Palmer

THE PUZZLE OF THE
  RED STALLION
THE PUZZLE OF THE
  SILVER PERSIAN
THE PUZZLE OF THE HAPPY
  HOOLIGAN

Craig Rice

HAVING WONDERFUL
  CRIME
MY KINGDOM FOR A
  HEARSE

Rex Stout

AND FOUR TO GO
BAD FOR BUSINESS
DEATH OF A DUDE
DEATH TIMES THREE
DOUBLE FOR DEATH
FER-DE-LANCE
THE FINAL DEDUCTION
GAMBIT
THE LEAGUE OF
  FRIGHTENED MEN
NOT QUITE DEAD
  ENOUGH
PLOT IT YOURSELF
THE RUBBER BAND
SOME BURIED CAESAR
THE SOUND OF MURDER
TOO MANY CLIENTS

Victoria Silver

DEATH OF A HARVARD
  FRESHMAN
DEATH OF A RADCLIFFE
  ROOMMATE

William Kienzle

THE ROSARY MURDERS

Richard Fleigel

THE NEXT TO DIE

M.J. Adamson

NOT TILL A HOT JANUARY

Max Byrd

CALIFORNIA THRILLER
FINDERS WEEPERS
FLY AWAY, JILL

R.D. Brown

HAZZARD

Sue Grafton

"B" IS FOR BURGLAR

Robert Goldsborough

MURDER IN E MINOR

Carolyn Hart

DEATH ON DEMAND

Ross MacDonald

BLUE CITY
THE BLUE HAMMER

A.E. Maxwell

JUST ANOTHER DAY IN
  PARADISE

Rob Kantner

THE BACK-DOOR MAN

Ted Wood

LIVE BAIT

Barbara Paul

KILL FEE
THE RENEWABLE VIRGIN

Benjamin Schutz

EMBRACE THE WOLF

S.F.X. Dean

DEATH AND THE MAD
  HEROINE

THE PUZZLE
OF THE
RED STALLION

Stuart Palmer

BANTAM BOOKS
TORONTO · NEW YORK · LONDON · SYDNEY · AUCKLAND

To
Nellie Secker Palmer
who gave me my first book,
and to Jay Sherman Palmer,
who gave me my first horse.

*This low-priced Bantam Book
has been completely reset in a type face
designed for easy reading, and was printed
from new plates. It contains the complete
text of the original hard-cover edition.*
NOT ONE WORD HAS BEEN OMITTED.

THE PUZZLE OF THE RED STALLION

*A Bantam Book / published by arrangement with
the author's estate*

*PRINTING HISTORY
First published in 1935
Bantam edition / February 1987*

ISBN 0-553-26150-9

Published simultaneously in the United States and Canada

Bantam Books are published by Bantam Books, Inc. Its trademark, consisting of the words "Bantam Books" and the por-
trayal of a rooster, is Registered in U.S. Patent and Trademark
Office and in other countries. Marca Registrada. Bantam
Books, Inc., 666 Fifth Avenue, New York, New York 10103.

PRINTED IN THE UNITED STATES OF AMERICA

O   0 9 8 7 6 5 4 3 2 1

No real persons or places are indicated in this book. The author desires to take this opportunity of thanking Dr. Ralph M. Crowley of the Sheppard and Enoch Pratt Hospital, and Mr. Reginald "Snowy" Baker of the Riviera Country Club for assistance given in their respective fields.

S.P.

Contents

1

Red Sky at Morning

If there are ghosts on the island of Manhattan they walk not in its garish midnights but in the long hour before sunrise. That is the time when life's tide is said to ebb, so that strong men weaken and sick men die—the hour of the false dawn when Hamlet's restless father returned to gibber on the battlements of Elsinore.

Manhattan slept, with no dead kings to haunt her turrets and no cheerful cockcrow to send them scurrying. Business had been so bad that night that Mr. Solomon Rosen slept also, his head pillowed on his arms across the wheel of his taxicab, lulled by the diminishing patter of rain on the roof.

He awoke with a start to find an apparition beside him—a remarkably solid apparition that weighed upon his running board. A low harsh voice spoke in his ear—"Follow that hack!"

Sol Rosen peered sleepily at a man in a badly fitting blue overcoat, a harried-looking young man whose breath was heavy with stale tobacco and whose eyes were weary and bloodshot. Sol had never won any silver cups for quickness of thought and at five o'clock of a wet morning he was slower than usual. He blinked and asked, "Why?"

"This is why!" The man in the overcoat displayed his cupped hand. It held a five-dollar bill, and not a silver badge as Sol had somehow guessed. The stranger was pointing across Broadway to the cab rank in front of the Hotel Harthorn. "Tail him—get going!"

He got inside and Sol kicked the starter. Then he noticed that not one but two taxicabs were pulling away from the canopy at the hotel entrance. "Which one," Sol wanted to know, "the Yellow?"

"Never mind the yellow one," his passenger ordered. "Tail the Checker, the one in front, and don't lose him."

Sol got his cold motor going, roared into an illegal U-turn

1

and rolled southward on Broadway about half a block behind the two other taxis. The rain had stopped and the murkiness of the night had paled to the point where his headlamps were almost useless. The taxis ahead passed Seventy-second, where around the deserted subway entrance the wind whipped listlessly at scattered newspapers. There were no stop lights at this hour and they went steadily on. Sol Rosen was just beginning to hope that this was to be a long and lucrative haul when the two cars ahead swerved suddenly eastward toward the park on Sixty-fifth Street.

Sol followed, with a screech of tires on the wet pavement. He put on his brakes as he saw that the foremost driver was slowing down in the middle of the block.

"Go on to the corner and pull up!" instructed his passenger hoarsely. Sol swung past the other taxicabs and stopped on the corner of Central Park West. The man in the blue overcoat stepped quickly out, handed Sol a bill and moved leisurely away. As Sol Rosen started cruising again he was wide-awake enough to notice that his recent passenger walked as one who did not want to get anywhere. He was strolling aimlessly along, pausing to scratch a match on a convenient lamppost and making it very clear that the last thing in the world which could interest him would be the passengers who were now piling from the checkered taxicab.

As soon as the door was opened a young man in full evening dress had plunged sprawling out, to the detriment of his silk topper. A fat man and a girl followed, she wearing her evening wrap of red velvet hoodwise over her blonde curls and loudly chanting that she "yoost come over from old countree."

There was loud laughter, but not from the tall young woman who now emerged from the crowded taxicab. She was incongruously dressed in a dark mannish riding coat and jodhpurs. Her auburn curls had been caught under a stiff derby and the silk stock at her throat was fastened by a gold pin in the shape of a polo mallet. She was thirtyish and pretty. She might have been more than pretty if she had taken time for a few hours' sleep, or even had lingered long enough at her dressing table to remove the make-up which still smeared her mouth and eyelids.

She stood alone on the sidewalk as the others began laboriously to pack themselves back into the taxi. "Good night, Violet darling," cried the blonde in the red wrap. "It was a lovely party!"

"Even if you did throw us out," chorused a feminine voice from within the taxi.

"Violet likes horses better than she likes us," cried a young man in a high tenor voice. "Violet's queer for long horseback rides in the rain!"

"Good night all," said Violet Feverel. She was sick unto death of her last evening's guests and her voice was thin and tired. She waved mechanically as the carload of departing merrymakers rolled away and then turned to face the second taxi which was pulling up alongside the curb.

This vehicle, too, was packed to the running boards. "Change your mind and come with us!" sang out a young man with a very red face whose whim it had been to ride beside the driver. Somewhere he had lost his black tie and somewhere he had found a milk bottle with a dime in it which he jingled as he spoke.

"No thanks," Violet told him. "Run along—the party ends right here as far as I'm concerned."

"It's our loss!" responded the red-faced youth gallantly. "Good-bye, then—— Come on, Eddie, say good-bye to Violet!" He leaned back and prodded at the protruding knee of a young man who was jammed in the corner of the taxi with a girl on his lap.

Eddie was softly singing a ballad of his own composition dealing with the further adventures of the notorious Miss Otis after she broke her luncheon engagement on account of being lynched.*

"When Miss Otis was dead and safely gone to hell, madam—
They found her a spot where the fires were hot—as hell,
As she writhed in the fearful heat
She gently rubbed her blistered seat and cried, 'Madam,
Miss Otis regrets she's unable to lunch today!'"

He was rudely shouted down by a chorus of demands that he say good night to Violet, good old Violet.

"Why should I?" demanded Eddie.

"Because Violet's going bye-bye on a big horsey!" cried

*See "Miss Otis Regrets," a popular song of the era.

the red-faced youth. "She'd rather ride a horse than make whoopee with us in Harlem."

"Violet," pronounced Eddie solemnly, "is nothing but a menace to navigation. Someday the Coast Guard will explode her with d-dynamite. She's an old frozen iceberg, that's what Violet is. But boy! Am I glad right now that it doesn't run in the family!"

Somebody nudged him quickly, but not quickly enough. Violet Feverel had heard. She came over and flung open the door of the taxi.

"Eddie—you swine! Did you let Babs sneak in here—as soon as my back was turned?"

The girl on Eddie's lap raised her head from his shoulder. Except that she wore a white lace evening dress and a last-season's bunny-wrap, she was just a later edition of the girl who now faced her accusingly. Babs had the same warm reddish curls, the same light-brown eyes. She also had youth, lots of it.

Now she laughed nervously. "Don't be like that, Sis!"

Violet Feverel bit her lip and her voice was thinner than ever. "I told you you weren't going on to Harlem with these—these soaks! I told you to stay home and go to bed. Now come out of there!"

As the younger girl hesitated Violet leaned forward and caught her wrist, half dragging her from the taxicab.

Barbara did not resist, but her face had suddenly gone white as chalk. "I'll pay you back for this!" she said softly.

Her elder sister still gripped her wrist with long painted nails that dug into the flesh. The young man known as Eddie started protestingly out of the taxi but Violet Feverel slammed the door in his face and told the driver to go on. There was a scream of gears and the yellow taxicab rolled on after the first one.

Barbara jerked her arm free. "I'm not a baby—I'm old enough——"

"Back in Syracuse you can do as you like," Violet snapped. "But here with me you'll do as I say. And I say you've had enough gay night life for one evening . . . and enough of fooling around with Eddie Fry. When I left I thought you were going to stay there and clean up the apartment, and then go to bed where you belong!"

"Eddie said he'd wait for me with the second taxi after

you'd started," Barbara protested. "It was going to be such fun—and now you had to spoil everything. We were going to a place in Harlem where a big colored woman fries chicken and sings songs. . . ."

Violet knew that chicken and those songs. "You're going straight home, my darling kid sister. You can get a taxi at the corner. . . ."

Barbara stared at the older girl, her lips hard. "I won't!" she flared. "You can't make me. I know—you're sour on everything because *you* went and made a terrific flop out of romance—"

Violet Feverel struck her young sister across the mouth as hard as she could.

The marks flamed red on white skin. "Some people would say I had that coming to me," said Barbara evenly. She turned and walked swiftly back down the street.

"Babs!" cried Violet Feverel. But the girl did not turn. After a moment Violet shrugged her shoulders. She wheeled and pressed a bell marked "Office" under a faded sign, "Thwaite's Academy of Horsemanship—saddle horses boarded and for hire."

There was no answer and she pressed again savagely. Then a mild and drawling voice sounded, close enough to startle her.

"You shore got a fast right hand, Miss Feverel."

She whirled to see a long lean young man attired in blue overalls who leaned upon the lower half of a divided stable door. He had sandy hair, a face tan as a boot, and a long sad upper lip.

"Nobody in the office yet—no use ringing," he told her. He swung the stable door hospitably open. "But come on in."

Violet Feverel eyed him. "Latigo! How long have you——" Then she broke off short. Coming across the cobbles into the dark and odorous warmth of the stable, she caught the scent of rank Burley tobacco.

"Does Mrs. Thwaite know you smoke in here, Latigo?" she asked.

Latigo Wells ground his heel upon a handmade cigarette. He flushed. "Not exactly, ma'am. But there ain't—there isn't any real fire hazard with these cement floors. I wasn't expecting any riders quite so early. You wouldn't tell her, ma'am?"

Violet Feverel pressed her lips together. "Saddle Siwash for me—quickly, please!"

Latigo nodded gravely. "Couple of minutes, ma'am. He hasn't been curried down yet."

"What? Where's that boy Highpockets?"

"Yesterday was Saturday and that's payday here," explained the other. "That colored boy just runs hog-wild when he gets a few dollars in his pants. That's why I had to come down and open up the stable this morning—that and because I figured you might be here to take your horse out. You see——" Latigo stammered a little. "You see," he began, "I wanted to explain about the other night. When you asked me up to your place, I sort of took it for granted——" Latigo seized a convenient pitchfork and sighted along the handle as if it had been a rifle. "I naturally figured——"

"So I noticed," said Violet Feverel shortly. Her wide eyes were expressionless.

"I didn't want you to think I was sore or anything," Latigo stumbled on. "I guess I must have looked pretty silly to you and your swell friends. If I'd known, why, I'd have fetched along the old guitar. . . ."

"Forget it—and get Siwash saddled, will you?" she cut in.

Latigo moved unhappily away down a long corridor. Here and there a horse thrust its long inquiring muzzle over the top of a stall. As always they were quick to sense the mood of the human they knew best.

On the last of the box stalls sacred in this stable to the boarded horses was a card ornately lettered "Siwash." Liatgo opened the gate and slapped roughly at the shoulder of the big chestnut thoroughbred who lay sprawled in the straw.

"Come on, Si—rustle out of the blankets!" As the big horse reared to his feet Latigo set about brushing the red-bronze flanks with a currycomb. "You would have to go and sleep laying down, you lazy stray," Latigo chided him. "More trouble than you're worth. If you were mine I'd have you sent to the refinery and boiled down for your grease!"

Siwash danced daintily sidewise upon tiny hoofs and then nuzzled at the man's shoulder affectionately. After a few moments they went out of the stall, when there took place a certain routine disagreement over whether Siwash was going to take the bit in his mouth or not. He finally gave in and champed on it dubiously.

"Next time I'll have it flavored with wintergreen for you," Latigo promised him sarcastically. A light saddle and pad were produced and tossed over the big red rump.

Siwash winced and then leaned back and nipped lovingly at the stableman's arm. He nipped again, harder this time, as Latigo tightened up on the cinch.

"You're a plumb locoed cannibal and you'll come to no good end!" Liatgo reached for the stirrup leather and then dropped it suddenly as Violet Feverel came up behind him.

She took the strap in her gloved hand. "I thought so!" she cried bitterly. "Maude Thwaite has been riding my horse, hasn't she?"

Latigo stammered a little.

"Don't bother to lie," she told him. "I'm not blind. I can see for myself that somebody had to have the stirrups taken up two holes shorter than I use them—somebody with short legs." The red mouth curved unpleasantly.

"It must have been Highpockets exercising your horse yesterday," suggested Latigo in the tone of one who does not expect to be believed.

"Him? He rides a longer stirrup than I!" She took the strap and snapped the buckle back into its proper place, then crossed behind Siwash and did the same for the off side, as Latigo moved too slowly to do it for her.

"When I come back I'm going to have a showdown with Maude Thwaite," Violet said. "I know she wants this horse to give a little class to her stableful of hacks, but she'll get him over my dead body!"

Siwash was led down the concrete runway. On the right peered forth the friendly faces of the boarders, whose owners kept them in the luxury of box stalls, monogrammed blankets and bins of carrots. Across the way were the dejected tails and the scarred rumps of the rent horses in their narrow cubicles—the horses who were kept here for hire, their mouths slowly growing callous under the pull of every inexpert hand.

Siwash clattered along the concrete, ignoring boarders and hacks alike, for he was an Irish thoroughbred and knew it. He lifted his arched neck and perked up his ears at the burst of fresh moist air which swept in through the open door.

Violet Feverel stroked his nose and then mounted with a snap of her heels. Latigo opened the door wide. "Take it careful today," he advised as she sent the thoroughbred out across the cobbled driveway. "Those paths are still soggy and I'd hate to see you thrown."

She did not answer. Latigo stared after her for a moment and then hitched up his pants. He turned suddenly to see a puzzled colorado-maduro face which had thrust itself next to his in the doorway.

Highpockets' voice was thin and querulous. "Mista Latigo, why you tell me to keep out of sight in the stall? If you're sweet on that white gal, why you tell her I'm too drunk to show up here, huh? Suppose she tell Missus Thwaite and I lose my job?"

Latigo began to roll a cigarette as the stableboy ran out of breath. The big eyes widened.

"Say, you better not let that white gal see you smoke in here—she'll tell Old Lady Thwaite on you!"

Latigo scratched a match on the seat of his overalls and applied it to the handmade cigarette. "That highnosed Miss God-almighty Feverel won't tell anybody—anything!" he pronounced with great finality. "Go on, Snowflake, get busy with the pitchfork. You got work to do."

"So has you!" Highpockets retorted. But he moved disjointedly away toward the stalls shaking his head. Latigo Wells remained at the door letting his cigarette ash fall from unheeding fingers.

As the hoofs of the big red thoroughbred rang out upon deserted Central Park West a man in a tight dark overcoat moved back into the shadows of a doorway, but Violet Feverel did not notice him. She was looking beyond the park gateway to see the glimmering of dawn in the sky above the towers of Fifth Avenue. She drew a deep breath of the damp sweet air and held it.

As they went up the slope into the park Siwash bent his heavy-sculptured neck and touched a velvet muzzle to his mistress's leg, leaving a wet mark on the jodhpur cord. He whinnied softly, remembering mornings like this in earlier and better days, when at Saratoga and Hialeah and Churchill Downs he had been breezed gloriously around the track with only stableboys and handicappers to watch, and with a monkeylike little man perched on his withers and crooning soft encouragements in his ear.

Siwash liked the soft feel of the mud underhoof. He tossed his head, wishing as always that the woman who straddled him would lighten the pull of the curb on his mouth. There was something about mud that always made Siwash want to go. During his four years as a race horse it had always been on a slow track with better horses floundering and slipping all around him that he had chalked up his victories. It was against mud that the power in those muscled red shoulders really came into play and the long trim legs thrust hardest.

He broke into an easy canter as his rider leaned forward and gave him a fraction more of the rein. Siwash was a horse who liked to get there—anywhere. Being only a horse he had no premonition of the strange destination toward which he bore his lovely but heavy-handed mistress this morning.

It seemed warm for this sunrise hour. Violet Feverel pulled the stock from her throat, trying to let her body swing easily with the rolling gait of the big thoroughbred. But she still held the curb hard against his mouth. Siwash knew, as horses always know, that his rider was afraid.

Across the green reaches of the park, beyond the towers of the Avenue, the sky was reddening with the sunrise. Violet Feverel remembered something from her childhood, a line she had once read in an old almanac—"Red sky at morning, sailors take warning. . . ."

Then, almost as if she heard the beat of invisible hoofs on the path behind her, she shivered and urged the big horse forward, so that they went galloping northward through the wet loneliness of the deserted path beneath the blind shuttered windows of the great apartment houses of Central Park West, as if in a wild effort to escape. But it was only herself that Violet Feverel wanted to leave behind that morning.

So horse and rider went northward at a full gallop, to keep an appointment in Samarra.

The sun was still well behind the towers of the Avenue when through the doorway of an old brownstone house on West Seventy-fourth Street emerged a small and bouncing terrier of the wire-haired clan. His nose was a black pin-seal button surrounded by shaggy whiskers which gave him an air of waggish respectability—an air belied by the twinkle in the hot brown eyes which peered through at the world. His shaggy white paws scrabbled over the doormat as the terrier sought to fling himself headlong down the steps to the sidewalk.

At the other end of a bright green leather lead he dragged a prim-looking schoolteacher of uncertain age and certain temperament, who wore at the moment a look of mingled sleepiness and resignation.

"Relax, you restless brute!" chided Miss Hildegard Withers as the little dog led her in irregular and undignified plunges down the street. She shook her head and her blue eyes twinkled. "It seems to me, Dempsey lad, that there ought to be at least one wisdom tooth among all those fangs in your mouth!"

Miss Withers was convinced that she preferred cats to dogs, just as she preferred a quiet scholastic life to the exciting adventures in applied criminology into which fate— and a longstanding friendship with an inspector at Centre Street—had drawn her so often.

Indeed it was as a climax to such an adventure* that Dempsey, along with several new-born brothers and sisters and a mother strangely misnamed "Mister Jones," had been dropped into the lap of the staid schoolteacher. The rest of the family had been found homes in the country, but Miss Withers had never been able to bring herself to the point of parting with this most bewhiskered and pugnacious puppy.

Life had been different and exciting since her acquisition of Dempsey—so called because of his pell-mell tactics as a warrior. The scamp had a habit of flinging himself fearlessly upon every male dog he met, and day after day his mistress saved him from possible extermination at the jaws of some massive bull or Alsatian. He gnawed her slippers and played rough games with her piles of neatly corrected examination papers, he rattled her bed as he searched himself for fleas in the midnight hours and roused her at the crack of dawn; but Miss Withers continued to view Dempsey with scandalized amusement.

This morning the little dog quite outdid himself by leading his mistress into the clutches of the law.

It happened as they rounded the corner nearest the

---

*See *The Puzzle of the Pepper Tree*, Crime Club, 1933.

park. Miss Withers was kneeling on the sidewalk in an effort to make Dempsey relinquish a particularly unsavory-looking bit of candy wrapper which he had discovered. Suddenly she looked up to see a little green roadster pulling alongside the curb. Two officers confronted her.

"Aha!" cried the foremost. He wore a jovial air, and the stripes of a sergeant.

Miss Withers drew herself up as haughtily as was possible with a dog and his leash wound around her long skirt. "What is the meaning of this, may I ask?"

"You're breaking the lawr!" said the sergeant.

"Indeed?" Miss Withers smiled icily. "I'll go with you quietly, so don't use the riot gun and the tear gas. And please, no third degree—I'll talk!"

"Talk!" The sergeant burst into a guffaw. "I'll just bet she will, eh, Shay? I can spot the talkers right away."

Officer Shay thought that was very funny. "Nothing else but, huh?"

Miss Withers saw that much to her disgust Dempsey was flagrantly betraying her by trying to lick the hands of both policemen at once.

They finally got down to cases. "It's your dorg, lady," explained Sergeant Greeley. "He ain't got no muzzle."

Miss Withers sniffed. "Besides the obviously bad grammar, that accusation is false," she announced. "My dog has a muzzle, an excellent muzzle. It's right here in my handbag." She showed them.

"Yeah, lady," explained the sergeant wearily. "But he's got to wear it on his face. City ordinance, it says so. Warm weather coming on, and you never know when a dorg will go mad and bite somebody."

"There are times when I would consider it in the light of a direct answer to prayer," Miss Withers snapped. Dempsey sat down unconcernedly and kicked at his left ear, remembering that a flea had annoyed him there once upon a time. He showed no interest whatever in the fact that his mistress was receiving a ticket instructing her to appear next Monday morning at West Fifty-third Street Police Court and pay a two-dollar fine.

Miss Withers was unable to refrain from pointing out that it was no wonder crime ran rampant and Bolsheviks flourished in Manhattan when police spent their time persecuting honest citizens for infractions of forgotten ordinances. If anyone asked her opinion——

The policemen started to get back inside the green roadster. "Lady," the sergeant told her earnestly, "you're lucky you don't have to wear the muzzle instead of the dorg!"

The official laughter at this sally was cut short by the sudden barking of the radio loudspeaker in the car.

"*Calling car 69—calling car 69——*"

"That's us!" yelped Shay. He kicked at the starter while the sergeant took out his notebook. Miss Withers, in spite of her excellent upbringing, listened shamelessly.

"*Calling car 69. . . . Go to Central Park bridle path opposite West Eighty-sixth Street. . . . See park attendant about a Code 44. . . . That is all——*"

"Let's go!" cried Sergeant Greeley. The little flivver whirled away leaving Miss Withers and Dempsey alone on the curb.

"*Code 44*"—she knew very well what that meant. On evenings when she had no papers to correct and when the inspector did not drop in for a fast game of backgammon, it was her delight to switch her radio over onto the police calls. One night, annoyed by the fact that all the real drama was hidden behind code numbers, she had hit upon the inspired idea of keeping a record of all calls together with the given address. Next day she checked them against the newspaper accounts of what happened at each address and thus solved the mystery of the codes.

"*Code 44,*" next to the general alarm embodied in "*Code 30*" (which Miss Withers had heard only during the capture of Two-gun Crowley), was the most exciting signal of all. It meant, as Miss Withers had discovered, simply—"*a dead body!*"

Miss Withers's nostrils widened and into her blue eyes for a moment there came the look of a small boy who has just seen the fire engines go past. Then she relaxed.

"After all it's not *my* dead body," she told the eager little dog. "I'm rapidly getting the reputation of being the most meddlesome woman east of Los Angeles, and there's barely time to get breakfast and take that spot out of my blue dress before church, and this is certainly one time when I ought to mind my own business!"

Dempsey quivered with delight as he sniffed the thousand odors of the green park across the street.

Miss Withers sniffed too. "After all," she remarked thoughtfully, "I have a perfect right to exercise my dog in the park if I wish—and those two flat-footed imbeciles are not the proper persons to cope with a *Code 44!*"

She started off at a pace which made Dempsey trot to keep up. "Not by a jugful," she concluded, and her nostrils flare as if from afar she had heard the note of a hunting horn.

2

Into Deep Water

Less than a mile to the north, where Eighty-sixth Street Transverse cuts across Central Park, four men stood in the shadow of the viaduct arch. Above them on the bridge the little green roadster of the radio police nestled against a long white ambulance from Bellevue. The men stood in the soft mud of the bridle path, looking down at what was left of Violet Feverel.

Her body lay sprawled in the path, with the auburn hair draggled and a red-brown stain about the mouth. Rather than fear or pain there was an expression of something very like surprised chagrin on her face, an expression rapidly being effaced by the last relaxation. About her body the earth was churned by small neat hoofprints, and in her dead and stiffening fingers Violet Feverel held a few coarse reddish hairs.

Sergeant Greeley wore a serious expression now. "How about it, Doc?"

The young interne shook his head. "Too cold for me," he said lightly. He shoved his fists into the pockets of his white linen jacket. "Too dead to interest anybody but the medical examiner and brother Campbell's head mortician. Deader'n a herring, in fact."

"I knew it!" burst in an elderly and unshaven man in the gray uniform of a park attendant. "That's why, soon's I found her laying here, I beat it over to the phone in the Reservoir office and——"

"Yeah?" said the sergeant. "Just how did you happen to find her?"

"I was coming to work earlier than usual this morning on account of how there's always a lot to be done around the flower beds after a rain. I was walking across the park—I live over on Lexington Avenue, lived there five years. You ask anybody if Ralph H. Simons hasn't lived there five years. I'm taking a short cut along the upper reservoir, and ahead of me maybe a quarter of a mile I see a woman riding hell for leather towards this viaduct here. I says to myself, She'll break her neck if she doesn't slow down! Naturally I watch to see if she slows down on the other side of the viaduct where the path comes into the clear again. But I don't see hide nor hair of her, nor the horse either, so I hurry on the rest of the way and when I get here all I see is this good-looking dame lying all mussed up in the mud. One look is all I need to tell me she's dead——"

"O-kay!" burst in the sergeant. "Sell it to the *Mirror.*" He waved the loquacious little man aside and looked down at the body thoughtfully.

"She must have went quick, eh, Doc? Get the funny look on her face!"

The interne nodded. "Tough—for a good-looking girl like that to go out with the taste of her own blood in her mouth. . . ."

Officer Shay, who had no stomach for corpses, winced a little. But the sergeant shrugged. "Good-looking or not, they all hate to stop breathing. What do you think killed her, Doc?"

The interne stuck out his lower lip. "Internal injuries caused by taking a dive off the nag, I'd say."

Shay dug his toe into the soft mud. "Say, can you really get croaked falling offen a horse? I've done it often enough as a kid and never got killed."

"Always a first time, my boy," the sergeant told him. "Bound to happen with these high-flying dames riding horses too good for them."

"Sure," chimed in Simons, the park attendant. "This dame, I see her here lots of mornings. Always on a big red horse too. She comes early so she can gallop the nag without

being stopped. After eight o'clock Casey's on the job—you
know, the big mounted cop who polices this path. He won't
let any of the riders go faster'n a trot."

Nobody was listening to him. "Say, Doc," the sergeant
asked, "you couldn't make out a death certificate, could you?"

The interne shook his head. "She was dead when I got
here."

Sergeant Greeley nodded. "Go phone the station, Shay,"
he ordered. "Tell 'em it's the works."

Shay began laboriously to climb up the bush-covered
slope which led to the top of the bridge, where the car was
parked. The way was impeded by a maze of bushes and
overgrowth. Suddenly he stopped and his perturbed face
peered through the foliage.

"Hey, Sarge!" he called. "What if they want to know
who the dame is?"

Sergeant Greeley pondered. "No handbag on her," he
said. "Wait, it stands to reason that the horse belonged in one
of the stables at the lower end of the park. Phone them a
description of the horse and they'll be able to tell you who
rode it out this morning!"

"Yeah? Description of what horse?" Shay objected.

They all looked at each other. "Can't have gone far,"
decided Greeley. "We got to find the horse before we can
find out who this dame is!"

Up on the bridge the ambulance driver was impatiently
honking his horn, but the interne still lingered, staring down
at the body. "You know, I've seen her somewhere," he said.
"That face is just as familiar to me as my own."

"Yeah? Say, on your way out, will you keep an eye open
for a loose horse?" asked the sergeant. "We can't have a
man-killing nag running wild through the park."

At that auspicious moment, heralded by a salvo of excited barks from the sidelines, the supposed man-killing
horse was led into the scene by a determined-looking spinster. Miss Hildegarde Withers was plodding along through
the mud, keeping as far as possible from the big beast at the
other end of the rein. Her terrier, suspicious and disapprov-
ing, darted hither and yon at a discreet distance as if trying to
work up courage enough to rescue his mistress from the jaws
of this ravening colossus.

"Were you looking for this, gentlemen?" inquired Miss

Withers calmly. "I found it trampling the flower beds and thought that perhaps—ugh!"

Siwash, suddenly noticing the limp horror in the bridle path, made an abrupt about-face, jerking the reins from Miss Withers's grasp and very nearly upsetting her.

She clutched wildly at him to keep her balance and the touch seemed to calm him. The big thoroughbred stopped, still trembling, and rubbed a wet and grass-stained muzzle against her shoulder as if for comfort.

Sergeant Greely stared incredulously. "Look who's here!" There was no appreciable note of welcome in his voice.

He turned toward Officer Shay. "Okay," he said. "You can phone in a description of the horse——" He stopped and looked critically toward where Miss Withers was gaping at the body. "You can tell which one is the horse, Shay," the sergeant continued heavily, "because the horse wears a bridle and the dame wears a hat. Get it?"

"Yeah," said Shay dully. He didn't feel appreciative with that girl lying there staring up at the sky.

Miss Withers sniffed, but she did not waste breath in argument. She was thoughtfully studying her hand.

The sergeant waved Shay toward the car. "Tell them to send out the medical examiner. But tell him he don't need to hurry—it's a simple case of internal injuries caused by falling offen a horse."

"Caused by *what?*" inquired Miss Withers wonderingly.

The interne, who was reluctantly tearing himself away from the scene, stopped and blinked through his glasses. "If it's anything to you, lady, this dame died of internal hemorrhage caused by a fall from her horse!"

Miss Withers looked again at her fingers where she had brushed against the big thoroughbred as he started wildly a moment before.

"Go on, Shay," urged the sergeant. "Get to the phone and make a report on this business so we can get home. That is"—he turned to Miss Withers—"that is, if it's okay with you, lady. No objections?"

"My only objection," Miss Withers announced calmly, "is to this!" She displayed her fingers, daubed with carmine. "If that young woman died from her fall I don't quite see why there should be a splotch of blood on the thigh of this animal!"

Sergeant Greeley came, swore mightily, and was convinced. "Blood on the horse—then it doesn't make sense. What does it mean?"

For a moment there was silence, broken only by the rasp of the park attendant's fingers across his stubby chin and by the faint tinkle of the interne's instrument case as he let it fall.

"It means," Miss Hildegarde Withers told them, "that this dead girl was *assisted* into the next world!"

Officer Shay was drawn, in spite of himself, into the scene again. "What's she talking about now?" he complained. "Come on, let's wash this up and get some sleep. . . ."

"Shut up!" roared the sergeant. "Can't you unnerstand plain English? The lady is saying that this dame was moidered!"

Miss Withers nodded approvingly. "There'll be an A-plus on your report card, Sergeant."

From that point on events came thick and fast. Miss Withers, who had dropped a stone into the figurative pool, now found herself carried farther and farther away from its center by eddying waves of officialdom. Seemingly, a small army had sprung up from nowhere to mass itself around the body of the dead girl on the bridle path.

Detectives from the local precinct station asked a great many questions and made laborious notations. Homicide Squad men in plain clothes asked a few questions and made no notes at all. Photographers flashed their blinding lights into the forever blind eyes of Violet Feverel, recording upon celluloid the tragicomic posture of her crumpled body. Fingerprint men wandered about and finally, for the lack of anything better, they began to dust their mysterious black and white powders over the saddle and bridle of the nervous thoroughbred. Siwash fretted in the grasp of two brawny patrolmen and wished he were elsewhere.

Forgotten, Miss Hildegarde Withers bided her time patiently. The moment arrived when little Simons, the park attendant, was finally permitted to stand aside and draw a few gasping breaths on a cigarette. He had been sucked dry by relays of questioners, and the little man was in such a state that he very nearly screamed when Miss Withers came up suddenly beside him.

He looked twice as guilty as sin and the perspiration streamed from his forehead. Miss Withers wore a more formidable expression than she realized as she confronted her intended victim, and the little dog who wriggled in her arms was embarrassed by the tightness of her grasp.

"I tell you I don't know a thing!" Simons exploded in Miss Withers's face. "I was just coming across the park to work like I always do—you ask anybody—and I seen her riding hell-bent . . ."

"Saw!" corrected Miss Withers absently. "Saw, not seen. Yes, of course you found the body by pure happenstance. Somebody had to find it. But you didn't see anybody running away?"

"No—I told the police, I told them a thousand times, that the park was deserted."

"You found the body dead, but still warm," she continued. "Was that before or after you heard the sound of a car driving away?"

Her clear blue eyes stared at him blandly, innocently. Simons's mouth dropped open.

"Say! It was after—I mean, there *was* a car!" He caught her arm. "You don't think . . ."

"Not yet," Miss Withers snapped. "But to return to that car—it was a big limousine, was it not?"

Simons shook his head and scratched nervously at his hairy neck. "Didn't see the car," protested the little park employee. "I just heard it—the engine starting up. I forgot it until just now, what with all the excitement and everything. Finding the body, I mean. . . ."

"And you have no idea from which direction the sound came?"

He shook his head sadly. "It might have been somewhere up there on the roadway," he offered. His arm swung in a vague circle. Then a sudden realization smote him. "Say, those cops are going to be sore! I got to go back and tell them about this!"

Miss Withers was not one to impede the course of justice. She nodded thoughtfully. "The detectives look very busy just now," she suggested. "Perhaps a little later would be a more auspicious time?" And with the little dog still clutched to her maidenly bosom Miss Hildegrade Withers faded quietly from the scene.

For a long time nobody missed her. Heavy brogans tramped this way and that in a wide circle around the body of

Violet Feverel. Then suddenly they all stepped back to clear a path. The uniformed men saluted.

From a squad car on the roadway above there emerged a gray and wiry Irishman with his hat cocked over one eye. This personage at once crashed down the slope into the scene of action, a dead cigar clamped in his jaws. As he approached the spot where the dead girl lay, he took the cigar out of his mouth.

"What is this, field day?" inquired Inspector Oscar Piper as he surveyed the assemblage.

A very large and bulging detective pointed down with a stubby forefinger. "There's the body, Inspector!"

"Right on the job, eh, Burke?" greeted Piper. "And you found the body already! You're off to a flying start, you are. A body—and it's dead! Anybody know why?"

"We haven't moved her, Inspector. The medical examiner says he'll be here when he finishes his breakfast."

"That's just dandy," said Oscar Piper. "Well, where's the weapon?"

"There ain't any, Inspector."

"Well, we can't have everything. Where's the wound?"

"There ain't any, Inspector!" Burke stared dubiously down at the stiffening corpse. "Must of been stabbed in the back, where it doesn't show. There was blood on the horse and that proved she didn't die from the fall like they thought at first. It seems to me——"

Piper grunted. "Don't tell me you figured this all out for yourself, Sergeant!"

The detective shook his head. "The radio boys gets the credit, Inspector. They said they figured it out just as soon as the old maid butted in leading the horse which had run away. . . ."

"Oh," said Piper. He lit a match and let it go out in his fingers as an expression of incredulous amazed wonder crossed his face. "What's this about the old maid? *What* old maid? Who are you talking about, and where is she?"

Sergeant Burke licked his lips. "Why—just a nosy old maid who was always butting in. Just another nut gone haywire about murders. So I told her to scram. . . ."

The inspector took his cigar out of his mouth and thoughtfully broke it into little pieces. He nodded in smiling approval. "Go on—so you figured she was a nut and you threw her out?"

"Yeah, Inspector. But we got her name and address!" Thick fingers fumbled in the pages of a tattered notebook. "Here it is—Miss Hildegarde Withers . . . Number 60 West 74th Street. . . ."

He discovered to his surprise that the inspector was chanting the name and address in unison with him.

Inspector Piper let it be known that he was annoyed. "Great work, Sergeant! She's just a meddlesome old battle-ax who happens to be the smartest sleuth I ever knew in or out of uniform!" By this time the inspector's collar was three sizes too tight and his face had turned a deep cherry red. "Burke, you'd have to go to night school for years to learn to be a half-wit!"

Burke gurgled and saluted mechanically. "Well," roared the inspector. "What are you waiting for? She can't have gone far—and if we don't bring her back I'll give you two weeks' duty cleaning spittoons down at headquarters!"

With the sergeant trotting at his heels Inspector Oscar Piper forced his way back up the bush-covered slope to the squad car. He motioned Burke behind the wheel and they drove on a little way looking for a place to turn around. But the transverse was well blocked with official cars and they found it no easy matter. "Back up, then," the inspector ordered.

As the roar of the motor died down they both heard the sound of a dog's frantic barking. "Wait a minute," said Piper. He swung open the door of the car and ran over to the stone railing which bordered the elevated transverse. For a moment he stared blankly down, his head cocked on one side like an inquisitive sparrow's. Then he wildly beckoned Burke to join him.

They looked down upon a little lake, hardly larger than a pool, which nestled here in the corner between the high slope of Eighty-sixth Street Transverse and the outer stone wall of the park. Here a cluster of young willow trees waved fresh foliage above its muddy waters. At the moment the quiet of this sylvan scene was being rudely shattered by a small and excited terrier who was leaping about in the shallow water near shore and barking at the top of his lungs.

Beside him, perched precariously upon a teetering rock

which threatened every moment to tip and hurl her headlong into the water, stood Miss Hildegarde Withers. She was engaged in poking at the depths with a thin willow switch.

Her voice added to the hubbub. "Go on, Dempsey, get it! Bring it to me, there's a good boy!"

Then the inspector leaned over the edge and shouted merrily, "Pearl diving, Hildegarde?"

The angular schoolma'am turned a startled face toward the heights. "Of all things!" she cried. But she was not one to waste time in idle badinage. "Oscar Piper—it's about time. Come here and come quickly."

In three seconds he was beside her, the grinning sergeant in the rear. "Hot on the trail, Hildegarde?" asked the inspector. "What do you expect to find in the pool—the mysterious Death-Ray machine? Or is it the feathered bamboo blow-gun filled with tufted poison darts of the Mato Grosso Indians?"

Nettled, Miss Withers pursed her lips. "Perhaps!" she told him. "The dog has found something anyway. If I only had a boat!"

Piper shook his head. "Now, Hildegarde, be reasonable. What could possibly be in that mud hole?"

"A gun, perhaps," Miss Withers told him. "The murder weapon! There's a spot of oil, fresh oil, in the roadway just in front of where you parked your car. Somebody let an automobile stand here since the rain—and the park attendant heard a car drive away just before he came on the body. It occurred to me that if the murderer wanted to dispose of anything he might very likely choose this pool—and Dempsey had scented *something!*"

The little terrier had finally cast himself into the water over his depth. He swam in circles around the middle of the pool, still barking. Now and then he thrust his whiskery muzzle under the surface.

"Okay," conceded the inspector. "Burke, get into your diving suit and see what the pooch is after."

Sergeant Burke protested that he was wearing a pair of almost new socks. But the inspector pointed a commanding thumb at the murky depths.

"Here goes!" muttered Burke, and threw himself forward. He landed up to his knees in mud and slimy water, and then, as if encouraged by the sight of reinforcements, Dempsey ducked under the surface only to come up choking and spluttering.

Beside him, Sergeant Burke rolled up his sleeve and plunged a massive hairy arm into the water. "I can't find anything, Inspector!" he bellowed.

But the little dog Dempsey was still confident. "Good boy," encouraged his mistress from the shore. "Go get it!"

In spite of himself the inspector was caught into the spirit of the affair. Wading a little farther into the mud he caught sight of an abandoned garden hoe among some other relics and took it up by the handle.

"Here!" he shouted to Burke. "Try raking the bottom with this." He tossed the hoe out to the dripping detective who caught the heavy implement and sloshed obediently at the bottom of the pool, stirring up great roils of mud. Then Dempsey barked, took a deep breath and dived out of sight, with his short legs churning the water like paddle wheels.

He was gone a long time. Miss Withers, who had been unconsciously holding her breath, let it go with a great sigh. She was just about to plunge in to the rescue when the little dog reappeared with a shapeless something gripped firmly in his jaws. Burke lunged for it, but the little terrier deftly avoided him and paddled toward shore.

"Good boy," called out his mistress. "Bring it to me!"

Dempsey obeyed cheerfully. He emerged from the pond, gave himself a brisk shaking which drenched the inspector's trouser legs, and then with an air of duty well done the little dog deposited at the feet of his horrified mistress a very sad-looking turtle.

There was a long and painful silence, broken by the splashings of an irate and bedraggled Burke, shoreward bound.

The inspector's eyes twinkled. "The murder weapon!" he exclaimed unkindly. "Somebody hit the girl over the head with a turtle. Or maybe the turtle chased her off the horse?"

Miss Withers, as was usual when at a loss for words, sniffed. Then she dragged Dempsey away from his prize in disgrace and started toward the roadway with all the dignity she could muster.

But Sergeant Burke was the type of person unable to leave well enough alone. "Look, ma'am," he shouted after her, "do you want I should bring the *murder weapon* along?"

Miss Withers turned to see him poking at the comatose

turtle with his hoe. She stopped and her eyes widened. She took a step closer and then suddenly let Dempsey slide to the ground.

"I don't suppose it would strike either of you two master-minds," she pointed out, "that the garden implement in the sergeant's hand is just a little—unusual?"

"What?" The inspector's gaze flickered from her to the hoe. His mouth dropped open.

The implement which had at first appeared to be an ancient and discarded garden tool now showed itself to be, as the schoolteacher had pointed out, a very unusual hoe indeed. The rusty blade had been bent sharply back and through holes punched in the iron, four screws held firmly to its lower surface a bright, unrusted horseshoe!

"Put there for luck, I don't think!" said the inspector.

Miss Withers reminded him that there were different kinds of luck.

"I only wish we knew what it meant!" Piper continued, studying the odd device.

"Come on and we'll find out," Miss Withers counseled. They went away from the pond, with Dempsey dragging back on his leash to gaze wistfully upon his turtle. That philosophical creature, sensing that all was quiet again, had miraculously sprouted legs and a beaked head and was ambling back toward the water—and out of Dempsey's life forever.

They returned to the scene of the crime to discover a new arrival bending over the body of Violet Feverel. This personage was lean and dyspeptic looking, and he affected loose English tweeds and a bowler which happened to be a size too small for him.

"Miss Withers," introduced the inspector, "meet Dr. Charles Bloom, medical examiner for Manhattan."

"I think we've already met," said the schoolteacher. "It was some years ago, at the Aquarium,* wasn't it?"

"Ah, the lady with the hat pin!" But Dr. Bloom had no desire to talk over old times. He tugged nervously at the wisps which remained of a once luxurious beard and frowned down at the body as if, by dying, Violet Feverel had incurred his displeasure.

---

*See *The Penguin Pool Murder*, 1931.

"You can move her any time you like," said the doctor. He scribbled upon a pad.

"But——" interrupted Piper. "What do you figure killed her?"

"Well," began Dr. Bloom cautiously, "as for wounds . . ."

"They crushed the back of the skull, and were *supposedly* made by a horse's shod hoof!" Miss Withers eagerly prompted. "Isn't that right?"

Dr. Bloom smiled wearily. His heavy-lidded eyes took in the hoe which the inspector dangled in one hand.

"You're suggesting that this was a murder fixed to look as if a horse had done it—and really involving a weapon improvised from a horseshoe?"

Miss Withers nodded eagerly. "There was a story in a magazine——"

"Dear lady," said Dr. Bloom patiently, "I read my Chesterton too. Though I must say that the device is well known to medical jurisprudence. There was a case in Calcutta—another in Texas. But this time I'm afraid the answer is no. There are no wounds on the body!"

"But—but she's dead!" protested Miss Withers.

"A superficial examination such as this is only enough to show that this young woman died from internal hemorrhage. As a matter of fact, blood filled her lungs and she strangled to death!"

"But it *was* murder?" the inspector hopefully demanded.

"Officially, I don't know," the doctor told him testily. "I can tell you better after the autopsy. My private opinion, however, is that if this is not murder I've never seen one!" And the medical examiner beamed like a happy child.

"I knew it was murder," Miss Withers chimed in. "Just as soon as I saw that splotch of blood on the side of the horse."

"Remarkable," Dr. Bloom congratulated her. "Particularly since the spot to which you refer is not human blood, but horse's. I had one of the officers bring me a sample on a bit of paper and applied a primary test." His firm white teeth clicked decisively.

"But . . . where was the horse wounded?" Miss Withers begged.

"That is just what worries me, dear lady," said Dr.

Bloom as he brushed mud from his trousers. "The horse shows no wound at all! And now, if you'll excuse me . . ." He took up his bag and scurried toward his car.

"Well, here we are!" said Oscar Piper. He hefted the oddly weighted hoe as if about to hurl it back into the shrubbery. "It was a swell idea anyway."

"Not so fast." Miss Withers stopped him. "I've just had another idea. Do you suppose that we could find one untrampled hoofprint in this vicinity and make a little comparison?"

The body of Violet Feverel was already being lifted into a wicker basket by two white-clad men from the morgue wagon. Perhaps a dozen feet from where she had lain, outside the trampled circle, the inspector caught sight of a comparatively smooth bit of path which showed the delicate circular mark of a horse's hoof.

He lowered the hoe so that the horseshoe fastened to the bottom touched the soft earth. It fitted the print, fitted with a microscopic exactness. "Well, I'll be——" He turned suddenly and found that Miss Withers was not beside him.

The squadron of detectives and police had begun to break up, but the angular schoolma'am still lingered over the spot where the dead girl had lain.

"Never mind looking for the missing cuff link," called the inspector over his shoulder. "It doesn't happen nowadays. Come over here, this is really important!"

Miss Hildegarde Withers did not answer. She took a quick look around to make sure that she was unobserved, and then bent down and hastily drew from the soft mud which still bore the impress of the dead body a warm and pungent-smelling object which she thrust into her handbag.

One glance had told her that it was a briar tobacco pipe, battered and blackened. As Miss Withers joined her co-worker her lips softly formed the words, "People's Exhibit A." She nodded prophetically.

3

If the Shoe Fits

"With this little invention a person could produce very credible hoofprints without requiring a horse," said Miss Hildegarde Withers. She had taken the weighted hoe from the inspector and was tapping gently at the muddy path.

"All the same time there *was* a horse," protested Piper. "You found him yourself, so what difference does it make?"

"This gadget was not made for fun," Miss Withers retorted. "And I'll bet you a bright new penny that the horse in question is going barefoot upon at least one hoof." She led the way to the spot where, still fretting and prancing, a big red thoroughbred was a prisoner in the grasp of two patrolmen.

"How does one look at the underneath of a horse's foot?" Miss Withers demanded. They showed her—and she was immediately confronted with the realization that she had lost her bet. Siwash wore all four shoes.

"And that is that," the schoolma'am decided. "By the way, Oscar—we might try a different tack. Have you identified the dead woman?"

Piper snapped his fingers. "I knew I'd forgotten something!" He turned and shouted toward the scattering detectives. "Boys, what's new on the identity angle?"

Sergeant Burke, who had been entrusted with the guardianship of Miss Withers's dog, ceased his efforts to make Dempsey sit up and beg. "Radio Officer Shay's been on the phone for half an hour, sir. But he reports most of the stables don't answer their phones, and the ones he's reached haven't sent out any horses this morning."

"Well, tell him to keep on trying," barked the inspector. "We can't have a murder investigation of an unknown dame."

But Miss Withers interrupted again. "We're only wasting time, Oscar. After all, the horse is supposed to be one of the most intelligent animals. Suppose we let this big red fellow lead us to his stable?"

"Huh? Will they do that?"

"They will," Miss Withers assured him. "In fact, the only time I rode a horse he turned around and galloped into the barn without giving me a chance to dismount. Just let him have his head. . . ."

"Come on, Burke," ordered the inspector. "Another job for you. Take this nag and see if he'll go home."

The sergeant put Dempsey down and gingerly accepted the reins. "You know, Inspector, I never rode anything except a motorcycle. . . ."

"You don't need to ride him, just walk along beside him and we'll follow," Miss Withers suggested.

Burke tugged on the rein. "Come on, Plug!" Siwash rolled his eyes a little and did not move.

Burke pulled harder. "Gitty ap, Napoleon. . . ."

"He's just balky, I guess," said the inspector. "Go on, you!" And he slapped Siwash smartly on the rump.

It was a mistake. Siwash seemingly performed the miracle of levitation. He reared with his front feet and almost at the same instant slashed out viciously with his heels. They whizzed past the inspector's face, neatly knocking the cigar from his mouth.

Miss Withers vented a surprised scream and Dempsey burst into a furor of barking. But Siwash, who had had too much of the whole affair for his liking, bounded over the prostrate figure of the sergeant and disappeared almost instantly around a bend in the path.

"Not so balky after all," observed Miss Withers quietly. "Are you all right, Sergeant?"

Burke climbed wearily to his feet. "Where is he, the misbegotten . . ." He stopped and smiled apologetically. "Guess he must of pulled a knife on me, Inspector."

"I'd like to get that big red plug alone . . ." Piper was muttering.

"Yes, alone in the back room at headquarters, with a bright light to shine in his eyes and a rubber hose to smack in his face," Miss Withers told him bitterly. "Anyway"—she pointed to the line of clear and definite hoofprints which led southward along the bridle path—"anyway now we can follow the horse and see where he belongs." Dempsey barked excitedly and tugged at his leash.

"Okay," agreed the inspector. "But let's get rid of the bloodhound. Burke, you know the address—take the pup home, will you?"

Then the inspector and Miss Withers set off together down the bridle path. They were barely around the second turn when the schoolteacher stopped and grasped her companion's arm. She was pointing down at the path. "Snakes!" she cried.

Sure enough, a serpentine trail wound along in the mud. "Oscar, what made it?"

"Relax, Hildegarde," he told her wearily. "It's the track of a bicycle tire, just a common, everyday bicycle."

"Oh," she said. "Odd place for it—one would think the rider'd prefer the roadway." They went on, trudging wearily along the path. After a while they came upon cinders, which made the going faster. Even here, still clearly marked, were the two lines of dainty hoofprints, going and returning, with the bicycle track between.

"Observe, my dear Oscar," pointed out Miss Withers, "that the light rain left the bridle path in excellent shape to give us a record of who—or what—passed here." She pointed. "First came the horse, running north. Then the bicycle, presumably in the same direction. Finally, superimposed upon the other prints, we have the hoofmarks just made by the beast on his homeward gallop."

Piper nodded. "Hildegarde, you should have been a Boy Scout."

She took that as a compliment. "But Oscar, how did the bicycle return? We haven't passed it anywhere. . . ."

Nor was there any sign of the bicycle as they left the park at the Sixty-sixth Street gate. Piper frowned. "I ought to know what stables are near here—walked this beat once. Thwaite's is closest, I guess."

He led the way one block south. "We'll ask there anyway. . . ."

But inquiry was not necessary, for outside the double doors of Thwaite's stood a big red thoroughbred patiently waiting for someone to let him in. He moved aside as the inspector somewhat warily edged past and pounded on the panel.

There was a long silence. "Open up, here!" roared Piper. He pounded again, harder.

Then the top half of the door opened and a round brown face peered through. Highpockets pointed at the other door across the driveway. "Office over there, mister man—just ring the bell——"

"I'll wring your neck if you shut that door," Piper promised. "Who's in charge here?"

"Mister Latigo Wells, he's the manager—only he's out to breakfast," Highpockets explained tremulously. "If you want to wait he ought to be back pretty soon, he's been gone a long time already!"

"Well!" said Miss Withers. "How long a time, young man—would you say forty-five minutes?"

Highpockets frowned in deepest concentration. Then he shook his head. "Not as long as that, ma'am—I wouldn't say he's been gone much longer'n an hour or two."

Miss Withers turned to the inspector. "Your witness," she said sadly.

Piper nodded. "What we want to know is—"

Intent upon questioning the colored boy, both Miss Withers and the inspector had quite forgotten the big red horse. They were now reminded of his presence as Siwash thrust a long russet-colored nose between them, over the top of the door. He nickered softly.

They jumped aside and Highpockets opened the lower part of the door.

"Look out—he's dangerous," warned the inspector quickly.

"Him?" Highpockets laughed gleefully. "I been taking care of this horse fo' a long time, boss, and I never see him dangerous to anything but a pan of oats!" And the colored boy grasped Siwash firmly by one ear and led him in through the door. Deftly he slipped off the bridle and loosened the cinch.

"Go on, git to your stall!" And Siwash obediently went back along the runway, meek as a kitten.

Highpockets turned toward the two who now ventured inside the stable. "How come you bring back Miss Feverel's horse all lathered up this way?"

"Feverel, eh?" Piper nodded. "Sounds like a phony—a stage name. But go on—where does—I mean where *did* she live?"

"Why——" Highpockets' face turned a sickly green. "Where *did* she live? You mean—she ain't living anywheres now?"

"Answer the question," pressed Piper. "Good heavens, if the woman stabled her horse here you must know her address."

But Highpockets backed away shaking his head. "I doan know nothing and I never had nothing to do with——"

"Anything!" Miss Withers finished for him. "Oscar, we're just wasting time. This place must have an office and the office must have records of some kind."

Piper nodded. To the boy—"You all alone here?"

Highpockets nodded. "Yes, sir. . . . I sleep on a cot in the back, so I'm always here. Mister Latigo, he comes in daytimes, and Mrs. Thwaite and her husband, they live in a flat upstairs. She owns the stables, but I doan like to disturb her unless we got to. . . ."

"Heaven forbid," Miss Withers cut in. "This is only a murder case, that's all. But which way to the office?"

Highpockets pointed with wavering finger toward a side door. "Down the h-hall," he offered.

It was a long hall with a sharp turn in the middle. Then they saw a pane of lighted glass in a doorway. As they came closer they heard sounds of distant, mournful song. . . .

"Hillbillies!" gasped Miss Withers. "But this isn't the hour for them to be on the air. Listen!"

The voice was untrained, but low and mellow. Its only accompaniment was the soft plucking of a guitar.

> *"Now I've got no use for the wimmen,*
> *They're greedy and graspin' for gold. . . .*
> *They'll love a man for his money,*
> *When it's gone they'll leave him co-o-o-o-old.*
> *My pal was an honest young puncher,*
> *Honest and upright and true. . . .*
> *Till he fell in love with a woman,*
> *With a woman known as Lou. . . ."*

The inspector's head was nodding in time with the wailing ballad of the plains, but such music was not to Miss Withers's taste. She flung open the door of the office.

Seated at a roll-top desk, with his booted feet high above his head, sprawled a tall, thin young man with a long sad upper lip. He clutched a battered guitar to his bosom and his eyes were closed as he sang.

He stopped and put his feet on the floor with a crash.

"Howdy," he greeted them, sliding the guitar quickly toward its place atop the desk.

"You're the manager here?" queried Piper.

"That's me—Latigo Wells. And if you're figuring to rent horses—"

"Don't be silly—do we look dressed for riding?" Miss Withers snapped. She smoothed her neat serge suit.

"You never can tell," Latigo Wells was saying. "I just had the dickens of an argument with a tough guy in a blue overcoat—he got sore when I wouldn't rent him a fast horse. I told him he'd have to wear boots or chaps to ride any horse out of this stable. And these hacks in the stable get a hard enough life without going out under that kind of a hombre."

"We don't want horses," the inspector cut in. "We're looking for—for a Miss Feverel. You know her?"

Latigo's gray eyes flickered. "Sure I know her. She's not here. And if I were you I wouldn't wait—she's likely to be gone for some time."

Miss Withers sniffed. "I don't suppose that you, working here, happen to know where she lives?"

Latigo bristled at that. "Sure I know—I been up to her apartment. Last Tuesday night, to a swell party. She lives in the Hotel Harthorn, up on Broadway." Then the westerner rose to his feet. "Say, what's it to you folks?"

"It's this," said Oscar Piper. He flashed his badge. "Miss Feverel was found dead on the bridle path about an hour ago."

Latigo didn't say anything, but his neck reddened and he grew oddly white about the mouth.

"Of course you've been right in this office all morning?" Piper continued casually.

"Sure," Latigo nodded. "Ever since I saddled her horse—that big red race horse she owns. I been sitting here . . ."

"Why didn't you answer the phone, then—and why did the colored boy say that you went out to breakfast?"

Latigo blinked. Then he smiled apologetically. "I told him I was going and then I changed my mind. I been sitting here, just singin' a little—and I guess I was too busy singin' to answer that phone. I just let her ring. . . ."

He began to roll a cigarette. "You say Miss Feverel's dead? Did the horse kick her?"

Miss Withers looked at the inspector and her eyelid dropped a fraction of an inch.

Piper nodded. "Looks that way," he said. "Dangerous horse."

"Sure," agreed Latigo. "Any fast horse is dangerous for a woman who can't ride better than her. I warned her—no race horse makes a good saddle horse without a lot of training. But she wouldn't spend the money to have the horse schooled right—I guess she was hard up. Didn't pay her board bill on time, neither. . . ."

"Mrs. Thwaite made a fuss about that, didn't she?" asked Miss Withers wickedly.

Latigo shrugged. "Not that I know of. They were great pals, Mrs. Thwaite and Miss Feverel. And the doc, too—that's Mr. Thwaite." He faced them, twisting his cigarette. "Everybody was pals with Miss Feverel—that girl was strictly aces."

"Not *quite* everybody," Miss Withers amended. Piper nodded.

"Well," Latigo admitted, "they did have their arguments. You see, Miss Feverel got the idea that Mrs. Thwaite wanted Siwash. She suspicioned that we were using her horse when we knew she wouldn't be around. . . ."

"And of course she was mistaken in that belief?"

"Well——" Latigo began.

"Of course!" snapped a brittle and decisive voice. A door had opened just behind Miss Withers, disclosing a stairway filled at the moment by a very wide woman and a rather smallish man who sported a large mustache. The woman came first in practically everything—as she made clear.

"I'm Maude Thwaite," she announced. "What's going on here?"

It was rare for Miss Hildegarde Withers to take an instinctive dislike to a person on sight. In fact, as experience had taught her, she was prone to the other extreme. Yet she felt an instinctive surge of loathing rise in her being as she looked upon the proprietor of this riding academy.

Mrs. Thwaite was wide and muscular—qualities not necessarily unattractive in a woman. But her eyes were small and beady, and her complexion was a gray-blue, heavily mantled with light powder.

She was dressed in formal riding attire—fitted jacket,

light jodhpurs and heavy shoes. In one hand she held a heavy crop with a silver cap and she switched herself on the ankles as she spoke.

"I said—what's going on here?"

"Yes, what's going on here?" echoed her husband. Even shaggy worsted failed to give him bulk, either physical or mental. He waxed his mustache as he spoke.

"Only a few questions about Miss Feverel," said the inspector hastily. "You know her?"

"Of course——" Rufus Thwaite began. His wife drowned him out.

"Yes, we know Violet—a very good friend and a valued customer," she said. "She has stabled her horse with us for the last six months."

The inspector was a great believer in direct frontal attack. "Well, she won't be a customer any longer," he remarked. He displayed his badge. "You see, she was killed about an hour ago on the bridle path."

"Murdered!" added Miss Withers, just to make it more definite.

Dr. and Mrs. Thwaite looked at each other. Then they both said the proper things.

"Naturally, you'll be glad to help us in the investigation?" Piper went on.

But the Thwaites were doubtful. "You see," explained Mrs. Thwaite, "we didn't know her except as a customer—a client, really. She was in the habit of coming very early in the morning to exercise her horse, before either myself or the doctor was up. . . ."

"Doctor, eh?" Piper looked at Thwaite. "Medical or divinity?"

"I am a veterinary surgeon," explained the little man. "As we were saying, we won't be able to help you much."

For once his wife agreed. "All we know is that Miss Violet Feverel lives—I mean lived—at the Hotel Harthorn." She sneered slightly. "No doubt Latigo here has told you more interesting facts about her—I understand he moved in her social circle. . . ."

Latigo Wells looked excessively uncomfortable. "I was only up to her place one evening, and then I only stayed a few minutes," he hastily explained.

"Well——" said the inspector.

Miss Withers nudged him. "Come on, Oscar—befor these people convince us that they never heard of Viole Feverel."

Dr. Thwaite opened the outer door for them. "If there any little thing you want to know, just call on us!"

"It's the big things that we want to know," Miss Wither told him. "We'll be back. Hotel Harthorn, you said?"

They passed out into the street and the office door close behind them. The inspector started toward the sidewalk, bu Miss Withers crouched beside the door, motioning him back

Together they listened. They heard Latigo being sent o into the stables with a message to Highpockets regarding rubdown for Violet Feverel's horse. Then, after a moment o silence, Maude Thwaite's voice came clearly, with a note o placid satisfaction.

"Well, my dear, *this* ought to settle the problem o Siwash!"

"There," said Miss Withers, as she led the inspecto hurriedly down the sidewalk, "there is a woman who woul eat her young!"

It was still early morning—particularly early for a Sun day morning—when they reached the Hotel Harthorn. T Miss Withers the place seemed a typical apartment hote identical with half a hundred others which lined Broadwa and the crosstown streets of the neighborhood.

But the inspector was more closely in touch with th city. "Hotel Harthorn," he observed as they stood outside th near-marble entrance. "Average monthly record—one racke teer arrested, two suicides of girls diving from high windows one dope peddler picked up and turned over to the Federals two complaints a week on noise or disorderly conduct charge . . . nice place. Mostly theatrical people. . . ."

" 'Nothing ever happens at the Grand Hotel'!" quote Miss Withers. "Shall we go in and start something?"

They found a dapper desk clerk hidden behind a Sunda newspaper scandal section. "Miss Feverel's apartment," sai Piper.

The clerk shook his head and turned a page. "She's out, he informed them.

"When did she go out?" Piper wanted to know.

The clerk shrugged. "Sometime before I came on duty," he said. He rustled the newspaper suggestively.

But the inspector and Miss Withers were not so easily discouraged. "Pry yourself out of that chair," Piper snapped. "And bring your pass-key."

The clerk's eyes widened as he saw a gold badge in the inspector's hand. "Oh—an accident?"

"There will be one if you don't get going," Piper told him.

The dapper man led them down a hall to a somewhat old-fashioned automatic elevator. He pressed the button and Miss Withers drew the inspector aside. "Not much use to question the night man, provided there was one and he wasn't asleep at the switch," she pointed out. Her finger indicated another hall which ran past a closed newsstand and opened into the side street. "Places with as many exits as this don't allow for much of a check on the guests."

Piper nodded and they rode creakily upward to the sixth floor. Then they went down the hall and the clerk took out his key in front of 607. By now he was thoroughly worried. "This is a respectable place, Officer—I hope there won't be any publicity."

The inspector reached out and took the pass-key. "You just trot back to your desk and everything will be just dandy," he told the clerk.

The man lingered dubiously. "If you're going in I'm supposed to go with you. . . ."

Piper shook his head. "There may be shooting," he hinted.

"Shooting? Oh—but——" He edged away, and then suddenly turned and made for the elevator.

"But, Oscar," began Miss Withers. The inspector hushed her.

"Mostly a bluff," he whispered as he inserted the key. "But I didn't want him around. And—— I think I hear somebody inside the place. . . ."

As he opened the door an odor of mingled perfume, stale tobacco smoke, mixed liquors, and massed humanity eddied against them. Yet light enough poured through the Venetian blinds at the windows to show that the long living room was empty.

It was a typical hotel apartment, with almost no evidences of the personality of the tenant except for a battered piano. Everywhere, Miss Withers noticed, were the usual flotsam and jetsam of a party's aftermath—bottles in the wastebaskets, glasses broken in the gas-log fireplace and making rings on the furniture, rugs piled against the wall and a large hole burned in one of the cushions of the davenport.

There was no sound of anyone in the place, though the face of the dead girl looked down from dozens of photograph frames. The intruders moved softly forward across the living room. Piper opened a farther door and stepped into a very frilly and feminine bedroom. This was in better order, in spite of the spilled powder and a silver evening dress tossed casually across a chair. The bed had not been slept in and here too the walls were covered with photographs of Violet Feverel.

Now Miss Withers realized why the dead girl's face had seemed so familiar. The photographs showed her lighting a cigarette of a popular brand, inspecting an electric icebox, and smiling brightly at a tube of tooth paste. "Lord," exclaimed Piper, "it's the Billboard Girl!"

Miss Withers peered gingerly into the bathroom, but that too was empty. Further investigation showed a tiny kitchen with more bottles and glasses. But that was the total. Miss Withers and the inspector moved back to the living room, and Piper went over to the window and drew up the blinds.

"We might as well have some light—" he began. Then both he and Miss Withers were startled half out of their wits by a hoarse cry from behind them.

"Hello, Eddie!"

The inspector whirled and one hand snapped to his pocket. "Stay where you are!"

"Nuts to you, Eddie!" came the voice again. The speaker had no choice about staying where he was. Miss Withers discovered him in a neat gilt cage under the piano—a tiny green-red parrakeet, far smaller than his voice.

He swung head downwards from a trapeze, his beak clicking rhythmically.

"Get out the handcuffs, Oscar!" Miss Withers suggested. They joined in nervous laughter—it was no pleasant task wandering among the belongings of the young woman whose body they had just seen laid roughly in a wicker basket.

Just then a key rattled in the door and quick as a flash the inspector dragged Miss Withers down behind the davenport. They waited, hardly daring even to breathe, as a girl and a man in evening clothes came into the apartment.

". . . because we've got less than no time at all! Just throw some things into a suitcase," he was saying, in a gay and flippant tone.

"Yes, Eddie," said the girl. They kissed in the doorway. As she moved with a nervous little laugh out of his arms the girl saw Miss Withers and the inspector rising up over the top of the davenport and her face froze.

"What . . . what do you want?" she demanded.

Miss Withers was as yet unable to speak, for the girl across the room was fearfully like, in face and figure, the victim on the bridle path. This seemed to be Violet Feverel come back to life—Violet Feverel as she had been ten years ago.

"I'm asking the questions here," Piper cut in. "I'm from the Bureau of Homicides."

"Yeah?" began the young man known as Eddie. But the girl at his side cut him short.

"I'm Barbara, Violet's sister," she said evenly. "Has something happened?"

The inspector nodded. "Something has. Your sister met with an accident on the bridle path this morning."

The girl nodded mechanically. "Yes . . . yes? She's dead, isn't she?" Barbara caught her breath and her teeth bit into her lip. "I . . . I can tell by your faces."

She sat down suddenly in a chair, but she refused Miss Withers's well-meant ministrations. After a moment she looked up at the inspector. "You'll want to ask questions?"

"Plenty," said Piper. He motioned Eddie into a chair. "You too," he ordered. He lit a cigar. "You're both dressed up for 8 A.M.," he continued. "Where you been?"

"Harlem," said Barbara.

"At Mabel's Inn on Lenox Avenue," added the young man. His fingers toyed with his evening tie, which by daylight showed blue in place of the conventional black. He wore blue socks and an orange handkerchief peeped from the pocket of his tight-fitting dinner coat.

"You made a night of it," Piper suggested. "I never heard of any place open there after sunrise."

"Well——" said Eddie thoughtfully. . . .

"For the last few hours we've been riding up and dow
Riverside Drive in a taxi," Barbara said, her voice even an
expressionless.

"Why?"

"Because I had to make up my mind," Barbara admitted
"About something private."

"About running away?" Miss Withers put in.

"Partly that," said the girl.

"She was trying to decide whether or not to marry me,
Eddie offered. "Imagine hesitating about a thing like that!
He grinned.

"*Will* you begin at the beginning?" Piper asked. He trie
vainly to find an ashtray with room enough left in it to contai
his cigar. Finally he used the rug.

"I've been visiting my sister for the past week," Barbar
recited, as if she had rehearsed it. "Tonight, I mean las
night, there was a party. For me, mostly, because I'm sort o
a sap from Syracuse. It broke up late and Violet got rid of th
last of the die-hards by changing into her riding clothes. Sh
said they could drop her off at the stable. . . ." She looke
at Piper through long lashes. "You've been to the stable?"

He nodded. "Well, I wasn't supposed to go on to Har
lem with the others," Barbara continued. "And I couldn'
ride with my sister because I haven't riding things. Besides
she said I ought to get to bed. . . ."

"Reasonable at that," Miss Withers pointed out.

"But she wasn't! You'd have thought Violet was m
mother, instead of a half-sister who never even wrote me
letter for ten years, and who took me in only because th
aunt I'd been living with in Syracuse had died and I didn'
have any other place to go. . . ."

She took a deep breath and went swiftly on. "So Eddi
knew I wanted to go on to Harlem with them all and hav
fun. He said he'd see to it that Violet got into the first cab
and I could come down and get into the second, and she'
never know. Only when we stopped at the stables Viole
found I was in the cab and we had a terrific fight. . . ."

Miss Withers's eyebrows went up.

"You hadn't heard about it?" Barbara bit her lip. "Tha
cowboy beau of Violet's was gawking through the door and
was sure he must have blabbed. . . .

"Anyway, Eddie had to go on without me, but I caught a taxi and told the man where the place was and I caught the crowd in Harlem."

"And had *fun*," Miss Withers nodded sympathetically. "You say that Mr. Latigo What's-his-name of the stables was friendly with your sister?"

Barbara shrugged. "She got a laugh out of him anyway. Even had him come up here one evening, but I guess he didn't look as interesting in his best clothes. He thought we were all laughing at him because we tried to make him perform—I think he went home mad."

"One more question," said the inspector. "Who was your sister's boy-friend?"

Barbara hesitated and looked sidewise at the young man beside her. He smoothed the very peaked lapels of his dinner jacket thoughtfully.

"Me, as much as anybody," he said slowly. "But we were just——"

"Just good friends!" interrupted Piper wearily. "I know, I know. By the way, what's your name?"

"Eddie—Edward M. Fry," the young man admitted. He seemed to retain his jovial air with a certain amount of difficulty.

"Business?"

"I'm a veteran in the army of the unemployed," said Mr. Fry. "Used to work around Coney until times got tough. . . ."

"And you support yourself in the style to which you had become accustomed—how?" Miss Withers interrupted.

He smiled apologetically. "I've been lucky out at Beaulah Park," Eddie admitted. "Guessing on the goats . . . horses to you, lady."

"But you weren't so lucky at love?" Piper pressed.

The young man hedged and Barbara saved him. "My sister Violet had an unhappy marriage," she told them. "She was divorced about a year ago and since then I don't think there's been any man who mattered."

"Married, eh? To a chap named Feverel?"

Barbara shook her head. "Vi and I were born Foley," she explained wearily. "She changed it to Feverel when she started her career as a model. But her husband's name was Gregg, Don Gregg."

"And she divorced him, eh? We'll have a hunt started for Mr. Gregg," said Piper quickly.

Barbara smiled on one side of her mouth. "You won't have to hunt very far," she told them. "He wouldn't pay up and Violet had him thrown into alimony jail."

"Jail, eh? Then there was no love lost between them?"

"Not on Violet's part anyway," the younger sister told them. "I'll show you just what she thought of her ex-husband." She rose from her chair and went over to the parrakeet's cage. "Look there!" she said.

The inspector almost gave vent to a guffaw, but stopped. In the bottom of the bird-cage, instead of the usual folded bit of newspaper, was a cabinet photograph of a blond and plumply handsome man of perhaps thirty years.

Barbara took up one of the larger ashtrays and dumped its contents into the fireplace. Here too, pasted on the bottom, was a smaller photograph of the same face, blackened and discolored by countless expiring cigarettes.

"Well, why don't you laugh, everyone does!" cried the girl.

There was only a stony silence, during which Miss Withers tried not to shiver. Then the parrakeet screeched shrilly and a ring came at the door.

The four of them stood immobile. There was another ring and a man's voice called, "Miss Feverel!"

Piper nodded at the girl. "See who it is—stall him!" She obediently went to the door, with the other three at Piper's gesture drawing back out of line with the doorway.

"Who is it?" Barbara cried, ear to the panel.

"It's Thomas, Miss Feverel—with a very important message from your father-in-law. . . ."

Barbara looked around and saw that the inspector was motioning her to open up.

The door swung and a man pushed hurriedly inside. He was neither old nor young, thin nor fat. Dressed in a musty and dampened suit of sober black, with a greenish derby clutched in one gnarled hand, he was the picture of an old family retainer.

"Mr. Gregg—he wants to see you," said the newcomer. His voice was fairly dripping with gloom. "Please get your things, Miss Feverel, and come with me . . . or it may be too late!"

"And *why* may it be too late?" interposed the inspector. Thomas looked past the girl and saw the others coming toward him. His mouth dropped open. . . .

"Excuse me, I didn't know. . . ."

"This is not Miss Feverel," Piper snapped. "It's her sister. Violet Feverel was murdered on the bridle path of Central Park this morning—"

He stopped at the look of blank surprise which had come across the worn and dusty features of the man in the doorway. He gasped twice, clutching the knob for support.

"Miss Feverel *murdered?*" he repeated. "No—it can't be! You're lying to me, you're trying . . . " He stopped, regaining control of himself. "But nobody would want to murder *her* . . . it's old Mr. Gregg they're after!"

Piper came closer. "What do you mean? Somebody's trying to murder who?"

"Mr. Pat Gregg, my employer," said Thomas. "That's why he wants to see Miss Feverel right away—she used to be married to his son, you know. The old man wants to talk to her before he dies—he knows he's going to die."

"Do you know it too?" rasped Piper.

"No man knows such things for sure," said Thomas sententiously. "It's not for me to say," his face darkened. "But I do know this—yesterday somebody poisoned old Rex, the police dog. It wasn't just ordinary meanness between neighbors either—for that dog was trained to take food from nobody but myself and Mr. Gregg!"

"And you think," Miss Hildegarde Withers asked quietly, "you think that anyone meaning harm to the old man would first remove the dog who protected him?"

Thomas nodded slowly. Then he turned toward the door. "I got to get back there," he said.

4

Chickens Come Home to Roost

The inspector hastily took up a commanding position against the door. "Not so fast, not so fast," he commanded. "What's all this about?"

"We might have a chance to find out," Miss Withers cut in, "if we follow the lead of this gentleman here, Mr.——?" She nodded inquiringly.

"Thomas," said the newcomer. "Abe Thomas, ma'am. Me and my wife Mattie have taken care of Mr. Pat Gregg twenty years come April. And now," he urged apologetically, "it's a thirty-mile drive to the place and I've got to get started. I wish you'd come with me. . . ."

Piper frowned. "I don't see what connection there can be between the murder of Violet Feverel and the fact that somewhere up in the sticks a dog got sick."

"Sick nothing! I tell you, Rex was poisoned. Some black-hearted hellion fed him ground glass in a biscuit, the cruelest death that a beast can die. Why, back in Australia, where I come from, I once saw a man run out of camp because he'd killed some dingoes that way—and the wild dog dingo is the most worthless creature in God's world. I tell you——"

"Save it," said Piper. He caught Miss Withers's eye and saw that she was nodding emphatically. "We'll go—but I'm betting it's a snipe-hunt."

Barbara, in the background, was now putting on her hat. The inspector shook his head. "Sorry, miss," he told her. "You'll have to remain in town and face a very unpleasant duty."

She looked up and nodded. "I know. I'll have to identify my sister's body, isn't that it?"

Her voice was controlled and even. Miss Withers noticed all the same that there were fine little lines of tension around her mouth and nostrils.

Piper nodded. "There'll be a departmental car to take

you down to the morgue. Better get it over with as soon as you can."

"I'm taking you down there, of course," cried Eddie Fry. He took his position jauntily at the girl's side.

Her slim white fingers touched his sleeve for a moment. "Please, no," she said. "I want to go alone."

"Don't weaken!" the young man told her anxiously. "You need me more than ever—we're still going to be sealed, aren't we?"

Everyone looked at Barbara. "I—I don't know," she breathed. "I don't think so. Isn't that funny, really? I was going to marry you just to run away from Violet, and now—and now I don't have to marry anyone. . . ."

She began to laugh, thin brittle laughter like the high notes of an untuned violin. Her wide eyes were misting over.

Miss Withers sniffed. "It's about time she had a good cry," said the schoolteacher softly. "Stay and comfort her, young man." Eddie nodded. He was already doing it to the best of his ability. "And don't worry over anything she says now; the girl is all upset," Miss Withers counseled as she followed the others out of the room.

Thomas, leading the way at a walk which was almost a trot, was halfway to the elevator, but the inspector lingered and grinned at his co-worker. "Well, if it isn't Miss Lonely-hearts!" he greeted her. "Still singing rah, rah, rah for moonbeams, Hildegarde?"

She made a wry face. "Don't be a sour old misanthrope, Oscar. Just because I've guessed wrongly in the past* is no reason why I shouldn't lend a helping hand to young love when I can. You know, Oscar, I feel sorry for that girl."

Piper lit his cigar, using four matches. "A harum-scarum piece she is, too," he observed.

"Nonsense! She's at an age when there's something sacred about having FUN, in capital letters. She was all starry-eyed and breathless about her good time in Harlem, and then it had to turn out this way!"

"You don't suppose," observed the inspector thoughtfully as they came out under the canopy, "you don't suppose that having FUN in upper-case type was so important

---

*Miss Withers's last appearance in the combined role of Hawkshaw and Cupid is recounted in *The Puzzle of the Silver Persian*, 1934.

to little Babs that she killed the sister who spoiled it for her?"

"I do not—at least, I don't think I do," Miss Withers came back. She was surveying, without enthusiasm, a rickety-looking station-wagon flivver which waited at the curb, with the nervous little Abe Thomas crawling behind the wheel.

"Oh, is this what we travel in?" she asked hesitatingly.

Thomas nodded heavily. "You'll find it rides comfortable as a hearse," he promised.

"How delightful," murmured the schoolteacher as she clambered aboard. The inspector swung in beside her and they were off amid a clatter of gears.

The summer sun seemed almost directly overhead by the time the roar of the engine died away. New York City was far behind them, lost over the rim of the horizon. Miss Withers drew a deep breath of the fresh country air. "Well," she asked the driver, "are we there?"

Thomas shook his head. "No, ma'am. I just turned off the ignition to save gasoline—had to fill the tank in the city, at seventeen cents a gallon. That's too dear to waste as long as the law of gravitation is still working."

The car was slowly gaining momentum down the slope, along a winding country road with branches whipping against the fenders on either side.

Ahead of them the road dipped and rose again, mounting toward a white house which sprawled over the farther hilltop. Thomas indicated it with his thumb. "We're nearly there," he said.

A rolling green pasture came into view on the right, and beyond the crumbling stone wall a fat mare raised her head inquiringly.

"Look!" cried Miss Withers, delightedly. The mare was galloping along the wall, keeping even with the car without difficulty. Behind her, manfully trying to keep up, a gawky red-brown colt cantered upon stilt-like and unsteady legs.

Thomas turned his head. "That's all there is of the Gregg stable," he said. "That Comanche colt—he's already entered for the Futurity Stakes. The old man's praying he'll turn out to be another Siwash, only better."

"Another *what?*" demanded Miss Withers.

"Siwash—the horse the old man raced for three years

and then gave to his daughter-in-law as a wedding present. It seemed like Mr. Gregg's luck went with the horse, somehow."

Miss Withers nodded. "I shouldn't say that Siwash brought much luck to his new owner," she observed. "Violet Feverel was riding him when she was killed this morning!"

Thomas nearly turned the car into the stone wall, awakening the inspector from a pleasant doze. "If she was killed, I'll tell you right now that it was through no fault of the horse," Thomas went on, regaining control of himself and the car. "That big red Siwash hasn't a mean streak in his body, or he hadn't when I handled him!"

The inspector was inclined to enter into an argument about this point, but Thomas put the car into gear again as they began to climb the steep slope toward the house.

"Well, well," Miss Withers ejaculated. It was veritably a house to gaze upon, built in a combination of the worst styles of the last century. The general effect was something like that of a dusty wedding cake, for in spite of the kind concealment of the towering elms, the house was an eyesore of gables, porches, porticoes, dormers and frescoes jumbled together, the whole thing topped with a somewhat precarious-looking cupola.

"The Gingerbread House!" gasped Miss Withers. "Oscar, when you were little didn't you ever read the fairy tale about the little boy and girl who wandered into the Gingerbread House and were turned into mice by the old witch?"

Oscar Piper looked at her intently. "Hildegarde, you need a strong cup of coffee," he returned. The car was swinging up toward a sagging porch, but before the wheels had stopped rolling their driver leaped from his seat, motioning for them to follow.

They had a glimpse of his thin legs dashing up the steps. Nobody in the world, Miss Withers noted, can run and keep his dignity, not even an old family retainer. Abe Thomas unlocked the door quick as a flash and disappeared inside.

"Say, that little man *is* worried," the inspector observed as he helped Miss Withers down. They hurried up the steps, but as ill luck would have it, an inconvenient gust of wind slammed the open door almost in their faces. The inspector rattled the knob furiously, but there was a snap-lock.

"A rousing welcome," Miss Withers observed. She pressed her forefinger against the bell while the inspector pounded on the panel. After a long moment the door was surprisingly flung open in their faces and the doorway filled by a very fat woman who seemed to have hastily hung wrappers, aprons, slippers and faded untidy hair upon her person.

Her small mouth put on a wide, ineffably sweet smile. "Good morning!" she cooed. "Did you want something?"

They both spoke at once. "Mr. Thomas . . ."

The fat face pouted. "Isn't that too bad! My husband, he went to New York early this morning and won't be back till late." At that moment she noticed the flivver still quivering noisily in the driveway. "You came in the car—then where's Abe? Oh——" She opened her mouth but the scream of anguish did not come. A faint crash sounded from somewhere in the upper reaches of the house. As the fat woman turned, the inspector and Miss Withers pressed past her. They glanced into a living room of the horsehair period and rushed on toward the stairs.

Halfway up they met Abe Thomas coming down, his face white as the proverbial sheet.

"Telephone . . . doctor. . . . Something's happened. . . . Mr. Gregg!" he mouthed. As they waited immobile, he burst past them and clattered down the stairs.

The inspector and Miss Withers stared at each other. "Something's happened to Mr. Gregg," she repeated softly. "Oscar, I'm not as surprised as I should be."

But Oscar Piper was sprinting down the hall toward an oaken door which now hung crazily upon burst hinges. In spite of his flying start Miss Hildegard Withers was neck and neck with him at the finish.

They burst into a wide and darkly dismal bedroom, its shades still drawn. The room was dominated by a bed of dark walnut, with a much-carved headboard rearing almost to the ceiling. On this bed, moaning feebly, lay a plump old man in a tangle of blankets.

The schoolteacher gasped and stopped suddenly—for all that could be seen of Mr. Pat Gregg was of an unearthly blue-purple shade, even to the crown of his bald head.

Whatever the inspector had expected to find, it was not this. He bent for a moment over the unconscious man. Then he looked up, his forehead puckered. "A stroke of some kind, Hildegarde."

Miss Withers shook her head doubtfully. In the silence

that ensued they could both hear the excited voice of Abe Thomas shouting into the telephone.

"I wonder if he smokes a pipe," Miss Withers murmured.

Piper stared at her. "The guy downstairs? What if he does?"

She shook her head. "I mean the man on the bed. But never mind, you wouldn't understand." The sick man was breathing more loudly now, expelling every gasp with a low moan.

"Shouldn't we be doing something for him?" Miss Withers wondered.

Piper shook his head. "Best to wait for the doctor, from what I know of first aid," he said. "He'll know what caused it—we'd better stick to our detecting."

"We'd better start detecting," Miss Withers snapped back. She carefully scrutinized the broken door. "Thomas had to force his way in, no doubt of that," she decided.

On a chair near the head of the bed were displayed scattered articles of masculine attire, including the trousers of a very loudly checked suit affixed to a broken pair of suspenders. "I'm too much of a lady to snoop," she told the inspector. "But as long as we have this fortunate interval, don't you suppose we might have a look in the pockets?"

Inspector Oscar Piper was not one to be over-delicate. The trousers held—besides a faded silk handkerchief, three dollars in silver, a penknife with a mother-of-pearl handle and a rabbit's foot—two identical keys on a ring. The keys fitted perfectly into the lock of the broken door.

"That's that," said the inspector. He replaced the belongings. Then he noticed that his companion had her head cocked on one side.

"Smell a herring, Hildegarde?"

"Several herrings," she told him. "Oscar, do you happen to notice that there's something gritty on the floor? Could it be sugar?"

"Sugar or sand," agreed the inspector. "Maybe the old man's been to the beach recently."

The schoolteacher nodded. She was wandering around the room, walking on tiptoe because of the old man who still groaned in his deep coma. She frowned at her image in the mirror and then upon an impulse she raised the window shades, permitting the cheerful noonday sun to come streaming in.

"Puts a different atmosphere on things, doesn't it?" the inspector asked.

She nodded slowly, looking over her shoulder. "It certainly does, Oscar! There's another entrance to this room!"

They both gazed upon a narrow stairway at the farther end of the room, an open stairway of unpainted pine which led to a trap door in the ceiling.

But before the two intruders could investigate this stairway, they heard Abe Thomas and his fat wife come rushing down the hall.

"He's gone, of course," cried Thomas, approaching the bed. "No—he's breathing! If he can only hang on a few minutes longer—the operator just managed to locate Dr. Peterson——" Thomas shook his head. "It'll be too late for him, that I know."

Mrs. Thomas quivered and a big tear rolled down either cheek. "The poor old man—to meet his end with no loving hand to stroke his forehead, and no loving voice in his ears . . . and me not dreaming that he wasn't right as a trivet, or anyways as right as his excitable nature would let him be. . . ."

"Has he been ill long?" Miss Withers asked.

Both Thomas and his wife loudly insisted that Mr. Pat Gregg had been in reasonably good health yesterday. "For a man of his age, that is," Thomas explained.

"And the last time you saw him, then, was it in the evening?" Piper questioned.

"Yes, sir. About seven o'clock, I guess. I helped him upstairs, because his rheumatism was bothering him more than usual. Then I heard him lock himself in—he had the only keys. You see, he was used to Rex sleeping under his bed and since the dog was poisoned old Mr. Gregg has been mighty nervous-like."

Piper nodded. Then he faced the fat woman, who was still staring toward the bed with an expression of mingled horror and fascination on her face. "Mrs. Thomas—remember carefully, and don't lie——"

She stared at him with a wounded expression. "How could I hold anything back from a member of New York's Finest, sir?" Her voice was very serious.

"Eh? All right, all right. You heard nothing, noticed nothing wrong last night?"

She shook her head, but chose to stare at a picture on the wall. "Not a sound, sir. But Abe and me, we sleep at the other end of the house. On Sunday morning, particularly when Abe goes away like he did this morning, I usually like to rest my bones in bed until Mr. Gregg rings for his breakfast. And this morning he didn't ring at all. . . ."

Miss Withers whispered something to the inspector. "Oh, yes." He turned back to Thomas. "Then it was last night that your employer told you to take the message to his former daughter-in-law?"

Abe Thomas hesitated, then nodded. "But I didn't leave until early this morning," he explained.

"And you have no idea why he wanted to see Miss Feverel?"

Thomas hesitated again, looking quickly from the man on the bed to his inquisitor. "I couldn't rightly say," he began. "But my own opinion would be that it had something to do with his son, young Mr. Don. You see, he and his wife were divorced with a lot of hard feeling, and when Mr. Don got behind with his alimony Miss Feverel—as she always called herself—had him put in jail. That worried Mr. Gregg, if I may say so." The little man's expression was pained, unhappy.

"I should think it would have worried young Mr. Don too," Miss Withers suggested dryly.

She was interrupted by the tooting of an auto horn in the driveway outside. "The doctor, praise be!" gasped Mrs. Thomas, and they heard her go pounding down the stair.

Dr. Peterson, unlike the general practitioner whom Miss Withers had visualized, was a crisp and tow-headed young man in his thirties. He came into the bedroom, frowned at the patient, and then tugged thoughtfully at his wispy mustache.

"Another attack, eh? Thomas, would you mind getting my kit out of the car? And one of you ladies get a pan of hot water. . . ."

Miss Withers wanted to ask why modern doctors were so disinclined to carry anything larger than a pad of prescription blanks with them. Her idea of a doctor was a large, untidy man with a worn black satchel in his hand and a stethoscope peeping out of his coat pocket.

But when finally equipped Dr. Peterson rolled up hi sleeves, displaying capable if rather hairy arms. "Outside, a of you," he ordered.

Thomas and his wife backed unwillingly through th broken door. Miss Withers hesitated and the inspector stoo his ground. "New York City Police," he said, displaying hi badge. The shield of gold had gone in and out of his pocket s many times that morning that he was half inclined to pin it o his vest. "I'm staying," he went on. "There's something funny about this business."

The doctor shrugged and looked toward Miss Withers "Is she the law too? Because——"

The inspector was about to spring to her defense, bu Miss Hildegarde Withers had had enough of the sickroom "I'll wait for you outside, Oscar," she said, and went quietl out of the room.

As he worked the young doctor kept up a running com mentary. "Simple enough case—cerebral accident or apo plexy," he said. "Probably bulbar—a rupture of blood vessel in the medulla oblongata. I was afraid this might happen. . . .'

"You've treated him before, then?"

Dr. Peterson nodded. "Two weeks ago—for a heart at tack. His blood pressure's away up in the clouds, due to hig living and taking such things as horse races too seriously. warned him—told him to stay away from the races."

The inspector moved closer, leaning over the bed. "Thi other attack—how did it happen?"

Dr. Peterson washed out his hypodermic needle with alcohol. "I was called in and found him unconscious on thi bed. Had a bit of bad news, I guess. Anyway he collapsed or the stair and somehow Thomas got him into bed and had sens enough to give him ammonia to sniff. That was all that kep him from going off then and there."

He bent his ear against the old man's chest and the shook his head. "If he comes out of this coma, he'll probabl be paralyzed on one side. I give him a hundred to one. . . .'

Both doctor and policeman jerked back as the sick man' mouth twitched open. "A hundred to one," he whispere faintly. Pat Gregg opened his eyes and stared up at them "I'll—I'll take fifty dollars worth of that bet. . . ."

Then his eyes closed wearily.

"He's reacting to the injection!" cried the doctor. H

pulled again at his mustache. "Funny that he isn't paralyzed—must have missed getting it by the skin of his teeth. . . ."

"Won—by a whisker," whispered Pat Gregg. "I was left at the post, pocketed badly on the backstretch, but I—I broke through and came to the front. . . ."

He tried to sit up in bed. The blue-purple tinge was receding from his face, remaining only in a spot beneath his ear.

"I had a funny dream, Doctor," he said, his voice coming more clearly now. "A regular nightmare it was. Bet you three to five you never had a dream like that. I dreamed I was the pendulum in that big clock out in the hall. And then I was a big red Barbary ape swinging in a tree, only the branch broke. . . ."

He stopped and looked up at the inspector. "Who're you?"

"Never mind," said Piper. "Remember anything before the attack—before you were sick? Who was with you and what happened?"

Pat Gregg shook his bald head. "Nobody was with me. My head's buzzing like a beehive, but I can remember. Thomas helped me up the stairs, and then I locked myself in and went to bed. . . ."

"You felt it was coming on before then, and sent for your daughter-in-law?" The doctor was making motions, but Piper kept on doggedly.

The old man's eyes filmed. "Sent for—Violet? Why should I send for that—that——"

"You told Thomas to bring her here first thing in the morning."

"Did I? And she came?" The old man was almost smiling.

"She didn't come—because she couldn't," Piper went on. "She was killed in Central Park this morning at sunrise."

A pleased, almost cherubic expression flitted across the old man's face. "How I'd like to have been there!" he murmured. Then, "So Thomas told you I sent for her? Police, aren't you? Then I can't blame him for discussing my business, can I? Police have to know everything. If a sparrow falls——Only my late daughter-in-law was no sparrow, she was a buzzard."

"That'll be all for now," Dr. Peterson interrupted. "I don't care if you're Sherlock Holmes himself, you can't give my patient the third degree now."

"'Okay," said Piper. "If you'll come out into the hall a moment, Doctor . . . "

They stepped through the broken door. "I'll make it snappy," said the inspector. "First, did you notice the mark on his neck?"

"Bruise," the doctor admitted. "Probably bumped something or hit himself during the attack. He's got bad ones on his shoulders too."

"It couldn't be anything else but an attack of apoplexy?"

Peterson shrugged. "I never saw that congestion of the blood vessels of the face and head in any other condition. I'll stake my reputation as a doctor that Pat Gregg has had a light attack of apoplexy, the logical follow-up to the heart attack two weeks ago. The next one—it'll kill him."

The inspector's eyes narrowed. "Could the attack have been caused by exertion—such exertion as going to New York and killing his daughter-in-law at sunrise and hustling back here?"

"It certainly could," Dr. Peterson remarked with a faint smile, "except for the minor objection that there's only one chance in a thousand that he'd be lucky enough to get home and have his attack in bed. It would almost certainly happen at the time of greatest excitement—presumably when he was engaged in exterminating his daughter-in-law. Besides, this attack appears to have come earlier than sunrise—at least an hour earlier."

"Okay," said the inspector. "It was just an idea anyway." He went swiftly in search of Miss Withers—so swiftly that he very nearly tripped over the fat Mrs. Thomas, who was crouching at the head of the stairs and weeping quietly.

"Turn 'em off," Piper told her, not unkindly. "Mr. Gregg is going to be all right."

"That's good," said Mattie Thomas brokenly, and the tears still coursed across her fat cheeks. The inspector shrugged and went on.

Miss Hildegarde Withers was nowhere in the lower part of the house, but knowing her distaste for such stuffy environs of the haircloth sofa era, he was not surprised. She was finally tracked down at the pasture fence, where she and the gawky red colt were studying each other in an interested fashion.

He told her of what had transpired in the sickroom. "So

the old man seems to have disliked his daughter-in-law—but there's no chance of his having been the one to do her in. Only a thousand to one that he'd be able to do it without having the attack then and there, the doctor says."

Miss Withers nodded. "A thousand to one—but Pat Gregg is a born gambler, Oscar. And he seems to have recovered mighty quickly, all of a sudden." She took Piper's arm. "But I haven't been wasting my time either. Come on. . . ."

Piper brightened. "Got something on the worthy Thomas at last? I knew he'd bear looking into."

She gave him a quizzical look. Then she pointed toward a distant hencoop where the man in question was busily engaged in liberating a large flock of squawking and excited white Leghorns. They gathered around Thomas, leaping at the pan of grain which he held in his hands.

"Breakfast is late for the hens this morning," Miss Withers pointed out. "It's probably due to the fact that Thomas was away in the city and his wife remained in bed."

"Yeah? Well, breakfast is late for me, too," Piper objected. "What's all this got to do——"

"Come and see," the schoolteacher told him. She led the way to an open shed at the end of the driveway. From the old number plates nailed on the walls, the grease and oil dried deep into the floor of pounded sand it was evident that here the station-wagon was kept. At the rear the frame of an ancient bicycle was peacefully rusting away.

Along one wall were piled three great iron drums painted red and marked "gasoline." "Evidently they save a cent or two a gallon by buying it wholesale," Piper suggested. "What's that got to do . . ."

But Miss Withers was pointing down at the tire marks on the sand. Over them, in an irregular tracery of webbed footprints, were the tracks of the chickens.

"What do you make of that, Oscar?"

He stared at her blankly. "Chickens mean nothing to me unless they're fried," he announced.

"Well, these mean something to me," Miss Withers retorted. "Those hens have been shut up all morning—and I never heard of a chicken searching for food after dark. At sunset they seek their roosts and presumably were shut up by Mrs. Thomas before she went to bed."

"Why not Thomas?" objected Piper.

"Because he wasn't here," Miss Withers exploded triumphantly. "He's lying when he says he took the car out of the garage this morning and drove into New York. It was last night—because there are chicken tracks *on top* of the tire marks!"

"Say!" said Piper. Then his face fell. "But the car might have been standing outside on the driveway all night. . . ."

Miss Withers shook her head. "You've talked with Thomas and you know he's not the type to let his employer's car stand out in the rain."

"That's right," agreed the inspector. "It did rain. And the hen tracks give us the real goods on Thomas. Say, I'm going to ask him a couple of questions. Where is that guy?"

But it was Miss Withers who found Abé Thomas coming out of the haymow with a hatful of eggs. And it was Miss Withers who asked the first question.

"By the way," she said casually, "do you smoke a pipe?"

Thomas stared at her suspiciously. Then he nodded and took from his coat pocket a blackened corncob. "I smoke it, but not around the barns," he explained.

"No, I don't mean that one," Miss Withers went on. "Haven't you got another pipe—or didn't you have one?"

He reached into his other pocket and produced a duplicate of the first, except perhaps a little more rich in color and aroma. "Never smoke anything but a corncob," he announced. "When one gets hot I switch to the other."

Miss Hildegarde Withers hung on like a puppy to a root. "And when both pipes get too hot to smoke?"

Abe Thomas retained his air of friendly helpfulness. "Now that's nice of you to be so interested," he told her. "When I run out of pipes I always chew gum or eat an apple. Nothing like an apple to freshen your mouth. It's early for 'em yet, but back in the pasture there's a Yellow Transparent tree that'll be worth shaking in a week or two. . . ."

Miss Withers relaxed. "I must try one whenever my mouth gets scorched," she said and started to move on toward the restless inspector.

But Abe Thomas followed her. "I got to know, ma'am—have you found anything yet? Did I bring you up here on a wild-goose chase?"

As she hesitated the little man kicked nervously at the dirt with his heavy shoe. "I know—you and him, you agree with that cocksure cub of a doctor that Mr. Gregg only had an attack of apoplexy. Well, I tell you he didn't—and he knows he didn't! You ask Mr. Gregg!"

"The old man has no idea of what happened," Piper vouchsafed. "I asked him."

Abe Thomas thoughtfully stuffed black tobacco into one of his pipes. "That makes it a lot harder, doesn't it?"

"A lot harder or a lot easier," Miss Hildegarde Withers concluded. She was staring over his head, up at the little cupola perched on top of the house. One of its four windows was open and the wind whipped at a chintz curtain.

She nodded and spoke very softly. "Or a lot easier," said Hildegarde Withers.

5

The Wings of an Angel

Dr. Peterson took his hat from the horns of the glassy-eyed deer head which haunted the front hallway. "The old man is not to be disturbed until he wakes, understand?"

Mrs. Thomas swore that she would guard her master's rest with every drop of blood in her veins.

"I'll be back later this afternoon with a nurse," continued the young medico. "I've given Mr. Gregg an opiate and he ought to sleep until then." He moved brusquely toward the door, stopping when he saw that it was barred by Miss Withers and the inspector.

"What I said goes for you too," the doctor told them. "No more third degrees."

But Miss Withers was interested. "A nurse for Mr. Gregg, eh? Is he as ill as all that?"

The doctor frowned. "Well—no. I don't think so. But there are some contradictory symptoms that I'd like to keep an eye on."

"In other words, you're not so sure that it's apoplexy after all?"

Peterson smiled wryly. "The one thing I'm most certain

of is that Mr. Gregg has had some sort of cerebral accident. But what worries me is the fact that it wasn't fatal!"

"I beg your pardon?" Miss Withers gasped, and Piper drew closer.

"I mean," he went on, "the attack was somehow arrested right in the middle, as if the hand of death slipped. That doesn't happen often—but it's a break for the old man. I've great hopes for his recovery now that he's dropped off to sleep."

"'To sleep: perchance to dream'!" murmured Miss Withers under her breath. "To dream of being part of a clock, poor man. If I were he, Doctor, I should try my hardest to keep very much awake." But the front door had with great finality slammed upon the doctor's heels. The inspector moved after him.

"And where are you going, Oscar?" demanded Miss Withers.

"Back to town," he told her. "Back where there's a hot trail. We're not buttering any parsnips out here."

"That," Miss Withers told him impolitely, "that is what *you* think!" But she was worried all the same. Absent-mindedly she patted the deer's nose and then whirled suddenly to face the inspector.

"Oscar Piper, I do wish you'd stop staring at the back of my neck . . ."

Her voice trailed away as she saw that the inspector was engaged in dropping his cigar ash in a convenient letter box.

He looked up and grinned. "Getting the jitters, Hildegarde?"

"Perhaps," she nodded. She stared down the hall, which ended in a dining room where the fat Mrs. Thomas was doing a bit of casual dusting. Overhead rose the ancient sagging balustrade of the stair leading to the upper hall, but that was vacant. Nobody was in the living room—there was not even a family portrait to stare down from the wall with narrow wicked eyes. That left only the deer head, unhappy symbol of man's interpretation of the idea of fellowship with the lower orders of life. Somehow Miss Withers could not believe that the silly glass marbles which the taxidermist had used for eyes could be responsible for the uneasy feeling at the back of her neck.

"Well, Hildegarde?" pressed Piper impatiently. "Coming back to the city?"

She nodded slowly. "It's noon, Oscar—and we've missed breakfast. Do you suppose that you could use your influence with La Thomas to get us a bite to eat?"

The inspector said that there was something in the idea, and when pressed, Mrs. Thomas admitted with only a second's hesitation that she thought she could find some cold baked beans and part of a lemon pie in the larder.

"Great!" cried the inspector. "Typical Bostonian breakfast—ought to suit you to a T, Hildegarde."

Miss Withers brightened. Just as many Hebrew gentlemen who have never been south of Chicago burst into tears when "Dixie" is played in a restaurant, the angular schoolteacher was a fervent New Englander in everything but birth. She had never quite forgiven her parents for migrating from Back Bay to Iowa a few weeks before her advent into this world.

But with her duty came first—even before the allure of baked beans and coffee. She sat down at the dining-room table, as it happened in a chair which stood very close to the wall. Suddenly she drew a sharp breath and cocked her head.

"Oscar, do you hear anything?"

"Sure," answered the inspector jovially. "I can hear chickens cackling, birds twittering, bees buzzing, and that she-horse in the pasture whinnying to her colt. This place is noisier than a subway station."

That wasn't quite what Miss Withers had meant. "Don't you hear noises upstairs—like soft footsteps?"

He listened. "Nary a footstep, Hildegarde. But what if there were? It's probably Thomas."

Miss Withers had forgotten the little man. After all he had a perfect right upstairs, and no doubt several good reasons for being there.

"Stop jittering and eat," counseled the inspector as Mrs. Thomas appeared with plates and cups. "Do you good."

Miss Withers nodded and tried to relax. But after a moment she rose suddenly to her feet, murmuring something about powdering her nose. The inspector stared after her wonderingly, for it was his belief that her somewhat prominent beak had not been powdered since the Taft administration.

She hurried up the stairs alone, trying to move as softly

as possible. But a chorus of squeaks from the sagging steps accompanied her, and she found the upper landing deserted. Even the face of a looming grandfather's clock seemed alien and unfriendly. It struck the half hour—eleven-thirty.

For a moment she stood stock-still, wishing for the comforting presence of the little dog Dempsey at her heels, wishing for the black cotton umbrella which had proved so useful a weapon in the past—even almost wishing that the inspector had accompanied her. She shrugged her shoulders and tiptoed down the hall.

There were three doors opening off this upper hall, three closed doors and the gaping space where a way had been broken into the old man's bedroom. She tried the handle of the first door. It turned, and she opened softly and peered within. Here was only a bathroom, grim and horrible. The streaked iron tub was mounted upon four lion's claws, and the washbowl bore the decoration of an excessively overpainted wreath of roses. For a moment she stared at her face in the uncertain mirror and then she closed the door. Nothing evil lurked in this room—nothing but that atrocity of a bathtub.

The next door opened on dusty hinges to disclose a room cluttered with worn-out riding boots, dusty saddles, countless bits of leather and harness, empty gun racks, and old trunks and suitcases spilling forth faded blue silks and mouse-gnawed horse blankets. There was a ripe rich smell of horses and leather and dust. Several spiders had set up extended engineering operations here, vast webs which swung from the ceiling and which were undisturbed as far as the schoolteacher could see.

She closed that door. There was only one left, the door nearest the broken door of the old man's room. Here, she decided, must be the room where Abe Thomas was pursuing his mysterious and furtive purposes.

Miss Withers drew a deep breath and turned the knob. Perhaps it was her fancy, but that knob seemed a few degrees warmer than it should have been, as if someone had held it in his hand a moment or two before.

She looked into a bedroom almost as large as the old man's, a long narrow room with windows to the south. Through the green shades, worn and tattered by the years, little pencil lines of sunlight radiated. The room was empty and airless, but as Miss Withers made a mental note of bed and bureau, table and chair, she wrinkled her nose at the faint but unmistakable odor of rich tobacco.

Quick as a flash she flung open the closet door, but found nothing more than a toy rifle, a very battered and empty suitcase, and a pair of riding boots, badly worn and scuffed.

Frowning, she surveyed the room again. This must, she felt, be Donald Gregg's room, or the room which had been his before his marriage. The walls were decorated with Rolf Armstrong girls torn from the covers of *College Humor*. Over the mirror, in a frame evidently intended for a much larger picture, was a photograph of a face which she recognized with a start. It was the girl who had called herself Violet Feverel, smiling a very wide and toothy smile and clasping to her very insufficiently clad bosom a tube of tooth paste.

But if Miss Withers was sure of anything at this stage of the game it was that the footsteps she had heard were not made by Violet Feverel. Turning aside from the advertisement she went out into the hall again. There remained only the room in which the sick man lay. Softly she tiptoed down the hall and through the broken door of the old man's bedroom.

The shades had been drawn again and the room was filled with the sound of heavy, irregular breathing. Pat Gregg's round, somewhat blurred face seemed as pale now as it had been livid before.

"If he's asleep I won't bother him and if he's awake it won't matter," she salved her conscience. Softly she crossed the room, while the man on the bed remained comfortably immobile. She went up the steep stairs at the farther end of the room, pressed against the trap door, and found that it lifted easily.

There was no sound from above, and risking everything on one rash plunge, she climbed into the cupola and let the trap door drop back softly beneath her. She found that she stood in a tiny room perhaps nine feet square, with a large window in the center of each wall. One window was open, and its chintz curtain flapped in the breeze.

She was alone—in spite of her certainty that here she would find the one who had padded softly up and down the hall.

From the walls, filling every available inch of space, half a hundred thoroughbreds looked down at her. It was horses, horses everywhere—horses in photographs, etchings, copies of paintings—and beneath each picture such deathless names of Exterminator, Sun Beau, Gallant Fox, Man o' War and Cavalcade.

Above the battered oak desk was a large photograph of a galloping horse with a monkeylike exercise boy perched on his neck. She recognized without difficulty her acquaintance of the morning, the big red horse called Siwash. Next to his was a smaller picture, a little out of place among so many thoroughbreds she thought. It was of a young man and woman coming down the steps of the Little Church Around the Corner—and the man's face was one that she had last observed on the bottom of a parrakeet's cage. The girl, of course, was Violet Feverel.

"Mr. and Mrs. Don Gregg," Miss Withers observed to herself. "In happier days than this, I'll warrant."

Besides the desk, which was a litter of racing charts, records of past performances and breeding histories, there was nothing in the room except a low stool and—surprising enough—a good-sized telescope mounted upon a tripod.

"Heavens," Miss Withers exclaimed. "The man's an astronomer!" She crouched down and peered wonderingly into the shining instrument, but only the absolute darkness of outer space met her eye. Then it occurred to her to remove the eyepiece and she had better results.

She found that the telescope had not been aimed at the stars of heaven, but through a gap in the elms and into a neighboring valley about a mile to the south. With a little adjustment of the knob, before Miss Withers's surprised blue eyes there appeared a portion of brown trampled earth. As she peered, she saw a massive red truck come momentarily into her field of vision, with a sharp-toothed drag hitched on behind. She could even see the clods of earth fly up from the soft track.

There was a pause, and then came a colored boy perched on a fat bay, one hand leading—or being led by—a prancing, eager race horse who wanted more exercise than he was being granted.

Miss Withers stood up and nodded. Of course—she should have remembered that Beaulah Park was in this vicinity.

"What an excellent method of saving admittance fees!" she observed.

But this was not what she had come to see. She poked busily among the papers on the desk but found little which seemed to have bearing on the case at hand. There were no letters, no signs of pipe or tobacco.

As a last resort she looked underneath the green blotter. Here was only a folded announcement of the forthcoming Beaulah Park Grand Handicap, to be run on the next Saturday. On the margin of the announcement, in shaky handwriting, she found notations which at first sight bore no meaning for her.

Roberman says maybe $500 at 25 to one, 5 more at 20. . . .
Toby Kyte will take any amt at 20 to one. . . .
Bard says up to $200 at 30. . . .

Somehow Miss Withers suspected that this had to do with gambling and for lack of a better clue she folded the announcement and tucked it into her handbag along with the muddy briar pipe which still tantalized her.

She was about to raise the trap door when another idea occurred to her. She went back to the window and studied the flapping chintz curtain. Then she peered out upon the shingles, which sloped steeply away toward the eaves. It would not be impossible for a man to descend, or even climb up along that route, given a ladder to reach from the eaves to the ground, but it seemed highly improbable.

"Dear me," observed the schoolteacher unhappily, "have I got to resort to the idea of a secret passage at my time of life? Yet otherwise how could that Thomas person have eluded me?"

She received another shock at that moment. Looking from the window she noticed that a lively bit of drama was taking place in the green pasture. There Abe Thomas with a bridle in his hand was endeavoring to capture the fat mare, who kept dancing tantalizingly out of his reach.

Beside her, kicking up his heels in sheer delight at being alive, the red colt galloped.

"Then who in heaven's name have I been stalking up and

down the halls?" the schoolteacher asked herself. She received no answer.

Trembling with excitement Miss Hildegarde Withers descended again to the bedroom. She felt like stout Cortez when with eagle eyes he stared at the Pacific. Only, she reminded herself, in spite of Keats it wasn't Cortez at all, it was Balboa. Nor did he recognize the ocean at which he stared. But the "wild surmise" part of the poem, that was genuine.

She tiptoed softly across the room. The irregular breathing continued, and suddenly she remembered something that she had once read. She turned and stood beside the bed.

"Fake!" accused Miss Hildegarde Withers.

The breathing changed into a surprised gurgle. "Eh?" gasped Pat Gregg feebly.

"I said 'fake,' " she told him, not unkindly. "When you try to simulate sleep, see that your breathing is regular."

"Well," said the old man calmly, "I had to get rid of that officious fool of a doctor somehow."

"Yes, of course," she hastily agreed. "Tell me one thing and then I'll let you remain alone with your thoughts. Just who in this wide world would have any reason to kill you?"

"Kill me?" Pat Gregg tried to rise up in bed. "I've been asking myself the same question ever since my dog was poisoned. There's only one answer to that—Violet Feverel!"

"But she's in the morgue!"

He nodded. "Makes me rest easier to know that. You see, she's the only person who could gain by my death. She knew she'd milked the last cent out of me that she could. My son couldn't pay her alimony and she had him thrown in jail."

Miss Withers was mildly amazed. "Jail for debt? I thought that went out with Mr. Micawber."

"Contempt of court they call it," he told her. "The judge decreed that my son should pay three hundred dollars a month alimony or a flat settlement of fifteen thousand. He couldn't pay the monthly rate, so she got a judgment against him for the fifteen. But none of it did her any good—not even putting Donny behind the bars. Because he gets nothing from me until I'm dead!"

He sank back on the pillows. "It cheers me up to think

that even if I do cash in my tickets one of these days, she won't collect at the pay-off window."

"You're not going to die," Miss Withers comforted him.

"No? Want to make a little bet on that? But not right away, I hope. Got a lot of things to do."

"What things?" Miss Withers pressed.

He smiled. "I want to live to see that red colt in the pasture romp home in the Futurity," he said dreamily. "Like poor old Siwash tried to do and couldn't. And I want to get Siwash back from that buzzard of a woman—only she's dead, isn't she? Anyway, I want to see him run again. And I want . . ."

"You're a rather horrible old man," said Miss Withers.

He laughed in her face. "You don't think that really," he croaked. "I know women—like I know horses. Pretty much alike when you get to know 'em. You got to master both, a bit of spur and plenty of whip. That was the trouble with Siwash, he was such a blasted pet that the jockeys never had the heart to whip him into front position. Siwash was beaten many a time by poorer horses. . . ."

"And that's why you gave him away?"

He shook his head. "Siwash wasn't as bad as that—he was known as the best second-rate horse on the track. I figured that Violet and my son would race him, maybe build up a stable around him. Only that vain peacock of a woman . . ."

"Buzzard, didn't you say?" Miss Withers corrected.

"She was both," Pat Gregg went on. "She insisted on having Siwash broken to be a saddle horse so she could look like a picture in the rotogravure section when she went out to ride. Bah!"

He turned his face to the pillow. "Now I'm going to sleep," he dismissed her. "Want to get rid of this buzzing in my head."

"Pleasant dreams," said Miss Withers. Swiftly she leaned down and felt of the slippers which lay at the foot of the bed. They were cold—and yet the footsteps she had heard in the hall were not those of bare feet. It was not until too late that she remembered that Pat Gregg might have jumped back into bed with his shoes on.

Downstairs she found a plate of cold and soggy beans awaiting her. Mrs. Thomas brought coffee, lukewarm and thin. Then, as the woman waddled back to her kitchen, Miss Withers leaned toward the inspector.

"I've found something, Oscar!"

"Yeah? Well, so have I!" Somewhat bitterly the inspector lifted a dank and unpleasant-looking hair from the uneaten portion of his lemon pie. "And I've listened to the inside story of the great romance between Mr. and Mrs. Abe Thomas. It seems that they got married last year after half a lifetime of both working for the old man—a love story fit for *Real Confessions Magazine*, according to the way the old girl tells it. And she calls him 'Ducky'!"

"Who?" Miss Withers asked absently.

"Him—the little guy who's been chasing that she-horse ever since you went upstairs. . . ." The inspector pointed out through the window.

"You listen to me," Miss Withers insisted. "Oscar, you remember the cupola and its open window? Well, it rained last night—but just now I sneaked up there and found that the curtain was dry and unstained, and the papers on the little desk the man keeps up there were not even disturbed!"

"Well?" The inspector pushed back his chair. "What of it?"

"*This!*" she snapped. "Pat Gregg was locked in his room where he had an attack of apoplexy sometime early this morning, according to the doctor. Anyway he had no reason to climb to the cupola and open the window. Yet the only entrance to the cupola is through that bedroom, and since the rain stopped the cupola window has been opened!"

"Huh?" The inspector frowned heavily. "Well, couldn't it have been Thomas who opened it, after he broke down the door?"

She shook her head. "There wasn't time enough, even if he had an urge for fresh air and a view of the countryside. We heard the crash of the door and only a few seconds later the little man burst past us crying for the doctor."

"That's right," Piper admitted. "But somebody could have hidden up there before the old man went to bed last night—somebody who waited until this morning after the rain, opened the window for some fresh air, and then slipped down and . . ." Piper's voice died away. "But why should a midnight prowler want fresh air, and how could he hand his victim a dose of apoplexy? It doesn't add up."

"It will, before we finish with this case," she told him. "We're at a dead end now and these beans are soggy. Suppose we go back to town."

Surprisingly enough it was Mrs. Mattie Thomas who protested most loudly against their departure. "I feel so much safer with you folks here," she insisted. "If you'd only stay the night—or at least until the nurse gets here."

The schoolteacher shook her head. "But the nurse should arrive soon——"

Mrs. Thomas bridled. "Dr. Peterson insisting that Mr. Gregg needs a nurse, with me ready and willing to smooth his pillow! I'd work my fingers to the bone for him." She waved a fat and languid hand in the air.

Abe Thomas, who had finally corralled his mare, was less insistent. "If you got to go, you got to go," he admitted. "All the same I don't like the look of things. I wish—I wish Master Don was home."

"By the way," Miss Withers pressed, "you both knew him as a child. What sort of person is Donald Gregg?"

"A fine young man," said Thomas quickly. "If only he could get the curse of gambling out of his soul. He'd gamble on anything, like his father. Only he's unluckier, if that's possible."

"Unlucky at cards, unlucky at love," observed the inspector dryly. "Young Gregg seems to have been born with two strikes on him."

"Doesn't he!" agreed Miss Withers. She faced Abe Thomas. "You say that you're not addicted to gambling on the horses?"

"Me?" He laughed. "I know too much about the game. It's a mug's racket. If a man could plunge once, win, and then stay out he'd be all right. But nobody can—it all goes back to the bookies." Mr. Thomas's face expressed a fine scorn for the sport of kings. "Look at the old man upstairs—doctor won't let him go to the races any more so he has a watchtower built and a telescope installed just so he can see the finish line at Beaulah Park. Me, I put my money where it belongs, in the bank."

"*Our* money, Ducky," corrected the fat woman coyly.

"Ours then," Abe Thomas amended. "Now if you folks want to be driven back to the station . . ."

As they climbed into the station-wagon again, Miss With-

ers looked thoughtfully back toward the Gregg house, h[
mind filled with question marks. Up the pasture slope s[
noticed a red colt standing under a Golden Transparent app[
tree and stretching his neck toward the unripe fruit. There wa[
tall ladder leaning against the upper branches, but you[
Comanche was not aware of the purposes to which a ladd[
might be put. Miss Withers, on the other hand, was.

A few minutes later she was jolting back toward the c[
in a half-empty day coach. The inspector was fretting. [
ought to have stayed in town," he insisted. "Lord only kno[
what the boys have been doing on the Feverel case. Just n[
luck to have some fresh newspaper laddie stumble on t[
thing and spread it all over the front pages. . . ."

"This case will not be washed up as easily as all tha[
Miss Withers pointed out. "Oscar, what do you know abo[
betting on the races?"

He looked at the schoolteacher with amusement. "G[
the bug, Hildegarde? Going to plunge on the big handic[
next Saturday? The best thing for you to do is to foll[
Thomas's advice and keep away from the bookies. Or if y[
must bet, put your money on the favorite to show and y[
can't lose much."

"Don't be silly!" was her rejoinder. "I just wanted [
know."

"Don't kid me," Piper told her. "You've got the yen, [
can tell. Better stick to teaching kids their A B Cs, Hildegarde[

"Indeed?" She glared at him. "If I did that, where wou[
you be?" And they rode the rest of the way into Gra[
Central in silence.

New York City stagnated under the weight of a Sund[
afternoon, with even the asphalt of its deserted streets si[
zling peacefully in the hot sun. The inspector was mu[
relieved to find that no extra newspapers were being hawk[
on the corners. Evidently the death of a solitary equestrienn[
had not awakened the curiosity of bored city editors. "Which[
said Piper fervently, "is a break."

Miss Withers found herself propelled toward a taxica[
"What next, for heaven's sake?" she queried.

The inspector lit a fresh cigar. "Hildegarde, haven't y[
begun to wonder, during the events of the forenoon, ju[
what, who, where and why is the lad named Don Greg[

Well, we're going to ask him a couple of questions. That's why I told the driver to take us to alimony jail. . . ."

They came down Thirty-seventh Street and drew up before a drab and ancient building—four stories of faded red brick which wore a tenement-style fire escape down its front and heavy iron lattice-work at every window.

"'A home away from home,'" quoted Miss Withers. "Cheery place, isn't it, Oscar?"

"You should have seen Ludlow Street Jail before the rats gnawed it to pieces," Piper told her. "The alimony-dodgers think this's a palace compared with that."

They went up the steps, through an open gate, and rang a bell.

After a long wait the door was opened by a guard in a blue uniform. He needed a shave and looked very unhappy.

"We want to see Donald Gregg," said the inspector. "And don't tell us he isn't in!"

The guard tried to shut the door in their faces. "This isn't visiting hours," he announced.

"I happen to know that it *is* visiting hours," Piper snapped back. "Come on, open up!"

"I—I'll tell the deputy warden," said the guard. The door closed and he was gone a long time. Finally he returned, looking more unhappy than ever.

Behind him was a man in plain clothes, equally unshaven and still more lugubrious of countenance.

"I'm the deputy warden," he admitted. "Sorry, but you can't see Mr. Gregg."

"And why the hell not?" demanded Piper, who had stood about enough. He flashed his badge.

"You can come in if you want to, Inspector," said the deputy. He swung the door wide.

The hallway smelled of strong soap, of cabbage, tobacco and humanity. They went up one flight of stairs and through a long room filled with uneasy easy chairs and tables. Here a few men in their shirt sleeves were playing cards or reading newspapers. They all looked as if they had headaches. In one corner a large blue-black Negro was singing to the accompaniment of a cigar-box ukulele:

> "Write me a letter,
> Send it by mail. . . .

> *Send it in care of*
> *Birmingham Jail,*
> *Birmingham Jail, love,*
> *Birmingham Jail,*
> *Send it in care of*
> *Birmingham Jail. . . ."*

All the eyes in the room focused upon Miss Withers an the inspector, vacantly yet defiantly. It was hard for Mis Withers to realize that these men were not criminals, tha few of them had ever stood before a judge and none of ther had seen a jury. They were locked up here because thei ex-wives had seized an opportunity to get back at them fo unpaid alimony.

At the far end of the recreation room was a tier of cells each fairly comfortable in spite of the open bars at the door The deputy warden indicated the farthest one, which showe only a shower curtain pinned across the door. On the showe curtain were lettered the words—"Do Not Disturb."

Piper lifted the curtain but the cell was empty. "Well where is Gregg?" he demanded.

The deputy warden swallowed. "That's what we'd like t know," he admitted. "He belongs in here. . . ."

"But he broke out?"

"Not exactly," the deputy hurried on. "You see, las night was Saturday night. I went out to a show and so di some of the guards. We left Milton, the guard who let yo in, in charge. 'Long about midnight, he says, a deputy sheri came to the door with a writ for Gregg's release. Seems hi alimony'd been paid up and it was okay for him to go. So Mi put the writ in the desk and let the prisoner go. . . ."

"But I don't see——" Piper exploded.

"Well—I came back after Milt had been relieved. checked up and figured everybody was here, on account o this curtain we let Gregg hang over his door to keep out th light. It wasn't until this morning that I found the writ and noticed . . . I noticed . . ."

From his pocket the deputy took an official-lookin document signed by a judge of the Court of Appeals. " noticed that Judge Bascom signed his name like he neve signed it before, and the seal——"

The inspector snatched the document and displayed it t

Miss Withers. "The seal," he announced sarcastically, "is made of pretty red wax, but it reads 'Sacred Order of the Sons of Ananias'! You can buy 'em at ten cents a dozen at any trick and magic store on Broadway!"

Back in the recreation room the blue-black Negro was mournfully singing:

> *"Oh, if I had the wings of an angel,*
> *Over these prison walls I would fly,*
> *I'd fly to the arms of my poor darling . . .*
> *And there I'd be willing to die. . . ."*

6

Horse of a Different Color

"Anyways," said the deputy warden, "he's flew the coop."

Inspector Oscar Piper drew a deep breath. "Did you send out a general alarm—notify all radio cars, ferryboats, railroad stations . . . ?"

The deputy warden shook his head sadly. "He got out of here about midnight, and by the time we discovered that the writ wasn't kosher he'd had plenty of time to get across the river into New Jersey. And there's no extradition for the offense of contempt of court. This is just a dis'plinary jail, not a penal institution," he went on to explain. "It's almost impossible to get out-of-the-state police to co-operate with us just to pick up a missing prisoner. Besides, we figured he might come back after he'd attended to some private business or other. . . ."

"How I should hate to remain sitting upon a red-hot stove until young Mr. Gregg wanders back to alimony jail," Miss Withers observed.

"Well," decided the inspector suddenly, "I'll authorize the general alarm for Gregg. There's extradition to cover the crime we want him for!"

"For which we want him," corrected Miss Withers absently. "But Oscar, even if Don Gregg is Suspect Number

One, I wish you'd make haste slowly. I have a feeling that he isn't far away, but if you make a loud noise you'll send him scooting."

"He's got to be found, all the same," insisted Oscar Piper.

Miss Withers told him that she would rather find the deputy sheriff who had appeared out of nowhere and freed the prisoner so handily. Piper seized upon the idea.

"Say, that's right! Who was he?"

The deputy warden didn't know. Milton, the hapless keeper who now awaited suspension or worse, was hardly more helpful. By dint of much questioning the inspector managed to build up a figure slightly less shadowy than nobody. It seemed that the stranger had been of medium height, had worn a hat and dark overcoat of blue or black, and was chewing gum. "That's all I remember," he insisted. "I wasn't feeling so well last night."

"Or were you feeling too well?" Miss Withers cut in. She remember her first impression—that the keeper and his charges had all appeared slightly hangoverish when she came in.

"Well," said Milton slowly, "we're not as strict here as most jails, and that's a fact. But it's my idea that Gregg knew he was going to be sprung, and he got the other boys to sort of cut up a bit and maybe get me rattled. They make a drink out of potater peelings and stuff, and they must have slipped some of it into the ginger ale I was drinking. . . ."

"Good thing you kept your eyes open," Piper said. "It was Saturday night in the jail-house and all of the boys were there raising merry hell, but still old eagle-eye here noticed that the deputy sheriff wore a hat and a coat. Wonderful!"

Milton frowned, scratched his head. "He looked like a deputy sheriff and he talked like a deputy sheriff—and he flashed a badge."

"We could pick him out of a million with that description," the inspector pointed out warmly. "Probably the badge was a tin shield with 'Chicken Inspector' on it. So all we have to do is to look for a medium-sized guy in an overcoat . . ."

"Who chews gum," Miss Withers concluded. "I'm surprised at that. I rather thought he'd have smoked a pipe." She gave Milton an innocent glance.

"A pipe? Say, that reminds me—he *did* smoke a pipe.

Threw away the gum while he was waiting for me to bring down the prisoner and lit a terrible-smelling old hod."

"Fancy that!" Miss Withers said softly and followed the inspector through the dismal portals and out into the street again. She put her hand upon his arm as he was about to dash off in the direction of the nearest telephone booth.

"Before you have young Gregg arrested for the murder of his ex-wife, don't you think it would be a good idea to find out if it *was* murder?"

"Huh?" That brought the inspector up short. "Good Lord, Hildegarde, you yourself tipped us off. . . ."

"I was only guessing, and I'm not the medical examiner," she reminded him. "How about getting a report from Dr. Bloom?"

The inspector spent a busy five minutes at the telephone. "The case is still pretty much at a standstill," he reported as he emerged from the booth. "No word from Bloom yet—we might as well drop in on him on our way uptown."

"After all, there's nothing like a social cup of tea at the morgue, is there?" Miss Withers agreed. They hurried to that grim building above the East River where life and death overlap.

There was a short wait and then Charles Bloom, veteran medical examiner for the Borough of Manhattan, came out of the back room and closed the door carefully behind him. Miss Withers wrinkled her nose at the faint odor of formaldehyde and wished she were elsewhere.

"Nice of you both to drop in," said Dr. Bloom, blowing his nose heartily upon a square of fine Irish linen which showed both a monogram and a ragged tear. "Just finished—want to have a look?"

Piper shook his head. "Well?"

Dr. Bloom nodded. "It was murder, right enough." He rolled something thoughtfully in the palm of his hand. "One of the neatest jobs I've seen for some time. I'm writing down the cause of death as internal hemorrhage caused by rupture of the main throat artery with—with this!"

He showed them what was in his palm—a tiny pellet of lead slightly flattened.

"What? Killed with a BB?" gasped Piper.

The doctor nodded. "Just an old-fashioned, ordinary BB shot, made to be fired from a kid's air rifle."

"But the wound—there wasn't a wound on her!" Miss Withers cut in incredulously.

"I didn't say there wasn't a wound, I said none was apparent," Dr. Bloom explained. "With a missile so small there's often no exterior bleeding, and the wound was no larger than a pin prick. But that's how the job was done, and death was almost immediate. Exact time of death—well, it must have been about three quarters of an hour before I first examined the body, say approximately quarter of six this morning."

Miss Withers was dubiously shaking her head. "It doesn't ring true," she insisted. "How could the murderer be sure he'd hit a vital spot with a toy weapon like that?"

Bloom was moved to laughter, stroking his wispy beard. "Vital spot? Dear lady, it's worse than that. I'll guarantee that there is no other spot on the body where Violet Feverel could have been shot with a BB and killed. Or even badly injured, except in the eye. No ma'am, that BB had to strike her throat just as it did in order to harm her. The killer played a long outside chance. . . ."

"And had hell's own luck behind him," Piper observed.

Miss Withers remembered something else. "Doctor, did you happen to notice that the dead girl had something gripped in her hand?"

Bloom nodded. "You have sharp eyes! Yes, there were a few reddish hairs, horse hairs I'd say offhand. Looks like she felt herself falling and grabbed at the horse's mane to stick on."

"That would mean that the shot was fired while she was mounted," Miss Withers said thoughtfully. "Which makes the marksmanship all the more remarkable, doesn't it? All the same . . ." She subsided.

The schoolteacher was somewhat annoyed at the inspector's jubilance as they came out of the morgue. "I see it all now," he somewhat optimistically announced. "Violet Feverel was in the habit of taking out her horse at that hour. Gregg knew it. And since all riders in the park take the same general route along the bridle path, he knew where to lie in wait for her. Somewhere he got hold of an air gun and as she rode up toward the viaduct he rose out of the bushes which cover the slope and—bingo! Then Gregg does a quiet sneak——"

"You're referring to young Don Gregg, I presume?"

"Who else? Naturally he had a grudge against the woman who had kept him in alimony jail for months. His first thought on getting out was to pop her off. He shot from the bushes and was out of sight before she hit the ground. . . ."

Miss Withers shook her head. "No, Oscar. The killer came down and stood beside the dying woman."

"Huh?" Piper was incredulous. "Then—there were footprints?"

She shook her head. "By the time I got there the path surrounding the dead girl was pretty well trampled by the flat feet of your radio officers."

"Then how in the dickens . . ."

But she didn't want to tell him, not yet. The briar pipe which reposed in her handbag was her ace in the hole, to be displayed at the proper time and place.

"Guesswork, Oscar," she said. "Where are you off to?"

"I'm going to take this taxicab to the nearest eastside subway station," explained the inspector wearily. "Then I am going to take a subway train down to headquarters. I am going to light a cigar, put my feet on the desk, and then send out a drag-net for Mr. Don Gregg that will bring him in if he's halfway to China!" He grinned. "Is that okay with you?"

"Godspeed," said Miss Hildegarde Withers. But she climbed swiftly into their waiting taxi. "You won't mind walking to the subway, Oscar?" she called out through the top of the door as she rolled away. "You see, I have an appointment with the only witness to this murder."

Somehow the excessive quiet of Sunday afternoon in Manhattan did not extend to the dark and aromatic confines of Thwaite's Academy of Horsemanship. In their box stalls the boarded horses moved restlessly, neglecting the hay which hung over the sides of their deep mangers. Across the alley the hacks fretted against the narrow sides of their stalls, pawing at the worn floor boards beneath their bedding. One of them, a sympathetic little gray mare known to her child riders as "Salt" because her disposition was that of the salt of the earth, raised her wise old head and whinnied shrilly.

Even Satan, the black tom whose manner usually indicated that he considered this stable his, from the tiniest mouse to the largest horse, had withdrawn after the unfathomable manner of his kind to the farthest corner of the harness room where he crouched beneath a saddle and waited.

Came the voice of Maude Thwaite: "Bring Siwash out, Highpockets!"

The colored boy quavered uncertainly: "I dunno, Mis' Thwaite. . . ."

"Bring him out, I say!"

"Now, Maude . . ." began the little veterinary surgeon placatingly.

"Hurry up!" commanded the woman, her voice harsh as broken glass. And Highpockets led the big red horse out of his box stall.

"Put that twist on his nose!" snapped Mrs. Thwaite. Highpockets protested again. "I can't do that, Mis' Thwaite. This Siwash horse and me—we're pretty good pals. . . ."

"Don't be a fool! Do as I say!"

Shaking his head, Highpockets slipped a curious instrument over Siwash's nose. It consisted of a short loop of rope run through a hole in the end of a stick of wood.

Still Mrs. Thwaite was not satisfied. "Around his upper lip, you fool. And twist it so he can't break away!"

Shaking his head again the colored boy tightened the twist. Siwash bobbed his head and his ears swung back against his neck. . . .

"Latigo, get the strap!" commanded Mrs. Thwaite.

But Latigo Wells shook his head. "I ain't paid to do that," he objected. "Besides, I—I got work to do in the front office." He stalked forward down the runway. As he reached the hall which led to the office he was almost trotting and beads of sweat stood out on his face.

Once in the office he threw himself down in the swivel chair. From the top of the desk he took his guitar and struck a very sour chord.

"Damn that old heifer to hell!" he prayed fervently. "For pure unadulterated meanness . . ."

He took a deep breath and shut his eyes. A succession of sad and weary chords sounded in the lonely room, and then he began—

"*Good-bye, old Paint, I'm a-leaving Cheyenne....*
Good-bye, old Paint, I'm a-leaving Cheyenne....
I'm leaving Cheyenne and I'm off for Montan' ...
Good-bye, old Paint ..."

In spite of the singing Latigo could hear the voice of his employer shouting, "Go on, do as I tell you!"

But Highpockets didn't want to wield the strap. "You don't understand," he was half sobbing. "This big sorrel horse, he's just like a brother to me...."

"Hold him then!" said Maude Thwaite through clenched teeth. "I've got to be the only man in this place, as usual!" And she thrust the rope twist back into the hands of the colored boy. Then she took up the strap which he had thrown aside.

Siwash, eyes staring, nostrils twisted away from his big front teeth, danced sideways. But the cruel rope around his lip tightened....

Sparks flew from the cement floor as he pawed with his front feet. "Kick, will you?" said Maude Thwaite. "I'll teach you to kick, you red bastard!" Which, to a horse whose ancestry could be traced back to one of the first Arab mares imported into England, was a singularly ill-fitting appellation.

She took up the length of heavy strap and with front teeth biting into her upper lip until she could almost taste her own blood, Maude Thwaite swung it across the rump of the red horse.

Siwash reared against the twist and vented—from injured pride rather than from the pain—a shrill and almost human scream.

"Maude, don't you really think ..." began her husband, backing against the farther wall.

In the front office Latigo Wells gritted his teeth and then swung more loudly than ever into the later verses of the ancient ballad of the range....

"*I'm leaving Cheyenne, I'm off for Montan'....*
Good mornin' young ladies, my hosses won't stand ...
Good-bye, old Paint——"

He broke off suddenly, glad of any interruption, and went to the front door. Back at the rear of the stable Maude Thwaite swung the strap again, with all her strength.

Siwash screamed and tried to lash out with his hind legs. Again the woman promised that she would teach him to kick. "Maybe with half the hide burned off your back you'll learn some manners," she gasped. Again she raised the strap . . . and Siwash winced in anticipation, half crouching on his hind legs.

But the brawny arm of Maude Thwaite stopped short in midair. "Hit him again," promised a cultured if not too calm voice just behind her, "and I—I'll stick this pitchfork into you!"

Mrs. Thwaite whirled to stare into the face of an embattled spinster whose blue eyes now flamed green and chill. In one hand Miss Hildegarde Withers held aloft a pitchfork as if it were a javelin, the sharp tines gleaming wickedly.

"I mean it," she finished. Latigo Wells, who lurked behind her still clutching his guitar, knew that Miss Withers spoke the truth. So did Thwaite, who backed still farther into the shadows.

For a long, long moment the two women stared at each other. Maude Thwaite spoke first. "At your time of life I'd think you'd learned to mind your own business," she said, her voice a little dry, a little throaty. Her eyes flickered doubtfully.

"I happen to be a member in good standing of the S.P.C.A.," said Hildegarde Withers. "Apart from that anything that involves a poor dumb animal is my business—*so put down that strap!*"

Maude Thwaite put it down.

Instantly Highpockets loosened the twist and Siwash burst past him and into his empty stall. His heels kicked twice against the side wall, sounding hollow as a drum.

Mrs. Thwaite smiled with a certain amount of difficulty. "I can understand how this looks to you," she said, her voice spreading with honey. "But there never was a horse who didn't need a sound beating once in a while. And Siwash just tried to kick and bite me at the same time when I was saddling him."

"Since his owner is dead," Miss Withers said evenly, still clinging to the pitchfork, "I don't see why you found it necessary to saddle him."

Mrs. Thwaite's smile was even more strained, but it still showed. "I was going to have some pictures taken mounted on Siwash," she explained. "For our advertising booklet. My husband rented a camera. . . ."

She pointed to a heap of wreckage which Miss Withers with difficulty identified as the remains of a Graflex and a flash-gun. "Siwash just missed my husband and got the camera," she explained. "I considered myself perfectly justified in using Siwash—after all, his board bill hasn't been paid in three months."

"He's still not your horse," Miss Withers pointed out. "He belongs to Violet Feverel's sister now, and I shall use my influence with that young lady to have him taken out of your hands at once!"

"Splendid!" said Mrs. Thwaite. "But first you can tell the young lady who has inherited this red demon that his board bill is over two hundred dollars!"

"One hundred seventy-five," said Latigo Wells feebly.

"Hmm," murmured Miss Withers. "That's a lot of money for a horse."

At last Mrs. Thwaite agreed with something. "Especially for an outlaw," she snapped. "Siwash is beautiful and he has lovely gaits, but he's just plain outlaw. . . ."

"Since when?" inquired Miss Withers, borrowing a phrase from her current crop of young hopefuls at Jefferson School.

"Well," said Mrs. Thwaite, "he's been worse today, but I always said he had a mean streak in him. Didn't I, dear?"

Thwaite hurriedly came forward, insisting that his wife had talked of nothing else but Siwash's hidden traits.

"You didn't happen to notice a spot of dried blood on his flank, did you?" inquired Miss Withers casually. "Today, I mean."

"Certainly not . . ." began Mrs. Thwaite. Even Latigo shook his head. But Highpockets burst in.

"I sho did, ma'am—and that big red horse, he didn't like it when I sponged him off, neither. . . ."

"Well, if all you experts will get together and make an investigation," Miss Withers snapped, "you'll find that Siwash is carrying a bullet under his skin. Which, though I admit I'm nothing but a rank outsider, would seem enough to make even a pet horse cantankerous when bumped."

"Nonsense . . ." began Mrs. Thwaite. But her husband had stepped into the stall and was gingerly approaching the nervous thoroughbred. He touched the horse's side and Siwash winced.

"Sensitive, surely," he muttered. "But there's no wound!"

"Blood doesn't drip from heaven," Miss Withers told him. "It comes from a wound—sometimes from a very tiny one."

Thwaite polished his glasses and tried again. "There's inflammation anyway," he announced. "Highpockets, go get my kit out of the office!"

"I know you'll do all you can for the horse," Miss Withers continued happily, "because of his late mistress. Miss Feverel was a very lovely girl, I understand."

There was a faint sniff from Maude Thwaite, but the little veterinary nodded. "Beautiful . . . charming . . ." he said. "One of the most——" He stopped short and licked his lips. "Or so she seemed. Not that I'd know . . ." he laughed nervously.

"Wouldn't you?" Miss Withers pressed on wickedly. Thwaite's neck had turned a bright red as he leaned against the horse, but his wife stepped into the breach.

"Whoever told you that there was anything between my husband and that Feverel girl was a liar," she said. The honey was all gone from her voice and the glance she gave Latigo was not pleasant. "They were seen together only during the time we were schooling Siwash to the saddle and naturally my husband rode out on the bridle path with Miss Feverel on the days when I couldn't go. . . ."

"Naturally," said Miss Withers. "By the way, Mrs. Thwaite, where were you at quarter of six this morning?"

There was another long pause, this time a pause which snapped and crackled.

"I was in my bed, in my bedroom upstairs," said Maude Thwaite angrily. "Where else would I be?"

Miss Withers looked toward Thwaite, who was already beginning preparations for the minor operation on poor Siwash. "Is that right, Mr. Thwaite?"

He looked up startled. "What? No—I mean yes. I really don't know, I mean to say . . ."

"Your windows, Mrs. Thwaite, open out on the street?" went on Miss Withers.

"Yes," snapped the woman. She looked longingly at the

strap which lay beside her as if she could think of another use for it.

"You didn't happen to notice that as usual your earliest rider was Miss Violet Feverel, did you?" the schoolteacher went on.

"I did not," snarled Maude Thwaite. "Not until I was awakened by the quarrel between Violet Feverel and her sister. They made noise enough to wake the dead."

Miss Withers digested this information. "Thank you very much," she said. "Oh, by the way, are you a good shot with an air rifle?"

Maude Thwaite suddenly went stiff as a poker. "I'm a good shot," she admitted through lips like cardboard. "But when I shoot I don't monkey around with popguns!"

"I got it!" Thwaite suddenly cut in upon them. He came out of the stall, rolling in the palm of his hand a tiny pellet of lead slightly flattened. "Nothing but a BB, after all. But it must have felt big as a cannon ball to old Siwash, for it was lodged in a nerve center." The veterinary seemed to find it very funny. "Haw!"

Mrs. Thwaite felt she had stood enough. She faced Miss Withers suddenly. "Are you a police officer?" she demanded.

"Not exactly. . . ."

"Then I must ask you to come back someday when we're not so busy," she was told. "Latigo, will you be good enough to show Miss What's-her-name out of here?"

Miss Withers put down the pitchfork which, until this moment, she had clutched like grim death.

"I'll be back," she said softly. And she followed the young man to the door.

He eyed her with respect. "Say, how did you get wise to that fact that Thwaite made eyes at Miss Feverel?" he wanted to know.

"Simple as A B C," Miss Withers told him. "Given a little man with a waxed mustache and a big dominant wife—let a beautiful girl come into the picture . . ."

"Listen," Latigo said seriously, "don't get Miss Feverel wrong. She may have lived a fast life among her own ritzy friends, but down here at the stables it was Siwash and nobody else she was interested in. There was never an icier dame in the world than she was. And she wouldn't have touched Mr. Thwaite with a ten-foot pole. . . ."

"Maybe his wife didn't know that," said Miss Withers. She leaned closer to the bronzed young westerner. "Promise me one thing, young man—if that woman tries any more whipping parties, let me know."

Latigo nodded. "But you don't need to worry, ma'am. Mrs. Thwaite knows her stuff. After she's got a horse well broken she never is very mean to him. Why, I've even seen her give sugar to her pets—oftentimes to Salt, that white mare over there. . . ."

Miss Withers looked where he pointed. "Hmm . . . one of the hack horses, eh? What a difference between her and Siwash!"

Latigo laughed. "You think so? Well, Salt came to this stable a year and a half ago looking better than Siwash does. She'd been a crack polo pony. But eighteen months of hacking sort of brought out her ribs and brought down her spirit. . . ."

Miss Withers's clear blue eyes clouded. "Life is rough on horses, as it is on people," she admitted. "We all have to be broken. Even that fresh-faced sister of Violet Feverel's—she has to face it. . . ."

The schoolteacher's gaunt and kindly face was bland. Latigo nodded. "Plenty of spirit in that little filly," he said.

Miss Withers smiled. "Then you did witness the scene between the two sisters! You know, I rather like you for not talking about it!"

Latigo fidgeted. "I got to be getting back into the stable. . . ."

"Of course you have," Miss Withers counseled. "I don't suppose you have much time for the gayer things of life—girls and so forth."

"Well, I dunno . . ."

"I only thought," the schoolteacher sailed calmly on, "that there's a little girl who is in need of a friend right now. I mean Barbara, of course—Violet's sister. I happened to find out that she thinks you're a pretty nice young man. . . ."

"Awk!" said Latigo. He rubbed one shoe against the other, staring thoughtfully at the ground. He gulped. "Say—that's right. Barbara didn't laugh, like the others did—at my Sunday suit. I mean, the night her sister asked me to come up to her apartment. I thought—well, I was mighty tickled with the invite. But when I got there I found out all they wanted was for me to sing cowboy songs and I didn't have my guitar."

"A word to the wise!" quoted Miss Withers happily and took her departure.

For a minute she hesitated on the corner. It was getting late in the afternoon, and her meals and toilet had been most sketchy this day. Moreover, she knew that at home a little muzzy-faced dog named Dempsey was by now awaiting her impatiently, with dinner and a long walk foremost in his mind. But something else came first. She was on the hot scent of murder and could no more turn aside than she could have allowed that strap to fall once more across the red thoroughbred's glossy back.

So it was that Miss Hildegarde Withers came hurrying into the lobby of the Hotel Harthorn. As she debated whether to be announced or to go directly to the apartment she noticed a brightly clad and familiar figure standing near the desk. It was Eddie Fry, puzzled and disconsolate.

"Miss Foley says she is so sorry," the clerk was intoning, "but she can't see anyone today."

Foley—of course, that was Barbara. Somehow Miss Withers liked the name far better than Feverel. She came up beside Eddie and nodded brightly.

"Never mind," she said cheerily, "the girl has had a great shock."

"Yeah?" Eddie looked dubious. "It shouldn't be such a great shock to lose a half-sister that you haven't seen for fifteen years or so. I can't figure what's got into the kid. She wouldn't let me go down to the morgue with her and now she won't let me see her. . . ."

Eddie thrust both hands deep in the pockets of his topcoat, which seemed to have been cut out of a material designed originally for horse blankets.

"G'bye," he said hopefully. But Miss Withers was not so easily discouraged.

"Young man," she began, "even if Barbara doesn't want to talk to you, I do." She half dragged, half led him toward a settee. "Don't you realize Barbara feels guilty about you? Her sister is dead—and Barbara took you away from her."

"Wait a minute," protested Eddie. "You got it all wrong. I was the boy-friend as far as going places was concerned, but with me Violet was always an icicle. Down at the stables among

her horsy friends she was different. But I never got to first
base. It was just see her to the door, that's all there is, there
isn't any more. So when I meet up with her kid sister, who is
as good looking as Violet ever was and friendly besides . . ."

"You wanted to marry her!" concluded Miss Withers.

Eddie shrugged. "I know," he began to apologize, "but
everybody gets married once in a while. And she is a cute
kid."

Miss Withers turned her blue eyes upon him. "As a
gambler you were willing to take a chance?"

He nodded. "Then," said Miss Withers, "I wish you'd
give me some advice about betting."

Eddie grinned. "You too? That's just what Violet said a
week or so ago. Seems like she got a tip on a certain horse
running at Beaulah next Saturday and she wanted to know
how to put down a lot of dough on him without spoiling the
odds. . . ."

Miss Withers dug in her handbag, finally producing the
announcement of the race with its penciled notations which
she had filched from the desk of old man Gregg. "Can you
tell me what this means?"

He frowned. "Bard . . . Kyte . . . Roberman. . . ." He
nodded. "That's easy. Those babies are big-time bookies at
the Beaulah track. No pari-mutuel up there, you know—all
bets are made with bookmakers. Evidently somebody was
interested in the big race next Saturday and spent some time
checking up to see which bookie would give the best odds on
a large wad of dough put down on the line."

"You couldn't tell me the name of the horse?" Miss
Withers pressed. Eddie frowned. "It's a long shot, certainly,
to get those odds of better than twenty-to-one." He was
thoughtful for a moment. "At present quotations I'd say the
horse would be Santa Claus, Prince Penguin, or maybe Wallaby. The others are all better nags and lower odds."

Miss Withers studied the list of horses on the front page
of the announcement. "Easter Bunny, Verminator, Toy Wagon,
Santa Claus, Head Wind, Tom-Tom, Good News, Prince
Penguin and Wallaby," she recited thoughtfully. "What kind
of horse is Santa Claus?"

Eddie warmed up a little at the idea of being asked for
expert opinion. "Lady, Santa Claus needs six reindeer to pull
him around the track," he told her. "If you're set on betting

in the handicap put your money on Head Wind to show. He's the favorite and you can't lose much."

"Was Head Wind the horse Violet Feverel asked you about?" Miss Withers went on.

Eddie shook his sleek head. "She had a wild tip on a rank outsider," he told her. "A plug that's never even raced on the flat in this country and one that hasn't done much since he fell down in the big English steeplechase. His name is Wallaby and for some reason or other Violet was set on betting her shirt on him. Seems like some guy who owed her some money paid it and then tried to borrow it back to bet on that horse, and so she thought she might as well plunge herself."

"I see," said Miss Withers, who did not see at all. "Perhaps Violet was fond of wallabies. As one race track fan to another, what horse would you advise me to plunge on next Saturday?"

Eddie was thoughtful. "Well, you see it's like this. . . . I'm betting Toy Wagon to place because when I was a kid I had a toy wagon and"—the young man grinned—"I'm not always such a scientific better after all. You got to play your hunches in this game."

"We all have to play our hunches," said Miss Withers thoughtfully. "Sometimes even when we haven't got any hunches." She looked up and saw that the brightly clad young man was moving away.

"Where are you going?" she wanted to know.

"I'm playing a hunch right now," he came back. "I think Babs really wants to see me and I'm going up and knock on her door. If I can talk to her . . ."

Miss Withers thought fast. "Young man," she said with one of her most meaningful glances, "do you want to help or injure the police in this murder investigation?"

He looked surprised. "Me? But what have I got to do with it?"

"Nothing, I hope," said Miss Withers. "But after all, you are a suspect. You were paying a good deal of attention to Violet Feverel and then suddenly you transferred your affections to little Babs. . . ."

Eddie's face hardened subtly, showing an expression of complete woodenness. "So that's how you figure it?"

"No," said Miss Withers heartily. "I'm just telling you

how it might look. After all, you and Barbara both claim to have been in each other's company at the time the murder was committed."

"Yeah?" Eddie countered.

"Yes. And so it would create a good impression if you co-operated with us all you can. Right now I'm faced with a problem which is right up your avenue, as the slangsters put it. I've got to know why it was that Mr. Pat Gregg made these notations about the odds on that horse race. And I want to find out if he placed the bets or changed his mind. Can you help me?"

"Well," admitted Eddie Fry, "I know Toby Kyte pretty well. He's a square bookmaker. He might tell me. . . ."

"Good!" said Miss Withers. She almost shoved the young man out of the lobby. "Don't let any grass grow under your feet and if you find out anything report to me at this telephone number. After all—if we discover anything that leads us to the real murderer, that will clear you—and Barbara!"

"Yeah," admitted Eddie Fry, still somewhat unconvinced. "That's right, it will, won't it?"

He wandered out into the street again lighting a cigarette. For a moment Miss Withers stared after him, shaking her head. Then she turned, and avoiding the clerk at the desk, she went back to the elevators.

Hesitating for a moment she pressed the bell of what had been Violet Feverel's apartment. She pressed it hard and long, the sound dying away in vibrating echoes. There was no answer, there was no sound of voices or of scurrying footsteps, and yet Miss Withers was ready to swear that the apartment was far from empty. There was an atmosphere of tension filtering through that closed door—an eerie air of poised and breathless waiting. . . .

She rang again, holding her thumb on the button for a long time. Then she knocked, calling softly—"It's I—Miss Withers. . . ."

Just as she was about to try for a third time the door opened in her face. There was Barbara Foley, innocent and smiling. She had changed from her white lace evening gown to some gay green and lavender pajamas which the school-teacher guessed had belonged to her sister Violet.

"Come in!" she invited. "I didn't answer because I thought

it was Eddie." The girl had needle and thread in her hand, and over her arm were a couple of light silk stockings.

Miss Withers entered the long living room and looked about her. The smile on Barbara's face was a little too open and a little too set.

The schoolteacher sniffed.

"I—I was smoking," said Barbara quickly. She crossed to the window and threw it wider. "Violet never liked me to, but my nerves are jumping like anything."

That was no lie, as Miss Withers could see for herself. She sank into a comfortable chair and took off her hat. "I thought it was time that you and I, child, had a heart-to-heart talk. . . ."

"Yes, of course," said Barbara. She drew up a straight chair and perched on the very edge of the seat. "I've been thinking and thinking, but I've told you all I know. Are you—have you learned anything?"

"I don't know, but I think so," Miss Withers said half to herself. She was staring at a near-by ash stand.

"It's not as if Violet and I had been brought up together," the girl was rambling nervously on. "I didn't know her very well, not really. And I wouldn't have come to her here if I had had any other home to go to. . . . All the same I've been trembling ever since I got back from that dreadful place where they took her."

Miss Withers nodded sympathetically. But her eyes were still glued to the ash stand and to what it bore in the tray. She looked over at Barbara, her blue eyes sad and doubtful.

"I hate to see a girl your age smoking," she suddenly broke in. Barbara looked surprised.

"Why—just a cigarette——"

Miss Withers got up and went over to the ash stand. "I didn't really think *you'd* been smoking this," she said taking up a still-warm tobacco pipe in her fingers. "At least not while you were doing anything as feminine as needlework."

There was a brittle silence, during which the girl took a long and shuddering breath. Her soft lips parted. "I wasn't smoking it," she admitted. "But——"

"Better ask the young man to come out of the closet," Miss Withers suggested sweetly. "We'll have a three-cornered heart-to-heart talk."

"There's nobody in the closet——" Barbara began. She

wasn't lying, because at that moment the kitchenette door opened and a man came into the room. He was a plump young man and might have been handsome if his face had not been so pale, and if his expression had not been faintly pouting. Over one arm he carried a dark and mud-stained blue overcoat which he immediately tossed onto a chair.

He kept one hand in the pocket of his jacket and his lips were pale and gray. Miss Withers blinked foolishly at him for a moment. This was a surprise. Even without getting up to look in the bottom of the bird-cage she recognized this young man. "Good afternoon, Mr. Don Gregg," she said. "It's high time you were joining us."

He didn't say anything but he took his hand out of his jacket pocket.

7

Bogey-Man

Miss Hildegarde Withers let the air from her lungs in a deep sigh of relief. She wasn't sure what she had expected the young man to pull from his pocket, but it certainly was not a harmless-looking tobacco pouch of yellow oiled silk.

His eyes flashed from the schoolteacher to Barbara, who was leaning stiffly against the back of her chair, and then back to the pipe which Miss Withers was clutching. "I'll take that if you're not using it," said Don Gregg. She gave it to him.

"This lady is from the police," said Barbara quickly—almost too quickly.

Somehow that set the key of the scene in the mind of the schoolteacher. Barbara wasn't looking toward Don Gregg. Her face showed no trace of softness or sympathy. Yet the single sentence had declared her colors as definitely as though a flag flaunted itself overhead. It was impossible, it was ridiculous—but so it was.

The three stared at one another. "Not exactly from the police," Miss Withers finally broke the ice. "If I were, it would be my duty to place you under arrest, young man."

"What for?" Gregg wanted to know.

"How do I know?" Miss Withers snapped back. "Jail-breaking, resisting an officer, parking in front of a hydrant, inciting to riot . . . possibly for murder. For the murder of Violet Feverel, in case you haven't heard. There's a warrant out for you now, or there will be in a few hours."

Don Gregg gave up trying to light the pipe. He made a sudden movement toward the front door and as suddenly stopped.

"This isn't a trap," Miss Withers said hastily. "So don't go jumping out of any windows."

"If it isn't a trap then who told you to come here?" And Gregg looked suspiciously at Barbara.

"Sit down, young man," Miss Withers ordered. "It's my turn to ask questions. The first one is—who or what inspired you to come here? I should think that after what happened this morning this would be the last place in the world where you'd want to be found."

Don Gregg didn't sit down but he leaned against the back of a davenport. "I didn't know," he explained. "I hadn't heard—until Miss—Miss——"

"Foley," said Barbara, not too gently.

"Miss Foley told me. About Violet, I mean. . . . Being found dead on the bridle path and all that sort of thing."

Miss Withers nodded. "So? You had no idea that your ex-wife was dead, so you dropped in to pay a social call? Naturally your first thought on getting out of jail was to pay your respects to the one person who would be most likely to have you sent back there?"

"I had to talk to her," said Don Gregg stubbornly. "So I came right up here. . . ."

"You got out of jail around midnight last night," Miss Withers reminded him. "And now it's five o'clock in the afternoon. Took you some time to get from Thirty-seventh Street to Seventy-ninth, did it not?"

"I've been here awhile," blurted out Don Gregg. "And besides, I didn't say I came right here after I got out of the hoosegow. I came here after I left the place where I slept last night."

"And where was that?"

"The Park Turkish Baths on Sixth Avenue, if you must know," Gregg told her. At Miss Withers's look of amazement he continued, "Were you ever in jail? No—well, you ought to try it. Even alimony jail is no Ritz-Carlton. The first thing I thought about when I got out, even before seeing Violet, was to get that place soaked out of me. The smell of it, and the feel of those gray blankets that they never wash, and the yellow soap that chaps your hands . . ."

"I can imagine," Miss Withers put in hastily. "You wanted to feel clean, is that it?"

She was watching, not Gregg, but the girl. Barbara seemed strangely uneasy, as if waiting for a bomb to go off under somebody's chair.

Gregg nodded. "After the steam and the rubdown I went to bed and pretty near slept the clock around. I left the place and came over here expecting to find Violet. . . ."

"I came upstairs after going down to—to the place where they've got my sister, and here he was," admitted Barbara. "I knew who he was but he didn't know me," she went on to explain quickly. "Violet hadn't ever told him she had a sister so much younger——"

"And named Foley," Miss Withers put in. "Naturally not. And what was the first thing Mr. Gregg here said to you?"

Barbara frowned. "The first thing? Oh—as I came in the door he rose up in his chair and said, "Vi, old darling, you're going to listen to me or I'll tie a knot in your white throat . . . !"

"Which would make it very clear that, like Mr. Thomas earlier in the day, this young man mistook you for your sister. And moreover that he had no knowledge, guilty or otherwise, of your sister's death."

"That's the way I figured it too," said Barbara Foley calmly.

Miss Withers stared at the girl sharply and then nodded. "For a young man who could break out of jail it would be no trouble at all to break into an apartment," she said.

"I didn't break in, I still have my key to this place," Gregg retorted. "And what makes you think I broke out of jail?"

"Why——" Miss Withers blinked. "The people at the jail seemed to have a suspicion that everything wasn't exactly 'kosher,' as they so aptly put it. By the way, who was the friend who posed as a deputy sheriff and got you out on a fake writ?"

A look of wide and complete surprise crossed the face of Don Gregg. "A fake writ? I don't know what's in your mind, but I tell you I never saw that guy before. They told me at the jail that everything was okay and I'd been sprung." He rose from his chair. "You mean—I wasn't legally freed?"

"Correct," Miss Withers snapped. She was growing a little annoyed with the complete and transparent innocence of everyone connected with this case. "And when this obliging stranger got you out of the jail where did he take you?"

"He left me at the door," Don Gregg insisted. "And drove—I mean rode away in a taxi."

"It must have been a Boy Scout doing his good deed for the day," Miss Withers remarked, not without a strain of sarcasm. "Of course, you can describe this Good Samaritan?"

Don Gregg tried again to light the pipe. "Sure—sure I can. He was a big, dark chap with a black mustache and a scar across his cheek."

"He wore horn-rimmed glasses too, did he not?" Miss Withers wanted to know. This young man avoided her eyes.

Gregg thought for a moment. "That's right, he did. But how did you know?"

"Everybody knows that," Miss Withers returned. "It's the same imaginary person who commits most of our crimes. Every witness sees a big, tall man with a mustache and a scar and glasses. It's the Bogey-Man, beyond a doubt." She paused. "The description is more than interesting, because until you gave it I was wondering if perhaps you had not borrowed that blue overcoat from the deputy sheriff who got you out of jail." She pointed to the coat on his arm. "It so evidently was made for a man much smaller than yourself . . . but if he was so tall and formidable . . ."

Don Gregg took his pipe out of his mouth and put it into his pocket. He rose suddenly, facing Barbara. "I'll be going," he said to her. "Thanks for the cup of coffee and . . . everything. . . ."

But Miss Withers also was standing. "Young man," her voice rang out, "you're lying like Baron Munchausen and you know it. But before you go, answer me one question and answer it truthfully. Remember, I'm a schoolteacher and I can spot a lie a mile away. Careful now; did you kill Violet Feverel this morning?"

"Of course he didn't!" Barbara put in indignantly.

"I'm not asking you, you're too good a liar," Miss Withers snapped. "Come on, young man!"

Don Gregg faced her without the slightest tremor of his eyelashes, without the slightest wavering of his gaze.

"I hated Violet," he said softly. "When I was rotting in jail I thought night and day about how I'd like to get my hands around her throat. But I don't mind telling you, or the police, or anybody else—as I told Barbara here before you came—*I did not kill her!*"

"Then you have nothing to worry about from me—or from the police either," said Miss Withers, gathering herself together. "I mean that, young man. If you're innocent I'm on your side of the fence and so, I'm sure, is this young lady." She shot a glance at Barbara ". . . Who, by the way," Miss Withers added, "had no sleep last night and needs it badly."

The schoolteacher stood beside Barbara, who began to protest. "But I'm not sleepy, really . . ." she began. The firm pressure of Miss Withers's hand on her shoulder broke off the sentence.

"Sure," said Don Gregg. "I'll go . . ." His voice too broke off. As he moved toward the door Miss Withers could not help noticing that there was a ragged tear across the lower part of his right trouser leg, a tear which had been somewhat sketchily mended with fine silk thread of a contrasting flesh color. The edges of the tear showed marks of black grease.

Gregg noticed her glance. "Caught it on the fender of a taxi," he explained. "I'm not used to traffic, you see." He displayed also a barked knuckle.

"New York traffic is terrible," Miss Withers agreed sympathetically, "particularly on a hot summer Sabbath when everybody is out of town." She sniffed. "Young man, I warned you not to attempt lying to me. But come on, let's take a ride."

Don Gregg stiffened. "What? Say . . ."

She faced him, still patient. "You're wanted for murder, are you not? And for jailbreaking besides. Well, it occurred to me that the best thing for you to do would be to come down to headquarters with me before you're arrested!"

Barbara rose to her feet protestingly.

"It'll create a good impression," Miss Withers urged. "And I have some influence with the police, a great deal of influence, I might say." She smiled brightly. "They'll be likely to ask you a few questions and then let you go."

Gregg nodded. "I'll go. But I don't know anything about what happened to Violet. She was probably mixed up with some gigolo, and . . . but that's not nice to say, is it?" He looked at Barbara apologetically. "So long, kid . . . and thanks for everything."

The girl followed them to the door. Her hair, to Miss Withers, seemed redder than ever and the pale skin more white. "Good luck," said Barbara Foley.

"Thank you, child," Miss Withers answered, though she knew that the wish wasn't meant for her. She let Don Gregg push on into the hall and leaned back toward the girl.

"You want to help solve this murder, do you not?"

Barbara stared at her. "Of course! But what can I do?"

"You can do a great deal," Miss Withers said. "Young men talk to a pretty girl very freely I've noticed. And when young men get jealous over a girl sometimes strange truths come to light. A word to the wise——"

"Wait!" cried Barbara. "I don't understand!"

"You have inherited a very pretty horse, down at the Thwaite stables," said Miss Withers. "Why not drop down and see Siwash one day soon. And keep your eyes open. . . ."

The girl nodded slowly, eyes narrowing a little. "Thank you," she said softly, and closed the door.

Don Gregg waited for Miss Withers down the hall. "I don't see why I have to——"

He was evidently a young man used to taking short cuts. "It is not necessary that you should," retorted Miss Withers. "I'm just a meddlesome old maid. But nobody ever got into any trouble through following my advice. And I'm advising you to spike the guns of the police—to come down to head-quarters with me. If you do, it will only be a short while before you're free to go up to the farm. . . ."

"What makes you think I want to go up home?" demanded Gregg.

"You ought to, if you don't," she said. "I have a feeling you're needed there."

Gregg laughed without humor. "My father's a great guy,

but he and I'd be in each other's hair inside of an hour," he said. "We don't get along."

They were going out through the lobby. "You seem to have trouble getting along with people, don't you?" Miss Withers went on. "I didn't want to ask you before that girl upstairs, but what was the real cause of your breakup with Violet?"

Gregg coughed. "She was an iceberg," he said slowly. "Violet only thought about dollars and what dollars could do for her. It's not nice to say now, but I'm not going to pretend I'm sorry she's dead. She'd been spoiled by seeing her own face looking too pretty in too many magazines."

"And you couldn't get along. . . . Was it another man?"

He shook his head. "I told you Violet was an iceberg. Funny we couldn't get along, at that. Because we had so much in common—we were both of us madly in love with Violet!"

He was still a little hesitant as they came out into the street. "You're sure this isn't going to get me behind the bars?" he asked. "I don't suppose they can hold me on the alimony rap now, with Violet dead. But the murder charge . . ."

"You leave that to me," Miss Withers assured him confidently. "If you're innocent you have nothing at all to worry about." And she waved for a taxi.

A car whirled up alongside the curb, but it was not a taxi. To Miss Withers's amazement it was a small green Ford roadster, the seat filled by two brawny officers and a riot gun hanging forbiddingly across the rear window.

Two officers slid out of the car with guns drawn.

"What, again?" the schoolteacher snapped. "Are you two hired to haunt me?" Miss Withers recognized her acquaintances of that morning.

But Greeley and Shay were starting a fresh shift on duty with evident intentions to cover themselves with glory. "We've got instructions to pick you up, Mister Don Gregg," the sergeant orated. "Also, anybody who's with you!"

Handcuffs clicked on Don Gregg's wrists and Miss Withers found her arm in a tight grip. "Get to the phone, Shay, and tell 'em to send the wagon," ordered the sergeant.

"But we're on our way down to headquarters . . ." gasped Miss Withers. "You can't do this to me . . . !" She fumbled in her handbag but as she did so she remembered that her silver courtesy badge was safe in a drawer at home.

"Just can't we!" snapped the sergeant. "I had my suspicions of you this morning, lady. You were trying to cover up for this guy, you and that cur of yours."

"Idiot!" Miss Withers retorted weakly. But there was nothing she could do. She subsided into a stony silence as they were led back into the hotel lobby to await the arrival of the wagon. A crowd began to form on the street, rising from nowhere, like worms after a heavy rain.

Don Gregg didn't say anything until the Black Maria pulled up outside and they were being hustled across the sidewalk. Then, as he politely stood aside to let Miss Withers mount the steps ahead of him, she heard a soft murmur: "So you're the lady who's got all this influence down at headquarters!"

There were the usual gasps and jeers from the crowd as the two unhappy prisoners ran the gauntlet of gaping eyes. Miss Withers tried to look her best but realized that in spite of herself she appeared extremely hangdoggish, with a general air of being Mamie, Queen of the Underworld.

"G'bye, folks," said Sergeant Greeley cheerfully. "See you over to the precinct station."

Miss Withers looked forward to that meeting, but it was not to be. No sooner had the wagon drawn up outside the green lights of the police station than hurried orders from a cop on the curb sent it southward again, cutting across town.

"Stop looking so nervous," Miss Withers told her companion as they jounced around on the hard bench. "You've got nothing to worry about."

"I'm worrying all the same," Don Gregg grunted. But there was a new note in his voice and the schoolteacher realized that their joint predicament had joined them subtly together—a pair of captured outlaws. She smiled faintly and resolved to make the most of it.

"The officer on the rear platform can't hear us in here," she said softly. "There's one other question I'd like to ask you. It's this: Why didn't your father pay your back alimony and get you out of jail?"

There was a faint suggestion of a sneer on Don Gregg's face. "You don't know my old man," he said. "He never forgave me because I let Violet make a saddle horse out of

Siwash. So when Violet and I had our bust-up, with alimony so big I couldn't pay it, he told me I'd have to take my own medicine. Said he was tired of buying me out of jams with girls."

Miss Withers edged a little closer. "Go on," she urged.

"Well, the alimony started to mount up and when it got to almost nine hundred dollars that I owed Violet, she and her lawyer got me thrown into jail. My old man sent word that it would teach me a lesson to rot there for a while. And Violet— she was willing for me to die there."

"And then . . ."

"And then my old man raised the nine hundred dollars and gave it to Violet in exchange for a receipt promising to have her lawyer drop the claim. That was just a couple of weeks ago—but just as I was walking out of the jail door, a sheriff's man nabs me and drags me back in."

"But I thought your alimony was paid up?"

He nodded. "That's the racket. It was paid up until the day I went to jail, but all that time it had gone on mounting up. So Violet had a great joke on the old man and on me. She had the nine hundred bucks and I was still behind bars. Nice girl, Violet. Don't you think so?"

"I think," Miss Withers told him, "that you'd better get a pretty smooth alibi for the hour of Violet Feverel's death . . . for you seem to have had something of a motive for killing her."

Don Gregg seemed to feel that he had said too much. "You could have found this all out anyway," he amended hastily. "I told you the truth when I said I didn't kill her."

"All the same," Miss Withers suggested sweetly, "couldn't you produce some witness who was with you at the time of Violet Feverel's death—somebody at the Turkish baths, perhaps? It would make a great deal of difference. . . ."

But Don Gregg shook his head. "No, I couldn't—I mean I can't do that." Miss Withers shrugged and relapsed into silence.

The wagon stopped and the oddly assorted couple were hustled out and up the steps of headquarters. They went up two flights of stairs and down a long hall, with here and there a man in uniform giving Miss Withers a cheery good afternoon. But the grip of the officer on her arm was not relaxed. At last they stood in an outer office, inside a door marked

"Homicide Bureau." There was a moment's wait while a young man at the desk spoke into a telephone.

The answer came clearly through the door. "Drag 'em in," cried a weary voice. "Hurry up, Georgie, both Gregg and the dame."

Detective Georgie Swarthout looked up in wonderment. Then he grinned and ushered the prisoners through into the inner office.

"Oh, hello, Hildegarde," said Inspector Oscar Piper. "How'd you get wind of this so quick?" Without waiting for an answer Piper turned toward the young man in the door. "Swarthout, where's the dame picked up with this guy?"

"I," interrupted Miss Withers coldly, "am the 'dame,' thanks to the efficiency of your much-vaunted radio police!"

The inspector snapped straight out of his chair, a look of delighted and incredulous wonder lighting his face. "You—you don't mean to tell me that you got dragged down here in the wagon?"

Miss Withers nodded solemnly.

"Well, I'll be a . . ." Unfortunately the rest of the inspector's remark was lost in the excitement as he chanced to place the hot end of his cigar between his lips. Spouting ashes and rich Tenth Avenue curses he was still being racked with howls of laughter when Miss Withers took her fingers out of her ears.

"Glad you find it funny!" the schoolteacher snapped.

"I know—I know," gasped Piper. "Hi-Hildegarde, this'll teach you to steal a march on me."

"As if I needed teaching to do that," she snapped. "Well, you wanted to question this young man and here he is. I've already given him a rather lengthy third degree and I tell you that if you arrest him now you'll make a terrible mistake."

The inspector noticed that her left eyelid was moving up and down.

"Eh?" he said. "Why, yeah—yes, of course. Just a bit of routine, Mr. Gregg. A few simple questions."

"You'll excuse me," Miss Withers interrupted. "I've had my fill of police routine for today." She stopped at the door. "Do try to remember someone who can vouch for your alibi, Mr. Gregg," she advised. "Good evening to you—and I'll join the charming Miss Foley in wishing you good luck."

"Thanks," said Don Gregg doubtfully. And it wasn't until

some hours later, during a brief respite in the inspector's attempts at a mild third degree, that the young man made a surprising discovery. Rapidly he had been going through his clothes and searching also in the pockets of the muddy blue overcoat which did not fit him. Now he rose indignantly to his feet.

"I don't mind answering your foolish questions 'til the cows come home," he announced bitterly, "but when it comes to having my pockets picked . . ."

"What's this?" roared the inspector.

"When I came in here," insisted Don Gregg angrily, "I had a pipe in my pocket."

As was his habit, Dempsey, the wire-haired terrier, aroused his mistress at an extremely early hour next morning (Monday) demanding an immediate walk. Miss Withers patted his crisp curly forehead and told him to have patience. She bathed, donned her sober serge suit and made a sketchy breakfast. She sipped her coffee, though Dempsey trotted beseechingly from her chair to the door and back again. Luckily it was vacation time and there was no roomful of unruly little hellions for her to cope with. "I'd rather face a murderer any day," Miss Withers had often said.

With Dempsey bouncing ecstatically around her she took down his lead and snapped it on. As an afterthought she added the muzzle which he hated so fervently, and thus equipped the two of them went out into the early morning sunshine.

Much to his surprise Dempsey got more of a walk than he had bargained for. By the time they reached Forty-ninth Street near Sixth, his tongue was hanging out so far he nearly trod on it.

Miss Withers paused under an odd sign which hung above the sidewalk. She had seen the sign many times, but now she stopped and stared up at it hopefully. Like a great misshapen comma it hung—somehow she felt at the moment that it should have been a question mark instead. The name was in gold letters—"H. JASPER."

The shop was as small as the sign was large. There was a partition midway of the place and a counter ran forward to the show window. Behind this counter a freckled blond young man drummed his fingers on the glass.

"A gift for a gentleman?" he inquired.

Miss Withers shook her head. She stared at the crowded shelves. "It's just an idea of mine," she began, "but I need a little expert advice. I was wondering . . ."

From the back of the shop came the whirring of a lathe. By leaning over the counter Miss Withers could see the rounded back of a fat little old man in a black linen apron. He was holding a tube of hardened rubber against a whirling brush, now and then raising it to the light to study the polish it was taking. Faintly above the sound of the lathe came the words of the soft old love song—*Du, du liegst mir im Herzen*. . . .

"I would like to speak to him," said Miss Withers abruptly.

The young man with the freckles looked hurt. He made it clear that he himself was more than able to take care of any of her needs. "My uncle is very busy," he explained.

"I'll speak to him all the same," insisted Miss Withers. At length the old gentleman was prevailed upon to leave his lathe. He plodded to the counter, wiping the dust from his spectacles and exuding a strong smell of powdered latex.

"Vat iss?" he demanded.

Miss Withers tried vainly to pull Dempsey away from a succulent cigarette stub which he had discovered on the floor. It was a taste which he had inherited honestly enough from his mother, a winsome terrier bitch who had enlivened Miss Withers's adventures in murder on lovely Catalina Island two years before. Finally dropping the leash, the school-teacher laid upon the counter two rather similar-looking pipes which had been safely wrapped in her handbag.

"You make and repair pipes," she said. "I'm trying to find out something which may make a great deal of difference to someone—it may send a man to the gallows or save him. To come to the point, is there any way you can tell whether both of these pipes have been owned and smoked by the same person?"

"Hmmm," said Mr. Jasper. Uncle and nephew both bent over the counter. There were minutes of whispered colloquy, much nodding and many shakes of the head. Dottle and half-burned tobacco were dug out of each pipe and placed in separate little heaps on the counter.

At length the old man came back to Miss Withers. "You say it iss a matter of life and death, this detective business?" he inquired. "I hope it gives life, then. Because—it is very clear, what you ask."

"Go on!" she gasped.

Jasper took up the first pipe. "This," he began, "iss the pipe of a young man—or a man who has not smoked a pipe long. First, it is a cheap pipe. There iss inside a patent tube and a patent gimmick and a patent whatnot, all intended to make smoking sweeter." There was fine scorn in the old man's voice. "Foolishness! Such gadgets only trap the dirt so that it sours the pipe." He held the pipe up to the light. "Notice the shape—not curved and not straight. That shape was not on the market until a year ago, but since then it has been sold in all chain tobacco stores. They even give such pipes away with half a pound of tobacco.

"But more than that," he continued. "This young man, he does not much like a pipe. He would rather smoke the cigarette, because he is always letting his pipe go out. Not only iss the top of the bowl blackened and burned, but the cake does not go halfway down on the inside of the bowl. Again and again the smoker has filled his pipe, lit it . . . and let it go out. Also, he uses a strong Latakia tobacco which burns fast and bites the tongue of the heavy smoker. He iss nervous, ja. He bites with his teeth very hard here. . . ."

"I noticed the marks on the mouthpiece," Miss Withers agreed brightly.

The old man glared. "Mouthpiece? There is a mouthpiece only on an Oriental hookah and on a Bavarian student pipe. Such pipes as this—they have a *bit!*" He tapped the hard rubber. "A bit, and a shank, and a bowl rising out of the shank; that is all. Again, we know he is nervous because he raps his pipe very hard on all kinds of hard surfaces to get rid of the ash. Notice how the top of the bowl is chipped and worn away?"

"By rapping on stone walls—the same stone walls which do not a prison make, according to the poet," Miss Withers said softly to herself. So much for the pipe which she had filched from the pocket of Don Gregg. "And the other?" she pressed.

The old man nodded and picked up the other pipe. He held it gently, almost tenderly, as he wiped away the faint remains of dried mud.

"This is a different kettle of fish," said old Mr. Jasper. "This is a *pipe!*"

"But can you tell me anything about the owner of it?" Miss Withers begged. "Anything at all?"

The old man smiled. "Nothing, mine friend. Nothing except that the owner of this pipe iss probably a man of middle age; that he has traveled abroad; that he iss a man of excellent tastes with money to spend; that he is by turns thoughtful and careless; that he appreciates the fine things of life; and that he iss a chemist or comes in contact with chemistry."

Miss Withers gasped. "Is that all?"

"Well," admitted the old man, "there iss one more thing. This man has a denture—what we call false teeth."

"Do you mind telling me how you figure all that out from a pipe which looks just like the other one?" demanded Miss Withers.

The old man was delighted. "First, this pipe bears the stamp of the very small but very famous London pipe-makers, Weingott. They are located in the Temple on Fleet Street where few American tourists ever go. Few of these pipes are exported—I can swear that this one was not, for it bears a serial number which I, without difficulty, can recognize as meaning that the pipe was made to retail in England.

"This is a straight-grain briar type of the finest. It must have cost twenty, perhaps thirty dollars or more. A man does not commission a friend abroad to purchase a pipe of such value, particularly when it is so much a matter of personal likes and dislikes. That is why I can say our unknown man traveled abroad; that he is a man of excellent tastes with money to spend."

"But how could you tell his age?" Miss Withers wanted to know.

"Very simple. After this pipe was purchased, which could not have been more than a year or two ago, the owner had a silver band put on it. Since silver bands have been obsolete for a long time he was evidently trying to make this pipe look like some old favorite of his. Young men, you see, are more inclined to follow the fashions of the moment." He looked at the other pipe.

"Band? I didn't notice any band," the schoolteacher protested.

"That is where the chemistry comes in," said the old man with a smile. "The silver is very discolored and black. Sulphur, acids, a hundred things will tarnish silver this way."

"And the rest of it?" she begged.

"The owner of this pipe has an appreciation of the finer things of life because he smokes one of the finest tobaccos in the world—not the most expensive, but one of the finest." The old man indicated a brown paper package on his shelf. "Mixture Fifty," he said. "Smells like vanilla, tastes like heaven. To continue, the smoker is by turns thoughtful and careless because he has kept the cake well cleaned from his bowl always, yet has allowed coal tar to thicken inside the shank, not to mention the corrosion of the fine silver band. As for the false teeth . . ."

"I was wondering about those," Miss Withers admitted.

"That is the simplest point of all." The old man pointed to the rubber bit of the pipe, which was wide and flattened at the end. "This is the only type of bit that men with dentures can hold in the mouth," he explained. "Every pipe manufacturer keeps these in stock for each of his pipes, and I mineself make a specialty of fitting them to the favorite pipes of those smokers who have had to lose their teeth. . . ."

He smiled. "That is all I can tell you. But you can rest assured that the man who smoked the gadget pipe never touched this one—for he would have left the mark of his gnawing teeth and his careless hand. Nor did Silver Band smoke the cheap pipe—the tobacco would have burned his tongue red, the patent devices would have maddened him, and most important, his manufactured teeth would have had to clamp so hard upon this round narrow bit that a serious jawache before the tobacco was well burning he would haf developed!"

"Thank you," Miss Withers said fervently. She took back the two pipes and then, much to the amazement of the pipe expert, she scraped up the refuse which he had taken from each and made separate envelopes with penciled notations.

"It iss so important as that?" queried the old man wonderingly.

"You don't," said Miss Withers, "know the half of it!"

She took a taxi homeward, paused only long enough to feed Dempsey and lock him in the kitchen, and then she sallied southward toward Centre Street.

She found the inspector poring sadly over the morning papers. "Did you see it, Hildegarde?" he was complaining. "The stories are all right—the boys only dared to print what we gave them and that was little enough. But the headlines . . . Get this. 'POLICE STUMPED BY BRIDLE PATH MURDER' . . . and the *Mirror* of course makes a crack about Lady Godiva, under a head, 'BEAUTY ON THE BEAST'!"

"Never mind your press notices," snapped the schoolteacher as she leaned over the official desk. "What did you decide to do with young Gregg?"

Piper frowned. "You know, Hildegarde, I had to turn him loose. There weren't any holes in his story that I could pick, and if he did kill his ex-wife you'd think he would have a better alibi than just to say he was in the sleeping room at a Turkish bath. Besides, I checked with the boys at alimony jail and they said he hadn't an idea in the world that he was to be sprung that night. He'd actually ordered breakfast sent in from outside. . . ."

Miss Withers digested the idea of breakfast. "Of course, if you think I ought to keep him in the cooler we can pick him up," Piper said doubtfully. "He's going up to his father's place, he says. . . ."

"Let him go," Miss Withers said shortly. "Because he didn't have anything to do with the murder. He doesn't fit the description of the murderer!"

"Yeah? And where did you stumble on an eyewitness?"

"Why, I——" Being able to stall no longer, Miss Withers played her ace. "Oscar, the murderer of Violet Feverel is a traveler, probably middle aged, with money and luxurious tastes—he is thoughtful with flashes of absent-mindedness, he has false teeth, and is probably a chemist by profession or avocation. . . ."

"What's his name?" broke in the inspector eagerly.

"I haven't the slightest idea," said Miss Hildegarde Withers. She produced the two pipes. "From one of these, which I found buried in the mud where the body lay, I deduced all those details. With the help of a pipe expert, of course!"

"You what?" the inspector demanded.

"Deduced—like Sherlock Holmes, you know," said Miss Withers belligerently.

The inspector shook his head. "Hildegarde, you'll be the

death of me—you and your concealing evidence and making deductions and what not! Besides—how do you know that pipe wasn't dropped there by accident?"

She smiled. "The long arm of coincidence, Oscar? Impossible. Besides, the pipe was in the mud *underneath* the body. And your own men testify that the body was not moved until the medical examiner arrived and took charge." She shook her head. "No, Oscar—the murderer dropped that pipe as he murdered the girl on the muddy bridle path—and it will hang him!"

"We don't *hang* people in New York. We use the Chair!" Piper snapped. "And I don't suppose there's a chance that you're wrong, but all the same—this sounds like reconstructing a dinosaur out of one of his fossil toenails. If you're right, of course, it simplifies our work—both the dames are cleared right off the bat."

Miss Withers agreed brightly. "But we still need the woman in the case, Oscar. That's pretty Barbara Foley. Three men are making eyes at her already—Eddie the gambler, Latigo the lonesome cowboy, and Mr. Don Gregg. If I can stir them up about her they're certain to conflict and something is bound to happen. . . ."

Piper lit his cigar. "Hildegarde, you're a holy terror. Always stirring up something. Dr. Bloom was describing you the other night—said you were what doctors call a catalytic agent, stuff that you put in with harmless ingredients to make them explode. . . ."

"What a nice compliment," Miss Withers was saying. The expression on her face showed that she was internally purring. "Now if I can only succeed in making somebody explode . . ."

Just then the telephone buzzed. Piper snatched it up, barking, "Who? WHO? Yes, put him on. . . . Yeah. . . . Okay, okay, sit tight."

He crashed the phone and rose to his feet. "Hildegarde," he said solemnly, "it looks like you've succeeded."

"In solving the case?"

The inspector shook his head. "In making somebody explode," he said. "That was Latigo Wells, the lonesome cowboy, on the phone. Wants me to send a man up to Central Park to watch Barbara."

"Barbara Foley? But why, for heaven's sake?"

"Because a few minutes ago the girl appeared at the stable demanding to take Siwash out on the bridle path. Latigo tried to stop her and was over-ruled by the Thwaite woman. The cowboy sneaked out to telephone because somehow he's got the idea that little Babs is riding in her sister's trail, straight for the Last Roundup!"

"Hold on to your hats, boys—here we go again," muttered Miss Hildegarde Withers as she climbed into the squad car.

8

Lightning Strikes Twice

As they went up the slope toward the park gate Siwash bent his heavy-sculptured neck and touched a velvet muzzle to Barbara's leg, leaving a wet mark on the old pair of flannel slacks which the girl had pressed into service as a riding habit. He whinnied uneasily, remembering another morning. . . .

Siwash liked the soft feel of the bridle path underhoof. He tossed his head and waltzed sidewise, whinnying. His rider's hand was heavy on the rein, heavy and uncertain. The big red horse tried to be philosophic about it, but the ache to run was making him fairly tremble. Months of bridle-path cantering had not sufficed to erase the memory of those glorious mornings of breezing around the track, those tense and wonderful afternoons with the crowd roaring in the grandstand. He had learned a lesson too well.

Then, miracle of miracles, it happened. His rider, that pleasant young female human, gripped his barrel with her knees so that her heels touched his ribs and at the same time the reins tightened and then fell slackly on his neck.

Siwash plunged as if somewhere a bell had clanged, bounding furiously ahead in the ground-covering leaps that his long red legs were born to make. There was a short cry, presumably of encouragement, from his rider and the heels pressed more tightly against his belly. Here was a rider after his own heart, an understanding human who loved to race against time! Siwash put his head down, since still there was no restraint from the bit, and really demonstrated what a race horse can do when he puts his mind to it.

There was no touch of the bit on his mouth, for the excellent reason that Babs had dropped the reins to adjust her unaccustomed foot in one of the stirrups. Now the leathers were flung wildly in the wind as the paralyzed girl clung to the pommel with both hands and prayed. . . .

On they rocketed northward through the cheerful stretches of Central Park in the sunny morning. Bleary men dropped their newspapers and stood erect on park benches as Siwash went thundering by. A woman screamed somewhere and a dog yapped sharply. Babs could hear the yap of the dog very loud and clear . . . she wondered if it would be the last thing she would hear, besides the thunder of those hoofs beneath her. . . . "And there are so many things I want to do with my life," she cried inwardly.

They rounded a turn without slackening speed and Barbara saw that just ahead a uniformed nursemaid was wheeling a baby carriage across the bridle path. There was a second of horror etched forever on Barbara's memory—centered in the white face and gaping dark mouth of the nurse who was frozen to the handle of the baby carriage. . . .

Barbara couldn't scream, but she managed to shut her eyes. If she didn't see it, perhaps the inevitable tragedy would have no real existence, remaining forever in the nightmare world to be forgotten when she finally awakened.

Siwash swerved to pass the unexpected obstacle, but on one side was the nurse, on the other two bystanders who were dashing forward in an attempt to seize the sleeping child. The big red horse had no choice in the matter. As Barbara clung blindly to his back she felt a sudden tightening of his muscles and then there was a long moment poised in the air and Siwash came down on his slim forelegs, well on the other side of the carriage. Barbara's cheek received a hard bump from an arched rising neck. They were over the hurdle—over and away.

The girl now had her arms tight around his neck, a variation in riding form which puzzled Siwash considerably. He was ready for a signal to collect his pace, sensing that something had gone wrong at that last crossing. But no signal came. Instead there were shouts from behind, human voices quivering with fear and excitement. Siwash didn't know what the voices were saying, but he immediately caught the note of hysteria. Someone was chasing him. . . .

He lunged forward, faster than ever. The girl on his back, daring to breathe again, felt for the stirrup she had lost. She found it, lost it again. . . . "Eddie!" she moaned softly. "Somebody . . ."

Just ahead was the arch of the viaduct. Siwash, like all horses running with his eyes on the ground, saw the curving dark shadow and remembered what had happened here only yesterday morning. He shied wildly.

Babs, her weight mostly on one stirrup, gripped at his mane with both hands. The big red horse rocked awkwardly—and then suddenly his rider felt herself going off over his side, saddle and all. She struck the ground directly underneath him, and a dark gray curtain came down over her brain.

Central Park was calm and peaceful in the morning sunlight as the squad car from headquarters came tearing up the parkway. "I don't see anything wrong!" the inspector was saying.

They were heading northward. "What you don't see would fill a book!" Miss Withers snapped. "Keep going—and faster!"

At Seventy-second they saw a horse and rider galloping northward along the bridle path. "There she is!" cried the inspector.

"Look again," Miss Withers retorted. "Barbara Foley doesn't wear a blue uniform." It was a mounted officer. Miss Withers had seen a lot of mounted police in her day, but she realized that until this moment she had never seen one whipping his horse.

"It's Casey!" cried the driver of the squad car. "He must have got wind of something. . . ."

Piper pointed to the left and suddenly the squad car left the parkway, smashed through a thin railing and rolled across a lawn. Then a sharp turn to the right and they were on the bridle path, the speeding car swerving dangerously as its tires spun in the dirt. A moment later they were alongside Casey and his fat brown horse.

The mounted cop shouted incomprehensible things. They could catch the words "runaway" and "girl."

"Come on," roared Piper. The mounted cop swung from his saddle to the running board of the squad car. His horse galloped after the car for a little way and then snorted indignantly as he found himself left behind.

"Girl—going hell-bent," Casey was gasping. "Tried to catch her, but my horse couldn't catch up."

"If you boys weren't so sentimental about those horses you'd have been transferred to motorcycles years ago," Piper snapped. They careened around a corner where on one side of the crossing a little crowd had gathered around a hysterical nursemaid and a crowing, gurgling baby in its carriage. But the squad car did not stop.

Eighty-sixth Street—and there was a screaming of brakes. The squad car skidded to a stop and the pursuers piled out to see a girl lying sprawled in the shadow of the viaduct, a small, helpless-looking girl with tossed auburn hair.

Standing almost over her body was a big red race horse, his curving neck bent as he nosed softly but impatiently at her shoulder. He pawed at the ground with one delicate hoof.

Siwash moved aside as the newcomers came closer, stepping gingerly over the fallen girl. The inspector flung himself to his knees, Miss Withers beside him. Casey caught the trailing bridle and led Siwash out of the way.

"Is she—is she dead, Oscar?" Miss Withers's voice was harsh.

Piper put his fingers on forehead and over heart, then lifted an eyelid. He held up his hand. "Smelling salts, Hildegarde!"

They were produced and waved under the pinched nose of the girl on the bridle path. "Come on, come on," the inspector was saying under his breath. "Takes more than this to kill anybody by the name of Foley!"

"Sure!" agreed Casey. Then—"Stop it, you red divvil. . . ." Siwash kept on rubbing his sweaty nose against the blue shoulder, which was rough and very comforting to a worried and unhappy thoroughbred. Besides, Casey smelled of horse.

"She's out cold," Piper was saying. "We've got to get her to a hospital. Come on, help me lift her. . . ."

The driver of the squad car bent to take Barbara's shoulder. But the voice of Miss Hildegarde Withers cut in rudely upon the proceedings.

"There he goes!" she cried sharply. "Get him!"

The officers looked up to see a rustling of the bushes on the slope above them. Casey and the police chauffeur lunged forward as one man, swarming up the slope.

It was all over in a moment. A young man in a light flannel ice-cream suit was plucked back just as he was about to clamber over the wall to the transverse above. He was dragged down again, thrust rudely before the inspector.

"Well, if it isn't Mr. Eddie Fry!" Miss Withers greeted him cheerily, moving away from the horse who was trying to rub his nose on the small of her back.

"What in blazes were you doing here?" roared Piper. The young man opened his mouth but no sounds came.

"He was waiting for a street car, Oscar," Miss Withers suggested.

Eddie Fry, somewhat shaken, was pointing down at the girl. "She asked me to come here!" he insisted. "She called me up early this morning and said I was to wait here because she was trying an experiment. . . ."

"An experiment? Talk sense." Eddie found himself surrounded by an accusing circle of unfriendly eyes. Even Siwash seemed to glare at him.

Still he insisted. "She said she was going to try to trap yesterday's killer by re-enacting the crime and I was to wait here in case anything did happen. . . ."

"The experiment seems to have been a success," Miss Withers put in dryly. "Too much of a success, in fact."

Piper caught the young man's shoulder. "Gambling on another long shot, eh? Well, go on with your story—what happened?"

Eddie wanted to do nothing else. "I waited here," he rushed on, "because it was here that Violet got hers. For a long time nothing happened and I was beginning to think that the people at the stable wouldn't let Babs have the horse after all. Then I saw her coming, but she was just managing to hang on. When they got almost here the horse jerked sidewise and she went off, saddle and all. Zowie!" Eddie gestured eloquently.

Piper turned toward the big red horse. "That plug ought to be shot before he kills anybody else. . . ."

"No!" Eddie protested. "You didn't see what I saw, hiding there in the bushes. When Babs went off she fell right under the horse, and I knew I was going to see her brains knocked out by his hoofs. Only he stopped spraddle-legged, so as not to touch her. Then he nosed her as if he was trying to say he was sorry. . . ."

"Stop, you'll have me crying," snapped the inspector. "Put the bracelets on him, boys. We'll let him think up a better story behind the bars."

"It happens to be true—what he's saying," came a soft voice from the ground. Forgotten for the moment, Barbara was sitting up and pressing both hands to the side of her head. If she had voiced the conventional "Where am I?" nobody had heard her.

She tried to rise but fell back with a little groan. "Breath knocked out of me, that's all," she said. Miss Withers and the inspector each gave her an arm, and she stood up. "Please let Eddie go," the girl begged. "He's telling the truth."

Piper nodded. "Yeah? Then if you're telling such a straight story, young man, why didn't you rush down here when you saw the girl go off her horse? Why didn't you try to help her instead of scramming?"

Barbara looked at Eddie with the same question burning in her eyes. He looked down at the bridle path as if he expected an inspired answer to be written there.

"I thought she was dead," he said simply. "I saw the police car coming and I—I thought I'd better beat it."

Barbara's eyes clouded and the inspector burst forth with "Why, you chrome-colored . . ."

Miss Withers stopped him. "Oscar, you mistake common sense for cowardice. If that bulge at Mr. Fry's armpit means what I think it does, he had every reason to make himself scarce. The neighborhood of a supposedly dead girl is no place for a young man with a gun in his pocket. . . ."

"Well, I've got a permit for it!" interrupted Eddie Fry ungratefully. "Of course I brought a gun along—suppose the murderer had appeared and made a pass at Babs?"

"Sir Galahad in a purple shirt," Miss Withers murmured. "All the same," she continued brightly, "things might have been worse. This young lady isn't hurt seriously and it all seems to have been just an accident. . . ."

But the inspector wasn't so sure. He faced Barbara. "Say, who knew you were riding up this way?"

The girl shrugged. "There's only the one curving path,"

she pointed out. "You either ride in a circle to the right or the left and come back at the same gate . . ."

"Yeah, but what person in particular——" Piper was saying. He was interrupted by the sound of galloping hoofs. Up the path came a small gray mare bearing on her back a heavy stock saddle trimmed with silver, and in that saddle a lean young man with a long sad upper lip. Latigo Wells was out of the saddle before the mare had stopped.

"Miss Barbara—you all right?" he gasped.

Babs pushed back a stray lock of auburn hair. Strange, Miss Withers thought, that the girl had been conscious of her appearance only when this young man came on the scene. Barbara was even managing a smile.

"I'm just fine," she said. "Only I went on my nose like you said I would."

"Oh, like he said you would!" Piper rasped. "Maybe we got a prophet in our midst!"

"Whoa, Salt old gal." Latigo dropped the reins and his mare stopped. He took in the situation slowly, as if making a mental note of everything. Particularly did he stare at Eddie Fry, and there was no love in that stare.

"Accident, eh?" said Latigo. "Maybe so. It's easy enough to fall off a horse, particularly a race horse that can't forget how he was trained. But begging your pardon, folks, it's not so usual for the saddle to go off too. Let's have a look."

They all had a look at the saddle which lay beside the spot where Barbara had fallen.

"Nice accident," said Latigo, kneeling down. In his hand was the webbed cinch-band, which happened to be in two parts. "Fine time for the cinch to break," he said heavily. "Worn out—have a look at it, Casey."

The mounted cop took the cinch-band as the others gathered around. He whistled.

"Looks like the wear came all in one place, don't it?" Casey remarked. Latigo nodded, biting his lip.

"That's the kind of wear that could be made with a piece of sandpaper or a knife blade," the mounted officer continued. "It sure looks like somebody *wanted* you to take a dive off that big red horse, miss." Again Latigo nodded.

The inspector thoughtfully fingered the webbing. "When the horse shied, there was an extra strain on the band and she snapped?" He turned to Barbara, who was watching wide-eyed. "Who saddled this nag for you?"

"Why—it was the colored boy, the one they call High-pockets. He saddled Siwash. . . ."

"Nobody else there?"

"Everybody was there," Barbara went on. "You see, when I called up this morning to say I was coming down and take Siwash out, Mrs. Thwaite wasn't very eager to have me. But she couldn't refuse, because legally the horse is mine. When I got there Latigo tried to talk me out of it. But I said I'd ridden lots of horses on farms back home. . . ."

"Why were you so determined to break your neck, young woman?" Miss Withers wanted to know.

The girl stared at her wonderingly. "Why—you gave me the idea! You told me when you left the apartment yesterday that I'd inherited a horse and that I ought to go down to the stables. So I took the hint!"

"That's true," Miss Withers admitted. "But I didn't mean . . ."

"Well, I thought you did. Anyway, I had an argument with Latigo and Mrs. Thwaite settled it by saying that if I wanted to ride Siwash I could go ahead. She advised me to tie up the snaffle rein and just ride on the curb—the hard bit, you know. And her husband said to keep him to a trot. . . ."

"Go on," Piper told her. "Did she make any adjustments of the saddle or anything like that?"

Barbara shook her head. "No, but Latigo let out the stirrups for me. Then he rushed away somewhere and Mrs. Thwaite showed me the way to the park gate. . . ."

"I went to telephone you," Latigo said to the inspector. "Then I was afraid something might happen all the same so I went back to the stable and saddled old Salt to try and trail Miss Foley. . . ."

"Then everybody had a hand in getting you started on the ride, didn't they?" Piper asked the girl.

Barbara nodded, but Miss Withers cut in with "What difference if they did? This cinch or whatever it is could have been scraped and frayed at any convenient time yesterday or last night——"

"Yeah," interrupted Piper. "Provided the person who did it was a clairvoyant and knew beforehand that this girl was going to ride today."

He moved over to the squad car and opened the door. "Come on, Miss Foley, we'll run you home. You've had a bad shaking up."

But Barbara hesitated. Eddie Fry sprang into the breach. "If I'm not under arrest," he said, "I'd like to drive Babs home. My old bus is right up on the roadway."

The girl's eyes wavered from his eager glance to where Latigo Wells was methodically gathering up the horses' reins preparatory to leading them both back to the stable.

Her red mouth tightened faintly. "Thanks, but I'm not going home just now," she said. She went over and took Siwash's reins from the ex-cowboy. "I'll walk back with you," she said.

"Returning with her horse or on it, like the Spartan youths," Miss Withers told the inspector. They watched the big red thoroughbred as he ambled quietly along in step with the little gray mare.

The inspector frowned. "Casey, you might trail along behind and see that no more accidents happen to Miss Foley on the way home." He looked toward Eddie Fry. "As for you . . ."

Miss Withers whispered quickly in his ear.

"Huh? Okay. . . ." The inspector climbed into the squad car. "Home, James," he grunted. They moved noisily away in the direction of the parkway.

Miss Hildegarde Withers found herself alone with a very nervous young man in a loud suit. "I just prevented your arrest, young man," she announced, stretching the truth a little. "You owe me some information."

"I told you . . ." he began.

"Wait," she said. "It's about that gun in your pocket, for which you have such a nice legal permit. It's an air pistol, isn't it?"

Eddie looked blank. Then he took the gun out of his upper vest pocket and showed it to her. "Better protection than any air gun," he explained. "I need an automatic, because sometimes I bring home a big wad of money from the race track."

"You're sure it isn't an air pistol?" insisted the dubious schoolteacher.

He shot out the clip and showed her the thick, snub-nosed cartridges. She nodded. "Very well, I'll trust you to drive me home. On the way you can tell me what, if anything, you found out about the matter of those race-track wagers I asked you to look up."

It was little enough, as it turned out. Eddie Fry seemed sorry. "I thought I was going to wash up this case like nothing," he began. "But your idea was a fluke, lady. I called up a pal of mine who works for Kyte, the big bookmaker. Finally he got the boss to come to the phone. But it was a false alarm. . . ."

"What? You mean Gregg didn't phone him?"

"He phoned him all right," said Eddie. "Old man Gregg called Kyte a couple of weeks ago and sort of finagled around trying to find out the best odds he could get for a big wad of dough on the nose of a nag called Wallaby that's running next Saturday at Beaulah. Only he didn't place the bet with Kyte or anybody else because, if he had, the odds on that horse would have dropped and as it is they're getting longer every day. A dollar bet on him will bring you thirty if he wins."

Miss Withers nodded brightly. "And if he doesn't win?"

"You'll get nothing, of course," the young man told her wearily. "Except the sleigh-ride."

"That," said Miss Hildegarde Withers, "is the trouble with betting on the races."

They rode on for a few moments in silence, Eddie Fry bent glumly over the wheel of his little roadster. His foot was flat against the floor boards as they sped out of the park and southward. . . .

"No hurry," Miss Withers finally ventured to remark.

"There sure is," Eddie retorted. "I don't mind dropping you off, but then I'm going to get down to see Babs and have a good talk with her. That kid has got a lot of screwy ideas in her head."

"I wouldn't go to see her right away," the schoolteacher suggested gently. "Let her cool off a little. Besides, I think it's likely that she'll have a caller at her home."

"Huh?"

"I'm not a gambling man," Miss Withers said, "but it seems a sure thing to me that Latigo Wells will take her home after they leave the horses at the stable. Just to make sure she's all right, of course."

"Latigo Wells!" said Eddie, managing to make the name sound like profanity. "His hair is full of hayseeds."

"Hayseeds?" The word reminded Miss Withers of something. She saw a drugstore on the corner of Amsterdam Avenue and hastily ordered Eddie to pull up to the curb.

"I won't be a moment," she promised. She rushed inside and sought a telephone booth. Luckily she had change in her purse, and without more than the usual delay she heard the clicking of receivers on a party line in upstate New York.

A distant operator rang four short rings, again and again. Finally a woman's cheery voice chirped "Hello!" and the operator enunciated a crisp "Here's your party!"

"Hello, hello," cried Miss Withers. "Is this the Gregg home—is that you, Mrs. Thomas?"

It was nobody else. "This is very important," said the schoolteacher. "When did your husband leave for New York?"

"What? You mean Abe?" Mrs. Thomas gave a muffled laugh. "Why, Abe didn't leave for no place, he's right here!"

So he was, for he took the telephone. "When did you get back from the city?" Miss Withers kept on hopefully.

"Me? Say, I haven't been anywhere. Not since I drove back with you folks yesterday." The gloomy little man seemed oddly annoyed by the suggestion.

"By the way"—Miss Withers tried a new tack—"how is the sick man?"

"Mr. Gregg is lots better," Abe Thomas announced.

"So much better that he left the house this morning?" prompted Miss Withers. She waited breathlessly.

"Say, what's—— I beg your pardon. Mr. Gregg is up and around, but the nurse won't let him out of the house."

"Could you call him to the phone, then?"

She learned that Mr. Gregg could not descend the stairs to the telephone, in spite of his miraculous recovery. Her shot in the dark had scored a clean miss. "Then will you please ask Mr. Don Gregg to come to the telephone?" she said.

This time Thomas hesitated for a moment. "Mr. Don Gregg," he said distinctly, "is not here."

"Where is he then?"

Thomas didn't know. He insisted that he had seen neither hide nor hair of his young master these many moons. "His father is mighty anxious to see him too," Thomas added.

"Thank you so much," Miss Withers told him. She put down the receiver and said, ". . . for nothing!"

Weary and disappointed she came out of the phone booth. "At least I have Eddie," she reminded herself. "And he knows more than anybody has been able to get out of him yet."

But it was distinctly not her lucky day, for when she came out of the drugstore she found that Eddie Fry and his little roadster were unaccountably missing.

She came upon the inspector at his desk brooding over a meager assortment of clues. There was the tobacco pipe with the discolored silver band, a slightly flattened pellet of lead which had cut a girl's throat, and a garden hoe with a horseshoe oddly fitted to its blade. These were all.

"Having fun, Oscar?" she greeted him. " 'And all my toys about me lay, to keep me happy through the day,' " she quoted. "How are you doing?"

He shook his head. "No prints on any of this stuff, of course. Water kills 'em; so does mud. Hildegarde, we haven't got anything yet."

"Haven't we!" She told him about the bets which Gregg had not made on the forthcoming race at Beaulah Park. "The old man was all set to put a small fortune on a certain horse," she explained. "Something or someone made him change his mind."

"And you figure *that* someone is our murderer?" Piper shook his head wearily. "I can't go out and arrest everybody who didn't bet his shirt on the big race, Hildegarde."

"I know you can't," she said. "Anyway, you'd do better to arrest all the people in this investigation who have false teeth!"

"What?" The inspector grinned. "Still harping on what they told you about the pipe, eh? Supposing your hunch is correct—I can't go out arresting people wholesale and making them show their teeth. There was a time when you could spot a set of phony teeth a block away, but not any more. They're making them better. And what a story for the feature sections—" Piper snorted. " 'POLICE SEEK KILLER WITH TEETH AS FALSE AS HIS HEART' . . . no, Hildegarde. . . ."

"There ought to be a way of finding out without arresting the suspects and tugging at their teeth," the schoolteacher came back. "But meanwhile can't we look over our list of persons involved and figure out who might fit the description of the man who smoked that pipe I found under the body?"

Piper cocked his head on one side. "Yeah? Well, everything was general except the part about the teeth. He might be middle-aged, probably a man with money, world traveler, very nervous . . . luxurious tastes . . ."

"It could fit the old man, Mr. Gregg," Miss Withers suggested. "Though I didn't find any signs of tobacco, not even a pipe cleaner, in his desk."

"It could fit that Abe Thomas," Piper told her. "At least, he's the right age. You know, I don't like that gloomy little guy. He's hiding something—and remember, he said he drove into town in the morning and we know he left the farm before sunset. There's a break he made."

Miss Withers nodded absently. "Thomas is lying, certainly. But so are a lot of others in this case. No, we can't solve it by spotting lies. . . ."

"Only I can't figure out how Thomas had a *motive* to kill the Feverel dame," Piper continued soberly. "Maybe it was loyalty to the family, only I can't quite swallow that. Old man Gregg had a motive and so did the boy who was in alimony jail. Only the old man could hardly kill her and have an attack of whatever it was all at the same time. And the boy—we've checked his alibi. He really was in the Turkish bath that night—he was sleeping soundly in one of the cots at the time the girl was killed."

"Really?" Miss Withers looked surprised.

Piper nodded. "Him and a friend of his—a little guy who fits the description of the phony deputy sheriff. They had their rubdowns about two in the morning and the rubber wrapped them up each in a sheet and put them to bed in adjoining cots. They were still there in the morning. . . ."

"And they couldn't have got up and gone out, together or separately—and then returned?"

"The people at the baths said not," Piper admitted. "But they admittted business was pretty slack that night . . . so they weren't on their toes."

"It sounds like a genuine alibi," Miss Withers admitted. "They could easily have faked a better one than that. I always suspect a watertight alibi, Oscar. All the same . . ."

"I don't figure Mrs. Thwaite as the killer," Piper went

on. "Even though she wants that Siwash horse pretty bad. Seems that she's set on riding him in horse shows or something. Besides, she wouldn't smoke a pipe. . . ."

"Her husband might," Miss Withers retorted. "He's the sort of man who'd do what he was told."

"And if Mrs. Thwaite wanted murder done, she'd do it herself," Piper snapped back. "She wouldn't trust it to the little vet. As for your little friend Eddie, he has an alibi. He was with Barbara, they both swear. And Latigo Wells—where would the motive come in? Besides, he rolls his own cigarettes instead of smoking a pipe." The inspector shook his head. "No, Hildegarde, this murder is tied up in seventeen layers of smoke screens."

"I'd cut through them quick enough if I knew just who in this case wears false teeth!" Miss Withers insisted obstinately. They were interrupted as the outer door opened and a frowsy, plump little old woman poked in an ingratiating face.

Over one arm she carried a basket. "Apples today, gentleman? Nice apples?"

Piper fished in his pocket and found a dime. "Keep the apple, Auntie," he said kindly.

But Miss Withers's face wore an expression of ecstasy. She snatched her purse and produced two dollars. "I want to buy all the apples you have!" she announced.

She said afterward that it was worth the two dollars to see the look on the inspector's face.

9

An Apple for the Doctor

"Anyway," Maude Thwaite was saying, "I'm going to try it."

She was stalking up and down the office, her hands stuck deep in the pockets of her well-worn riding breeches. Her husband was engaged in the delicate operation of squeezing pomade from a tiny lead tube, which he then daubed thickly upon the twisted ends of his mustache. He leaned closer to the wall mirror.

"I don't know," he said dubiously. "He's not a jumper."

"Any horse can be broken to the jumps," the woman told him. "If he can't be schooled into form enough for the horse shows there's still the steeplechase meets. With his speed . . ."

"He's light in the leg," Thwaite reminded her. "That horse is racing bred—needs heavier bone to make jumps safely."

"If he breaks a leg it's his hard luck," the woman said. "You can't make an omelet without breaking an egg or two. Anyway I'm going to take that Siwash horse in hand and see what I can make of him."

"Wait until you get him, my dear," counseled her husband.

She nodded. "I'm going to get him, all right. Who's to stop me?"

"Who indeed?" broke in a clear New England voice. "Except perhaps the owner of the animal."

The Thwaites whirled to see Miss Hildegarde Withers framed in the doorway of the inner hall. "I hope I'm not intruding," she went on cheerily as she entered the office and sank gratefully upon a chair, depositing her bundle in her lap. "I went into the stable looking for Mr. Latigo Wells, and not finding him there . . ."

"See here!" began Thwaite angrily. But his wife gave him a look.

"Sorry I can't help you—because there's nothing I'd rather do than aid the police in this investigation," she intoned rather speechily. "But you see, Latigo asked for the rest of the day off. I think he said something about going to the dentist."

"Really?" Miss Withers smiled brightly. Her mild blue eyes peered around the room, noting the blank space on top of the desk. "How thoughtful of Mr. Wells to take his guitar along—I'm sure his dentist must appreciate the musical accompaniment."

Maude Thwaite looked at the desk top and then back at the schoolteacher. There was surprise and annoyance in her eyes and the faintly blue tinge of her complexion was deepening.

"I wouldn't be surprised," she remarked conversationally, "if Latigo sang himself right out of a job one of these days."

Miss Withers nodded. She could understand that. "I suppose you are a little annoyed with Mr. Wells for being so quick to point out that the cinch-band had been tampered with this morning," she said. "Casts certain reflections on the stable, doesn't it?"

Mrs. Thwaite smiled, showing a great many excellent teeth.

"Possibly," she admitted. "Provided there was tampering, which I won't admit until the police let me look at the saddle. But of course it must have occurred to the police that Latigo was awfully quick to notice things—almost miraculously quick unless he knew beforehand. . . ."

Miss Withers stared at the little veterinary who was twirling his mustache full steam. "Yes, I think that occurred to the police," she said.

"Well, it's clear enough," Thwaite broke in. "If you'd asked me I could have told you! Latigo's mixed up in this whole thing. Probably tried to get rid of the girl this morning because he thought she suspected him of the job yesterday. He was always making calf's eyes at Violet Feverel, until he found out she only looked on him as a stable boy. . . ."

"Rufus," said Mrs. Thwaite patiently, "did I tell you that Boots has a saddle sore? It needs attention."

He nodded. "In a moment, my dear. I tell you, that crooning cowboy could have killed Violet Feverel out of jealousy—he's not as innocent as he looks. You should have seen him gaping at her when she happened to wear a tight sweater one morning. . . ." There was a reminiscent look in the veterinary's eye.

He caught his wife's glance. "All right, I'm going," he said, taking up an instrument case from the floor. "But remember what I say, all the same."

Miss Withers promised that she would. "Have an apple before you go," she offered, opening the bag on her lap.

Dr. Thwaite took the red fruit, shined it on his trousers, and then, much to Miss Withers's disappointment, put it into his pocket. He said, "Thanks—not between meals," and hastily departed. Mrs. Thwaite declined an apple, but that was no disappointment to Miss Withers.

"You're awfully anxious to add Siwash to your string of horses, aren't you?" the schoolteacher plodded on.

Mrs. Thwaite was making visible efforts to be pleasant.

"Yes, I am," she admitted. "Not that he could ever be worth anything as a sprinter again—unless he was given a spot of heroin on the tongue before each race, and the judges are getting wise to that. But there's something about him . . ."

"You just naturally love him, don't you?" Miss Withers looked at the Thwaite woman and they both remembered the episode of the strap.

"I don't *love* any horse," snapped Mrs. Thwaite. "And nobody can say that I'm unkind to 'em either. When they begin to break down at hacking, I sell 'em to the glue factory, which is quick and merciful. Siwash has two or three years as a top saddle or show horse ahead of him and then I can hack him for a couple more. . . ."

"Perhaps Barbara Foley will have something to say to that," Miss Withers put in.

"Perhaps she will," Maude Thwaite retorted. "But I haven't seen any signs on her part of paying the back board bill. And when she led him in a little while ago, after he tossed her off, she swore she'd never ride him again."

Mrs. Thwaite made no effort to conceal a look of satisfaction. "Was there anything else?" she inquired.

"Not at the moment," Miss Withers answered. She rose to her feet. "I must be on my way."

"I wonder if you'd mind telling that detective out in the street," Mrs. Thwaite suggested, "that if he wants to shadow this place he might as well come right inside. He makes me nervous lurking out there."

"Really!" Miss Withers resolved to speak to the inspector about this blunder. Then from the outer doorway she saw that the man who loitered so inartistically across the street was not an operative at all—it was Mr. Don Gregg.

She withdrew hastily. "I think after all I'll go out through the stable," she said. Maude Thwaite stared woodenly after her as the schoolteacher hurried down the passage into the stable.

Highpockets went past her, carrying an armful of straw. Miss Withers asked him the whereabouts of Dr. Thwaite and the colored boy nodded in the direction of the rear stalls.

The veterinary was leaning over the gate of Siwash's stall. He looked up and grinned as the schoolteacher approached. "Watch this, it's going to be good," he said.

In one hand he held the apple which Miss Withers had

hoped to see him bite—or refuse to bite. "Here, boy, here you are," he was saying.

Siwash tossed his head dubiously and skittered sideways. "Come on, eat it!" commanded the doctor.

Siwash came closer and then danced away again. "Finicky, eh?" Thwaite tossed the apple into the horse's feed box. "He wouldn't take it from my hand, but watch him now!" said Thwaite.

Miss Withers, puzzled but pleased at this unexpected evidence of friendliness, drew closer. She saw the big red thoroughbred nose the apple, then pick it up daintily between his teeth and munch. . . .

"Watch him!" gasped Thwaite, bubbling with repressed laughter. "Just watch him, that's all. . . ."

Siwash chewed. Suddenly he stopped chewing and the apple fell in slobbered fragments to the floor. His ears waggled and he shook his head savagely. It is impossible for a horse to spit, but Siwash came as close to that act as he could. His teeth ground together and he reared high in the air. Great tears rolled out of his brown eyes.

Thwaite was roaring with laughter. "Quinine!" he finally managed to explain. "A tablespoon full of quinine stuck into the core of the apple. . . ."

Miss Withers looked blank. "I didn't know he was sick," she said.

"He wasn't—but he is now!" Thwaite gasped. "Did you see the look on that nag's face?"

Thwaite didn't see the look on Miss Withers's face. "You mean that was a practical joke?" she asked calmly.

He nodded. "That red horse is so particular about what he eats you'd think he was human," Thwaite explained. "It isn't often I can fool him."

"Hmm," said Miss Hildegarde Withers. "By the way, where did you attend public school?"

Thwaite looked blank. "What?"

"You were never a pupil at Jefferson School, on the east side?"

He shook his head. "Too bad," said Miss Withers, somewhat wistfully. She was thinking of a two-foot rule that she kept in the top drawer of her desk.

"By the way," said Thwaite in a low voice, "no use saying anything to my wife about this, you know. She's an excellent woman, but she does take everything too seriously. . . . I have to break loose once in a while. . . ."

"We'll just keep it a merry little secret between us two," Miss Withers promised. "Won't you have another apple . . . for yourself?"

"Thanks," said Thwaite, and took one. Miss Withers waited a little while longer and saw him bite into the fruit. Finally she went away, vaguely surprised and disheartened.

Highpockets was sweeping the runway as she came back toward the front of the stable. On an impulse the schoolteacher stopped. "Young man," she said accusingly, "I want to ask you a question."

"Yas'm?" Highpockets immediately became the picture of guilt.

"Were there ever any—any carryings-on between Dr. Thwaite and Miss Violet Feverel—that you happened to notice?"

The eyes rolled. "Tha's what Miss Thwaite like to know, I bet you!"

"That doesn't answer my question," snapped the schoolteacher, who realized that she was very close to being a meddlesome busybody. Yet she supposed that the end justified something or other.

"Well," decided Highpockets, "I wouldn't say yes and I wouldn't say no."

"Didn't Dr. Thwaite like Miss Feverel?"

Highpockets could answer that. "Yas'm! Everybody like Miss Feverel. She was a mighty fine lady—gave me a red-hot tip on that big race next Saturday. She tell me how to win myself a barrel of money."

"And you're going to bet on the horse she suggested?"

"I sho am! That is," he corrected, "if that Wallaby horse has the right number on him. I can't bet on no two or three—but if it's seven or eleven! Zowie! Miss Feverel was always lucky."

Miss Withers thought of Violet Feverel as she last had seen her and shivered a little.

"Thank you," she said, preparing to depart. She saw the colored boy staring hopefully at her paper sack full of apples. "Oh—have one?"

"Yes, ma'am!" said Highpockets. He took a large red apple, opened his mouth very wide and bit it in two. Both halves disappeared almost instantly. He grinned.

Miss Withers looked gratified. "Too bad you're not on my list of suspects," she said cryptically. "I could cross you off."

She went out of the stables into the street again, stopping long enough to have a good look all around. But there was no sign of the young man she had expected to find lurking there. It had not been her intention to warn him off—indeed, the more the various characters in this mixed-up affair spied upon each other the better she liked it. This broth needed a good deal of stirring.

She hurried over to Broadway, descended underground and rode past three subway stations, and came up into the daylight again. Yet as she approached the bulk of the Hotel Harthorn Miss Hildegarde Withers had a vague feeling that the daylight was not as bright as usual. "I'm getting the fidgets over nothing," she scolded herself. "This is no work for a person with nerves." Yet all the same she kept looking over her shoulder.

The desk clerk knew her by now. "Miss Foley came in about an hour ago," he proffered. "With a gentleman. Shall I announce you?"

"Take your hand off that telephone," Miss Withers told him, "or I'll see that your announcing days are over." She flounced on toward the elevator. Once she stopped and waited behind a pillar, but nobody seemed to be following her.

The hall was deserted except for a fly which buzzed noisily in the slanting ray of sunlight which poured through a narrow window at the farther end. There was a small table beneath this window holding a vase and a number of dusty wax flowers, evidences of a spasm of interior decoration on the part of a previous manager of the hotel.

For some time Miss Withers hesitated near the doorway of the apartment which had been Violet Feverel's. There was a narrow transom above the door and it was slightly open. Through this opening faint sounds of voices came.

"It would be a shame to interrupt them," said Miss Withers to herself. Her glance lit upon the table beneath the far window. It was but the work of a moment for her to put vase and flowers on the floor and to move the light table to a vantage point directly in front of the door of the apartment. She drew a deep breath and mounted upon the table, teetering unsteadily and praying that no guest or employee of the hotel would come down the hall at this inopportune moment.

By clutching the edge of the transom with her fingers she was able to draw herself up to a point where she could see a chandelier and some ceiling of the living room inside. It was Latigo Wells who was speaking, for she could recognize that soft drawl anywhere. Miss Withers strained her ears for all they were worth, but she could barely make out what the young westerner was saying.

"There's some that go in for yodeling," he was telling his invisible audience. "But me, I don't yodel. Though I don't say I couldn't learn to yodel. . . ."

"Sure you could!" It was Barbara, her voice vibrant, ringing with misplaced enthusiasm.

"Anything to get away from the job I got now," Latigo continued. "You know, I'm so sick of horses I hope to die if I ever see another horse. . . ."

There was an exclamation from the girl. "But Mr. Wells—I thought all cowboys loved their horses."

"You been seeing Tom Mix," Latigo accused her. "Besides, now that we're pals I don't mind telling you that I never was no real cow-puncher. My old man, he run a livery stable in Butte for a while. . . ."

There was a faintly disappointed "oh" from the invisible girl. Then, after a short pause, a chord was struck on the piano. A guitar chimed in and Latigo's voice boomed out in the lugubrious strains of a ballad bewailing the fact that "He won't see his mother—when the work's all done next fall. . . ."

Miss Withers, frowning, tried valiantly to open the transom a little wider. Then she started violently as a voice spoke just behind her.

"A true music-lover!" said Mr. Don Gregg.

She slid off the table, hoping that the noises inside the apartment would cover the sound of her descent. "And what, pray, are you doing here?" she demanded.

Gregg shrugged. "I could ask you the same thing, couldn't I?"

Miss Withers told him somewhat sharply that he was in no position to ask questions. "So it was I and not the Thwaites whom you were shadowing!" she observed as she drew the young man out of the vicinity of the apartment door. "Might I ask why?"

The pouting expression was gone from the pale and untanned face of Mr. Don Gregg, though his eyes were still a little flitting, a little evasive.

"I had to know if you were suspecting Barbara," he admitted evenly. "I—I just had to know."

"Really?" Miss Withers sniffed. "Well, young man, I don't see how it concerns you. But I don't mind telling you that as far as I am concerned, I'm willing to give Barbara Foley a clean bill of health in this murder investigation."

"In spite of this?" said Gregg, motioning toward the table on which she had perched.

"In spite of that. But what difference would it make to you?" Miss Withers went on. "I had my own reasons for snooping. Supposing I did suspect Barbara, suppose even that she were arrested . . ."

"She didn't do it," said Gregg breathlessly. "And if you did seem about to arrest her, I was going . . . well, I intended . . ."

"Not a confession, surely?" Miss Withers prompted.

He stared at the faraway window. "No, of course not." He was suddenly a thousand miles away. "I don't suppose there's any use my asking you whom you do suspect?"

Miss Withers surprised him. "You, of course!" she said brightly.

Don Gregg turned two shades lighter than his prison pallor. "Did Thomas tell . . .?" His voice trailed away to nothing. "Don't pay any attention to what I've been saying," he told her bitterly. "I'm what they call stir-crazy—you get that way, rotting in jail. I'll just be pushing along now. . . ."

"Whither?" Miss Withers called after him. "I mean, where to?" Don Gregg turned and faced her.

"I've got to get home," he said. Then he hurried on, out of sight.

"For a young man who's been rotting in jail he was slow enough in deciding to seek the shelter of the family estate," Miss Withers told the inspector half an hour later. "Could there be a reason?"

They were sharing limp drugstore sandwiches and a can

of coffee across one corner of his official desk at Centre Street.

Piper took a large bite of bacon, lettuce and tomato. "Who cares about him?" he mouthed crumbily. "If there's anything in common with this pipe clue of yours you can give Don Gregg a clean bill of health. Because the pipe you found under the body had no points in common with the one you filched from him."

Miss Withers shook her head dubiously. "That pipe clue bothers me, Oscar. Besides, I forgot to offer young Gregg an apple."

"Apple? What's that got to do . . ."

Miss Withers didn't tell him. She pushed aside her coffee with an air of decision. "Oscar, the police aren't getting anywhere with this case!"

The inspector grinned. "You'll be glad to know that two of 'em are: Greeley and Shay, the boys who stepped out of line and arrested you along with young Gregg yesterday." He picked up two green slips of paper from his desk. "Here's orders jerking the boys off radio car duty and bouncing them out to walk beats among the vacant lots of Brooklyn."

Miss Withers rose up in her wrath. "Oscar! Of all the senseless things!"

The inspector looked exceedingly blank. "But I thought you were thirsting for their blood?"

"Countermand that order, Oscar Piper, or I'll take my doll rags and go straight home! Those men were doing what they imagined was their duty."

"Okay," said the inspector with a shrug. "It's your dignity, not mine." He took up the two green slips of paper and tore them across the middle. "You're still on the case, Hildegarde."

"I am, and I haven't begun to fight!" she said belligerently. "You know, Oscar, it strikes me that it would be a good approach to this case if we cracked down on the most obvious liar."

"Hm! You mean Don Gregg?"

She shook her head. "I was thinking of the hen tracks up in the country."

For a moment the inspector stared at her. "Abe Thomas, eh? You know, I was intending to go up there and quiz him. I've been wondering about that guy all along. . . ."

He stuffed a handful of cigars into his pocket. "Come along if you like, Hildegarde. Yes, sir, it's a great idea and I'm glad I had it. We'll solve this case or bust!"

"In the bright lexicon of youth there's no such word as 'bust,' " Miss Withers corrected him. "Or in any other lexicon, by the way." She followed the inspector out of the office, smiling gently.

Enthusiasm fired by what the inspector fondly imagined to be his own idea, they rode slowly northward through the busy afternoon traffic of Manhattan. Piper himself had supplanted the usual uniformed driver of the little squad car. "I hope the Commish doesn't get wise to my taking departmental property out of the city," he observed. "But the next train isn't until five this evening."

Miss Withers was leaning back in the seat, her eyes closed. "You know, Hildegarde, I've been thinking about that pipe clue of yours," he continued. "Maybe you're right, but somehow I got a hunch that the pipe is nothing but a red herring drawn across the trail. Maybe somebody planted it there to get us looking for a guy of such and such description with false teeth. Maybe . . ."

He stopped as he realized that his companion was peacefully sleeping. Miss Withers slept all the way up to the Gregg farm, a pleasant and much-needed nap.

It was too bad, as she admitted later, that she had to wake up to hear the alarming music of a bullet whistling past her ears.

10

Target Practice

The car had come to a stop in the driveway of the Gregg home, and the inspector was frozen half inside and half on the running board. His mouth was unbecomingly open.

Miss Withers blinked at him. "Oscar, what was that?"

"Keep your head down or you'll find out!" he returned, drawing himself somewhat under cover. "Sounds like a declaration of war to me," he added.

"Sharpshooting, eh?" Miss Withers peered toward the
ingerbread House in an interested fashion. "But I didn't
ear a shot!"

She heard one now—a sharp spat like the clapping of
nds. Again she heard a sharp z-z-zing in the air overhead.
his time the aim of the invisible marksman was either worse
infinitely better, for a fat sparrow who had been quarreling
isily with his fellows in the clear air overhead now did a
rfect double inside loop and then shot away toward the
stant thickets, leaving only a couple of silvery feathers to
at lazily down upon the inspector and Miss Withers.

The face of a man presented itself momentarily at a
droom window and was withdrawn. Piper straightened up,
gained his hat.

"Wasn't shooting at us, after all," the inspector admitted.

"He had the range closely enough to make me feel
comfortable," the schoolteacher returned. "Come on—in
e immortal words of the poet, let us storm their redoubt!"
e led the way toward the porch of the Gingerbread House
d pressed a resolute finger on the bell.

"Somehow," she observed during the ensuing silence,
omehow, Oscar Piper, I have a feeling we are getting
rmer."

Mrs. Mattie Thomas opened the door and greeted them
long-lost friends. But behind the vast smiles her eyes
nted warily.

"We want to see——" began the inspector, and stopped.
ay, Hildegarde, who do we want to see?"

"Everyone in the household," Miss Withers prompted.

"You can't see Mr. Gregg," the woman told them. "He's
lot better, but he can't see anybody. He even sent out the
irse to say he couldn't see his own flesh and blood."

Miss Withers's eyebrows went up. "Then—his son is
re?"

Evidently Mrs. Thomas had made a mistake. "Who?
hy—no, ma'am. . . ." She managed another smile. "He
is—but he's gone. . . ."

He hadn't gone far. Don Gregg was coming down the
ircase holding a rusty air rifle in his hand.

"Hello," he said. "Owe you an apology, I suppose. But I
n't think anybody would be in the driveway." He held out
e little gun. "Stumbled on this in my closet when I got

home a little while ago—haven't seen it for years. I wa
practicing shooting out of my bedroom window. . . ."

"You're quite a good shot with that thing?" Miss Wither
hinted.

Young Gregg smiled. "I used to be—but it took tw
shots to get that sparrow. When I was a kid Thomas woul
have given me the raspberry if I didn't do it first crack."

"Oh—so the efficient Mr. Thomas taught you to shoot?
Miss Withers went on.

"Him?" Gregg laughed shortly. "No, Thomas could neve
hit anything. Bad eyes or nerves, I don't know which. H
could miss the barn when shooting inside the haymow. Bu
that didn't stop him from encouraging me."

"A shot with the air rifle, eh?" Piper cut in. "Wel
Hildegarde, that's as good as . . ."

He was going to say "confession" and then sudden
realized that as yet the newspapers had carried no accura
information as to the way in which Violet Feverel had die
Also, his partner was shaking her head violently.

"So you haven't seen your father yet?" Miss Wither
asked. "Is Thomas with him?" Young Gregg shrugged.

"My husband has gone to the village," said the fat woma
from her vantage point in the doorway of the dining roon
"Abe ought to be back pretty soon, if you want to wait. H
had important business at the bank."

"Really?" Miss Withers started for the stairs. "We'll ju
have a word with Mr. Gregg's nurse while we're here."

Mrs. Thomas protested, but the schoolteacher stalke
resolutely up the stairs, followed by the inspector.

There was nothing wrong with the nurse. Miss Withe
realized that point as soon as she gazed into the sensibl
freckled face of the woman in the white uniform. Ther
couldn't be anything wrong with this nurse. Dr. Peterson ha
chosen well, for her name was Rogers and she stood fou
square upon her heels, a Gibraltar among nurses.

Miss Rogers had moderate respect for a gold badge. Sh
closed the repaired door of the sickroom behind her an
came into the hall.

"He's better," she pronounced. "Doctor was here a litt
while ago and said he could get up."

"Rather surprising in a case of supposed apoplexy, isn
it?" Miss Withers asked.

The nurse nodded. "It was a very slight attack, the slightest I ever saw," she said. "If it weren't for the bruises on his neck and shoulders, Mr. Gregg would be practically a well man. He seems to have had a very hard fall."

The inspector frowned. "Just bruised up a bit, eh? Probably had convulsions in the attack. Yet is he really too sick to be seeing his only son?"

Miss Rogers's face was impassive. "He isn't," she said shortly. "Mr. Gregg could see anybody he likes if they'd promise not to talk about horse races."

"But why did he send word . . ."

"He doesn't wish to see his son," said Miss Rogers finally. "There seems to be some family feeling which I cannot discuss. . . ."

"Of course," agreed Miss Withers. "Then may we go in?"

The nurse nodded. "Not a mention of horses, mind!" She opened the door.

Old Pat Gregg was sitting on the edge of his bed reading a newspaper. He was dressed in underwear, trousers and shoes, and smoking a cigar. When he saw the nurse he threw the cigar away.

He stood up to greet the newcomers. "I'd have given ten to one that you would be back," he said. "You can't leave well enough alone—got to be stirring up trouble about a killing that was pure and simple a break for humanity."

"We wanted to ask," Piper began casually, "a question or two about your attack yesterday morning. Can you remember anything more—anything you haven't told us?"

He shook his head testily. "Nothing only that one minute I was laying in my bed sleeping, and then I had me a flock of bad dreams and finally woke up mighty sick."

Piper frowned. "Then how did you get the bruises?" he demanded.

"Dr. Peterson says I must have thrown myself around and hit against the floor. . . ."

"Yes," Miss Withers cut in. "That's probably right. Only it's odd that you managed to fall up into bed again—for that was where Thomas found you."

The old man pressed his hand to his forehead. "Well, I don't remember. . . ." The nurse signaled that they had gone far enough with that line of pursuit.

"All right, all right," said the inspector testily. "There's only been a murder committed, that's all. We don't expect anybody to give us any help, but we would like a few questions answered."

"It might avoid a second murder," Miss Withers added. "Because I'm almost willing to wager that there'll be . . ."

Gregg's face lit up at the word "wager." He motioned them closer, out of hearing of the nurse who had taken her position by the door and was beginning to look impatient.

His hands were hairy, trembling. Undoubtedly the man was torn by some inner conflict, some shadowy fear.

"If I tell you——" he began and broke off short.

"Yeah? Go on!" insisted the inspector. "What do you know?"

"Nothing, yet," whispered Pat Gregg. "But you may as well know that there won't be any second murder until after the big race Saturday!" His voice dropped. "If you'll come to see me afterward—as quick as you can get here after the race—I'll give you a hint. And it's a hint that will knock you right off your feet, I'll bet a dollar to a tomato." He leaned back weakly.

"But don't wait, man—tell us now!" Piper pleaded.

He shook his head. "I might be wrong and I wouldn't want to go getting anybody into trouble."

"Not *much* he wouldn't!" Miss Withers said to herself.

But that was all they could get out of Pat Gregg. The round-faced old man subsided into a stubborn but meaningful silence.

On an impulse Miss Withers proffered to the invalid the paper sack which she had carried for so long. "Won't you have an apple, Mr. Gregg?"

He looked up surprised. "What? Why, this's mighty nice of you, bringing fruit to me. I do get hungry for apples 'long about this time of year." He accepted a red apple from the sack, sniffed of it appreciatively, and grinned. "A cold-storage Jonathan, but mighty good all the same," said he. Then, to Miss Withers's badly concealed disappointment, he took a large bite out of the apple.

Miss Withers moved toward the door. "I'm glad to see you better, Mr. Gregg."

"Better?" he laughed. "I'm well—only for this foolishness of having a nurse around all the time."

"Well enough to see your son, who's waiting downstairs?"

"What?" Pat Gregg stood up to his full five feet five. "My son downstairs? Nurse, why didn't you tell me? My boy has been away for months and you don't tell me when he comes home!" Miss Rogers opened her mouth, but before she could speak he cut her short. "Have Don come up here, at once! At once, do you understand?" His head moved slightly in negation even as he spoke. The nurse put her hands on her hips and sighed.

Piper left the room and after a last look at the invalid Miss Withers followed him. She smelled a rat—several rats—but she couldn't say just where.

At the foot of the stairs Don Gregg waited. "I'm surprised that you left town when the charming Miss Babs Foley is there, alone and unprotected," the schoolteacher suggested.

"That kid?" said Gregg. "She can take care of herself. Besides—I've had enough of that family, call it Foley or Feverel or whatever you please. Her sister made life hell on earth for me. . . ."

"Half-sister, wasn't it?" Miss Withers corrected. She held out her paper bag. "Have an apple, young man."

"But I don't like apples!"

"Have one anyway," cut in the inspector on general principles. If Miss Withers was going crazy he was going to stick with her.

Don Gregg took an apple rather gingerly.

"Bite it!" insisted Miss Withers. "It isn't poisoned or anything like that."

Don Gregg drew a deep breath and looked at the ceiling. "O-kay!" he said wearily. He bit into the apple. Immediately he became unhappy; he was staring at the remainder.

"A worm!" he cried.

"You're lucky that it isn't half a worm," Miss Withers told him. "And now we must be running along. By the way, I think your father would like to see you."

"Did he say so?" Miss Withers nodded and Don Gregg went swiftly up the stairs. They heard him go hurrying down the long hall, heard him knock upon the door. There was the murmur of voices and then the door closed with a slam. Don Gregg came back down the hall at a slower pace.

"The old man changed his mind again," said the inspector as Miss Withers drew him through the door and out into the afternoon sunshine.

"Yes," she nodded in agreement. "That's obvious. But *why* did the old man change his mind?"

Even as Piper frowned over that riddle the answer came from the doorway behind them. Don Gregg stood there, his face pale and impassive.

"Because my father wants to ask me a question and he's afraid of what the answer might be!"

Miss Withers didn't need to ask what the question was. She nodded slowly. Perhaps that was it—and yet at the same time a very interesting and intriguing alternative presented itself.

"Hmm," she remarked. "Well, Oscar, we'd better be getting back to the city."

The inspector looked surprised. "Why, we haven't——" Then he caught her glance and stopped short.

"If you're waiting to see Abe Thomas, you ought to know that he won't be back until late—much later than his wife thinks," said young Gregg hopefully.

"Well, then——" said Miss Withers as if it didn't matter. She nudged the inspector.

"You'll be here in case we want to find you, just as a matter of routine?" Piper put in.

Don Gregg nodded. "Until Saturday anyway."

He stood on the porch, watching, as they got back into the police car and turned around. "I'd like to know why he's so anxious for us not to question Thomas," the inspector said.

Miss Withers looked at him. "I wonder if it could have anything to do with a forged writ and a fake badge?" she idly suggested.

They drove slowly along the pasture wall while the fat mare and the red foal called Comanche galloped companionably on the other side. "Poor little fellow," Miss Withers observed. "He's got to grow up and have his legs raced half off, and then probably he'll pass downhill from owner to owner as a hack and finally on a junk wagon or somewhere. . . ."

The inspector said that that was the life of a horse. He stepped on the gas and then as they reached the corner of the pasture he slowed down again.

A station-wagon was rattling and roaring up the hill toward them with Abe Thomas at the wheel. "Let's chat a moment," Miss Withers told Piper, and as the two cars came abreast she leaned out and waved her hand.

Thomas shoved in his clutch so that the flivver stopped with its motor roaring louder than ever. He peered out dubiously and then tried to shout. There was no sound though they saw his lips move.

"Shut it off—we want to talk to you!" Piper called.

Light dawned in the little man's gloomy face. He spoke a silent "Okay" and then moved the gas lever up so that the motor died away to a low rumble. "What d'you want to talk about?" he asked warily.

"Plenty!" said the inspector before Miss Withers could cut him off. "You lied when you said you went into town Sunday morning to take a message to Miss Feverel, didn't you?"

Thomas blinked and nodded. "Sure I did."

"You went in early so you could get Don Gregg out of alimony jail on a fake writ, didn't you?"

"Sure I did," repeated the little man. The faintest suggestion of a smile flickered across his face.

"And you went with him to a Turkish bath?"

Thomas nodded. "Sure I did. He said he'd been dreaming of how good that steam room would feel all the time he'd been cooped up. After the steam room we were taken to adjoining cots in the sleeping room and there we slept!" Thomas did not exactly add "Make something of it!" but the phrase was implied.

"You slept there until when?" Miss Withers put in.

"Until about eight, when I went up to Miss Feverel's apartment and met you!" insisted Thomas.

Miss Withers looked mildly triumphant. "But if you came into town to free Mr. Don Gregg instead of bringing a message to Miss Feverel, just why did you get up at the crack of dawn and go to her apartment?"

Thomas seemed to shrink, but he did not speak.

"Was it because you discovered that in the night Don Gregg had slipped out of the place—and you were afraid he might do some violence to the woman he hated? Was it because you wanted to warn her?"

Thomas seemed to shrink still smaller behind the wheel of the flivver. Automatically he fumbled for a blackened corncob.

"Too much been said already," he muttered.

Miss Withers and the inspector exchanged a glance of

mutual congratulation. "By any chance," continued the school-teacher quietly, "did you leave this station-wagon in the street outside the Turkish baths—with the ignition key in its place?"

"You think Mr. Don——" began the little man. He shook his head violently. "I left this flivver in the Park Central parking lot—and it was there in the morning!" His mouth snapped shut. "That's all I'm saying!"

"That's enough," the inspector remarked pleasantly. "Let's go, Hildegarde. . . ."

But she shook her head. "Make haste slowly, Oscar." She noticed that Thomas was knocking the tobacco from his pipe and making a wry face.

"Pipe getting sour?" she said conversationally. "Didn't you say that there was nothing like an apple to sweeten the mouth?"

Thomas nodded suspiciously and then caught one of the red globules she tossed into the front seat of the station-wagon.

He stared gloomily at the apple. "Thanks—but it's nothing like the apples we have 'Down Under.'"

Miss Withers looked up. "Down under *what?*"

"Australia, where I come from," said Thomas. "That's a country where the police solve murders instead of pestering innocent bystanders. . . ." He took a big bite out of the apple and Miss Withers's heart sank.

"We might as well go," she told the inspector.

"You mean back—to arrest Gregg?"

She shook her head. "He'll be there if we want him. By the way," she called to Thomas as he was about to start away, "what did Don Gregg mean by telling us he would be here until Saturday?"

The little man shrugged. "How sh'd I know? Probably the young fool expects to make a killing on the big race and then . . ."

"And then decamp?"

Thomas gnawed at the core of the apple. "Don't worry, he won't," said the little man. "Nobody ever beats the races, but they all try. I like to go and watch 'em—screaming and gasping with excitement and then, when their horse trails in, you should hear 'em wail."

Abe Thomas let off the emergency brake. "I've got to get home to my chores," he said. The station-wagon moved protestingly on up the hill toward the Gingerbread House.

"Well," said the inspector cheerily, "now we're getting somewhere!" He started his motor.

But Miss Hildegarde Withers wore a face that was very long. "Oscar, it's possible to make good time in the wrong direction," she said thoughtfully. "Racing full speed down a blind alley . . ."

The inspector said he didn't get her. "You're mysterious as a fortune-teller," he complained. "And all this stuff about apples! What's behind it?"

She shook her head sadly. "Oscar, what do you think of a mystery in which the murder was committed by a person who didn't appear until the climax?"

"In a book I'd say the author was cheating and in real life I'd say that the police weren't on their job!" he came back.

She nodded. "Such a lot of lovely suspects and I've cleared every last one of them!"

"Cleared 'em? How?"

"The man who smoked the murder pipe had false teeth," she explained. "The rest of the description was guesswork, but that was certain sure. So I had a wonderful inspiration— knowing that you can't take a good healthy bite at an apple with false teeth. Yet every suspect—even the big red race horse—passed the test!"

There were two small hard apples in the bottom of Miss Withers's well-worn paper bag. As the police car started up she tossed them over the fence into the pasture where the mare and the red colt were standing as interested spectators.

One apple chanced to strike the mare smartly on the rump, and as Miss Withers rode away she saw the plump matron leap into the air, kick savagely at nothing, and then race wildly homeward with the surprised colt staring after her.

11

Off to the Races

It was on the following Thursday evening when Miss Withers, thoughtfully engaged in washing some of her best Wedgwood, nearly dropped a priceless cup as a shrill ring came at the door.

Dempsey plunged to answer it, and as the door opened the little dog threw himself up and almost into the inspector's face.

"Down, Gilmore!" said the caller. Dempsey gave a very un-lionlike bark and wriggled with ecstasy. He escorted the caller into the living room and then returned to his mistress's side. When she sat down Dempsey curled beside her and hung a whiskery chin on her shoe, from which vantage point he benevolently surveyed the room.

"You haven't showed up so I thought I'd dig you out," Piper began. "Deserted us, Hildegarde?"

She shook her head. "I've been thinking, Oscar."

"High time somebody did," Piper told her cheerily. "This Feverel case is still up in the air higher than a kite. And the Commissioner has had a few things to say." After dinner the inspector allowed himself a cigar much fatter and more greenish-brown in color than during the rest of the day. He lit one now and expelled the fragrant fumes. Miss Withers and Dempsey crossed the room and brought him a saucer to use as an ash tray.

"Thanks," he said. "Thinking about anything special, Hildegarde? I mean, have you got any new ideas?"

"I've been thinking about pipes," said the schoolteacher. "About pipes and air guns and bicycles and horses, but more especially about pipes."

"And the result of your thinking . . ."

Miss Withers smiled wryly. "No result as yet." She prodded Dempsey with the toe of her shoe and he kicked sleepily at his ribs. Then he rolled over and held up white paws at the ceiling.

"We've been running around in circles trying to find another man in Violet Feverel's past," the inspector went on. "A man with false teeth maybe. But we didn't find one."

"With or without teeth?"

"Either way," said the inspector. "She was a funny girl, that Violet Foley who changed her name to Feverel. At the studios where she posed they all insisted that she was icy-cold when working—but, they all hinted, she must have been a gay damsel off duty. Such casual friends as the race-track gambler Mr. Eddie Fry swore that Violet was a very conventional lady at home—but that she cut loose at the stables. Down at the stables everybody swore that she was hot stuff with her friends, but strictly business when riding. And to sum it all up—if Violet Feverel ever had any man in her life except her husband it was the Invisible Man. Her only love——" Piper made a dollar sign in the air. "Everybody admits that Violet did love to get money, and spend it."

"So much for the murderer with the false teeth," Miss Withers admitted. "Go on."

"We checked up on that guy Thomas too," Piper said. "Anyway on his car, because those rubbers at the Turkish bath don't know which end their head is on. And we found out that Thomas was telling the truth when he said he parked the station-wagon at the Park Central parking lot. He left it there at about eleven o'clock Saturday night . . ."

"I didn't think he'd be foolish enough to risk having it spotted in getting Don Gregg out of alimony jail," Miss Withers put in. "But when did he get it again?"

"The men at the lot go off duty at midnight and come back at six in the morning," Piper explained. "We've proved that the flivver was there at six—because Thomas had left word to have it filled up with gas and the oil changed. The boys swear they were working on the car at the exact hour that we know Violet Feverel was killed!"

"Hmm—then the car heard by the park attendant was not Thomas's!" Miss Withers seemed only mildly disappointed.

"Thomas showed up for the car about eight—a few minutes before he arrived at the Harthorn," Piper finished.

Miss Withers was frowning. "There's something wrong with this murder, Oscar," she pronounced. "Something slipshod and unfinished. I have a feeling this was a very clever plot that miscarried—perhaps Violet Feverel wasn't even the intended victim! Or maybe we've been seeing it backwards. . . ."

She didn't explain. "I've got a list of questions," she told the inspector. "You can have them for what they're worth. If they fail and if the murderer doesn't make a mistake, we're finished. I thought for a while I could start something by mixing up Barbara and the three young men—out of such a quadrangle we might have struck a spark or two. . . ." She let the metaphor fall mangled and left it there.

"Let's have the questions," said the inspector without eagerness. Miss Withers had them all neatly typed out.

"Try to have the answers before Saturday," the schoolteacher advised as he got up to go. "Before we leave for the races."

"Races? What races?"

"You and I," she told him, "are going to be at Beaulah Park this Saturday. We are going to keep our eyes open and pray that the murderer will make a misstep. That's your method anyway, isn't it, Oscar? To sit tight and wait for the other team to fumble?"

"Yeah—but what makes you think the murderer will be there?" protested Piper.

"I'll bet——" began Miss Withers. Then, "Why should the killer be any different from the thirty thousand people who will be there? Besides, can't you see that every trail leads straight in the direction of that race track—and that day?"

The inspector didn't see it at all, but he nodded. A drowning man will clutch in desperation at a straw, and Miss Withers had proved herself more than a straw in the past. "It's a date for Saturday," he said. Meanwhile he could hang his teeth onto the questions.

The Farmers and Merchants Bank of Beaulah village was not in the habit of giving out information about its depositors. The inspector had to telephone his old friend, Captain Joel Tinker of the state police, in order to find out what he wanted to know.

He finally learned that Mr. Abe Thomas had a savings account with the bank to the amount of thirty-one dollars and sixty cents. He also discovered that the mission of Thomas on the preceding Monday had been to solicit a personal loan to the amount of five hundred dollars.

"When we couldn't let him have it without security he wanted a hundred," explained the cashier. "He wanted it pretty bad and said he'd repay the loan on Monday, certain sure. But—we couldn't see our way clear."

It turned out that Mr. Pat Gregg also had an account at the bank to the amount of twenty-three dollars. Mr. Gregg had also made strenuous efforts, in recent months, to solicit a loan. It was of no avail because he hadn't been paying the interest on the mortgage upon his place. "Nor anything else around this town," said Captain Tinker.

Heinrich Jasper, pipe-maker and repairman, gave it as his official opinion that a pipe could remain warm to the touch not longer than twenty minutes after the smoker had put it down. "And only if the pipe was very hot to start with, and put down in a closed place out of the draft, could it remain hot more than ten minutes," he added.

A. V. Leonard, plain-clothes officer assigned to homicide duty, working out of the 7th precinct, reported that one "Latigo" Wells had been discharged from his job at the Thwaite stables on Sixty-fifth Street. The officer reported that Latigo had been discharged in a forcible manner which included the smashing of his guitar and that since Wednesday the young man had divided his waking hours between a park bench on Lincoln Square and the Hotel Harthorn.

B. L. Armstrong, also a plain-clothes officer assigned to homicide duty out of the 7th precinct, reported that Miss Barbara Foley had succeeded in having herself appointed executrix for her deceased sister, and that on Thursday Miss Foley had drawn seven hundred dollars from her sister's account at the Manufacturers Trust Company, leaving a balance of forty-four dollars and eight cents.

Also on Thursday, Miss Barbara Foley had purchased a twenty-dollar guitar from the Conn Music Company. Miss Foley had entertained Mr. Wells, presumably with the twenty-dollar guitar, on the evenings of Thursday and Friday respectively.

"They were singing," reported Officer Armstrong. "I listened awhile outside the transom and it sounded terrible."

D. B. Trent, sergeant, headquarters homicide division, reported that Mr. Edward Fry had locked himself in his room in the Hotel Amsterdam since Tuesday night, emerging only for meals. From time to time bellboys brought him reading material, mostly dealing with the race track. His phone bill was more than five dollars a day. "One call was to a dame named Babs, and she said yes, she'd love to go with him Saturday. . . ."

A. V. Leonard, in addition to his report on Latigo Wells, supplied information to the effect that on Wednesday Mrs. Maude Thwaite had been seen posing for a large number of photographs in Central Park, mounted upon a large red thoroughbred. Her husband had been left in charge of the stables.

"The husband had a good grouch on too," added Officer Leonard.

"Abe never rode a bicycle in his life!" insisted Mrs. Mattie Thomas when discreetly questioned by Captain Joel Tinker of the state police. "Wouldn't risk his neck on one of the things—but there is an old wreck of a bicycle around the place somewhere that used to belong to Master Don."

Nurse Rogers, when diplomatically questioned by Captain Tinker, gave it as her opinion that Mr. Pat Gregg needed a nurse as much as a cat needs two tails. "Whatever he had he's over it now," she said. "The old man would outlive us all if he'd only make some effort to quiet his nerves."

Nurse Rogers denied any interest in the big race. "I've heard my patient talk about horse racing until I'm sick of it," she said. "When I leave this case Friday night I'm going to sleep twenty-four hours. I always sleep twenty-four hours when I go off a case."

Sergeant J. A. Howe, assigned to desk duty, headquarters, reported that there were no automobiles stolen on Manhattan Island between the hours of midnight Saturday and 8 A.M. Sunday. "Nothing bigger than a bicycle," said the sergeant. "Some Western Union kid claimed his bike was pinched outside an apartment house on Central Park West while he was delivering a message. The bicycle was recovered in a smashed condition on the parkway in Central Park at noon on Sunday. Probably he smashed it up and then claimed it was stolen so the company wouldn't hold him responsible.

"We did have a report of one stolen car, but it was a phony," added the sergeant. "A hackee left his cab outside a Coffee Pot on Fifty-seventh early Sunday morning. He found it an hour later a block away, down the street—probably some other driver noticed the key was in the dashboard and played a joke on him."

On Friday afternoon Officers Brown and Ruseck of the Special Operations squad dragged thoroughly and with much profanity a small muddy pool hidden away in a corner of Central Park near the Eighty-sixth Street Transverse. The results were:

One turtle (comatose)
Four rusty tobacco tins (empty)
One man's shoe (minus sole)
One wedding ring (Woolworth non-tarnishable)
One whisky bottle
Two pop bottles
One small target-type air pistol (retail value three dollars and a half at any shop on West Forty-second Street)

This booty, with the exception of the turtle, was carefully turned in as per instructions to the desk of Inspector Oscar Piper, Homicide Bureau, Centre Street.

At the hour when the rest of the world was sitting down to its evening meal sportswriter Francis Xavier McCarthy removed his shoes, yawned, and moved sheets of yellow paper into his typewriter. He typed the heading "MAC SAYS—"

He lit a cigarette, threw it away and continued: "Today war news, quintuplets and upside-down stomachs move off the front page to let the sport of kings get into the headlines. Even yesterday's murder is cold potatoes compared with the mystery of what nag is going to poke his nose first across the finish line at Beaulah Park.

"Head Wind, Mrs. Julius B. Higginbotham's temperamental beauty king, is going to be an odds-on favorite comes the word from the insiders. But the big sorrel is the bookie's delight, because until the starting bell sounds nobody on earth knows if Head Wind will run his race or sulk.

"If he feels like galloping he'll have to run sideways to keep from flying. But that's a big IF, boys and girls. He'll either be first or last, there's nothing halfway about Head Wind. And if he cuts up at the post the way is clear for any one of the other eight nags to come home with the bacon. Pick 'em by name, pick 'em by post position, or fold your program and stick a fork through it—you're likely to make a pile for yourself.

"Don't forget there's Verminator, that grand old veteran. Maybe his legs won't hold out, but if they fail him he'll run on his heart. Easter Bunny too is a filly that never quits and who may take it all at a price. Toy Wagon likes the distance and saves ground at the rail. And if you want a long shot, where your dollars will come home—maybe—by the basketful, you have your pick of Prince Penguin, the California-bred six-year-old who's won five out of his last eight starts; you have Good News, who's backed by a great stable; you have the gallant but erratic Tom-Tom; the great sprinter Santa Claus; and the ex-steeplechaser Wallaby, who looks like a horse and may not run like a duck today.

"They're all going to be in there trying. Nine great horses thundering around the mile and a sixteenth in a minute and forty seconds or better. Maybe it'll be Head Wind in front, but if this humble observer is any guesser at all it'll be one of the long-shots who'll come thundering down the home stretch in the lead—to gladden a few hearts with winnings in telephone number prices.

"The weather man says it'll be a clear day and the track at Beaulah Park is in perfect shape. A crowd of thirty thousand is expected and if that thirty thousand doesn't see a track record (and maybe an American record) broken, your guide and mentor will eat his hat.

"And if that record isn't broken by Verminator the hat is all your uncle Mac will have to eat, because the week's wages are going down on the nose of that grand old thoroughbred who's out with a chance to top all stake-winning records if he knocks down this fifty-thousand-dollar purse. . . ."

The inspector was reading this aloud to Miss Withers from the *Herald-Tribune* as they rode northward in a crowded Race-Track Special on Saturday morning. The train was a madhouse of excitement, massed humanity for this little while freed of its worries and fired with the chance—the wonderful, elusive chance—of Something for Nothing.

Oscar Piper wore a binocular case on a strap and was making notations on the margin of his newspaper—"As long as I have to be there anyway," he said. Only Miss Withers remained aloof from the contagion, for deep in her heart she knew that there was more than money at stake in this race of races.

"What are the odds on murder?" she kept asking herself.

12

The Short End

"You can't go in there!"

A tall and soldierly figure suddenly stepped forward to bar their way as Miss Withers and the inspector were heading for the turnstiles of the west gate. They stopped, startled.

"This park is for sports, not for bloodhounds," said the big man severely. "I got instructions to keep all suspicious characters out and that means you, Inspector. Haw!" He extended a hamlike hand.

Piper's face lit up. "Tinker! You old horse-thief! Haven't seen you since you picked Judd Gray off the Albany train for us. Miss Withers, meet Captain Joel Tinker who stands for law and order in these parts. Think you'll let us in, Cap?"

Miss Withers shook hands stiffly. "I wouldn't have you think I'm a race-track tout," she informed him. "We're here on serious business."

"Me too," said Captain Tinker hastily. He drew the inspector aside. "As long as you're going in put five on

Easter Bunny for me—to show. My kids always like Easter bunnies. See you here as you come out?"

"Sure!" said the inspector, accepting the five dollars. He led the way through the gate. "Awful jam in here," he told Miss Withers. "You'd better grab hold of my arm or you may lose me."

"You mean *you* might lose *me!*" she corrected. But she took the proffered arm all the same.

"They're running some of the preliminary races now," Piper explained as they moved toward the grandstand with the hurrying mob. "We may as well slip into the restaurant for a bite of lunch while we have a chance."

Miss Withers was looking over his shoulder. "I said we might as well have some lunch!" he shouted.

"Lunch? I couldn't swallow for love nor money," she said. "I'm too excited."

"Excited over the race, Hildegarde?"

"Over the murder," Miss Withers told him. "And over my number-one clue."

Piper grinned. "You mean the pipe? You've finally managed to fit it into the picture?"

She shook her head. "I can't fit the pipe to the murder and I've tried to fit the murder to the pipe. No success yet—but before this afternoon is over——" Again she peered over his shoulder. "You go and eat," she advised him. "I'll meet you by the door of the restaurant in half an hour."

"Wait!" cried the inspector. But Miss Withers was already out of sight in the scurrying crowd.

In a corner near the stand devoted to the sale of hot dogs, beer, and postcard portraits of the horses Mrs. Maude Thwaite was haranguing her husband.

"I said put the whole bankroll on Verminator to show!" she was saying. "The old champion always tries—look at the form sheets. And form is everything."

The little veterinary was protesting. "I tell you that horse is running on nothing but his nerve!" he argued. "His legs are gone, all gone. Let's put the money on a horse that's got a chance . . . on Tom-Tom, maybe!"

"You're a fool, Thwaite," the woman said angrily. "You have no guts. I know form in a horse when I see it. . . ."

"And I know legs!" interrupted the veterinary.

"You're more than a fool," began his wife furiously, her

face purple underneath its heavy coating of powder. But she broke off and her mouth cracked into a sort of smile as a cheery voice interrupted them.

"As I live and breathe, the Thwaites!" said Miss Hildegarde Withers. "Could you give me a tip on the big race by any chance?"

"Yes——" began Thwaite. His wife nudged him.

"Of course—bet—er—bet on Prince Penguin," she said. "You can't go wrong. We have a hot tip right from the stable."

"Thanks, I'll remember it," murmured Miss Withers as she moved away. She looked back at Maude Thwaite and sniffed. "A sneak!" said the schoolteacher. "A clever, cautious sneak!"

Yet for all that Miss Withers sought out a bookie, drove the frog-faced little man frantic for ten minutes with questions, and finally put down a modest bet of two dollars.

As she put the slip carefully away in her handbag a low and discreet cough sounded behind her.

"You too!" said Abe Thomas, his face alight with a gloomy sort of triumph. "Gone dizzy with the itch for gambling, eh? Can't you see where it leads?"

Miss Withers stared at him. "No, not at all clearly." Then she smiled. "I'm surprised to find you here."

The man of all work at the Gregg farm took a blackened corncob from his pocket and filled it with coarse tobacco.

"My wife's looking after Mr. Gregg," Thomas said. "I like to come here. I like to watch the fools tossing their money away!"

"Any advice on how to bet?" Miss Withers hinted.

For a moment his face brightened and then he looked at her discouragingly. "Advice? Sure I'll give you advice. Leave your money in the bank like I do. Then nobody'll get it away from you. Spend it for balloons and stick pins into them— even at that you'll have something for your money. But don't hand it over to the bookies!"

The crowd surged forward and against her will Miss Withers was carried along. She heard a burst of cheering and knew that out in front of the grandstand another race had swept to a climax. She found herself afloat in an unfamiliar sea with vast tides carrying her hither and yon, helpless as a floating cork. All around her shipping clerks, bank presidents, colored chauffeurs, chorus girls and stenographers surged, some screaming tips to each other, some secretively huddled over programs and racing forms.

It was a new element—beyond Miss Withers's depth. "I can only try to tread water and pray for enlightenment," she said.

She found a moment's respite in the shadow of the staircase which led to the upper levels of the grandstand. Yet even here she was not safe from the contagion of the race-track madness.

A fervid and perspiring young man in a light-colored ice-cream suit suddenly seized upon her. "Toy Wagon!" he gasped in her face.

Miss Withers looked mildly amazed. "I beg your pardon?"

"Don't forget what I told you about Toy Wagon—it's red hot, straight from the feed-box!" cried Eddie Fry. "Bet him to win, place, or show, or straight across the board. I tell you, you can't lose!"

"To show what?" Miss Withers wanted to know.

"Show means to come third—place means second," the young man explained. "Across the board means all three. Follow my tip and you'll coin dough. This is my lucky day!"

Miss Withers raised her eyebrows. "Lucky? I don't see pretty little Babs Foley on your arm. I thought you were bringing her here?"

Eddie Fry shrugged. "That kid? She—well, it was just a pipe-dream, just a pipe-dream. I'm not the marrying kind anyway. Besides, Babs hasn't got the pep that her sister had." He moved away, humming a cheerful lyric of his own composition.

> *"When Miss Otis was asked, at the last great Judgment Day, madam,*
> *'Are you pure as the driven snow?' They heard her say,*
> *'I was pure as the driven snow!*
> *But I drifted far and I drifted wide, and so, madam—*
> *Miss Otis regrets——' "*

"A strange young man," Miss Withers said to herself. "But he was very definite about that horse." Almost in spite of herself she sought out the bookmaker, studied the mysterious notations upon his slate, and made two more bets. "Just to make sure," she said to herself.

She found the inspector near the door of the restaurant nervously gnawing at a cigar. "Too much of a mob to get anything to eat," he admitted. "I finally grabbed a hamburger and let it go at that. Let's go back to the paddock and see if the horses are being led out," he urged. "No use wasting our time in this mob."

Miss Withers denied that she had been wasting her time. "I've been making a decision."

"Yeah? What about?" Piper grinned. "I suppose you've got an idea who's going to win this race?"

She nodded seriously. "I was given a hot tip—right from the horse's haymow," she said.

"Right from the what?" gasped the inspector.

"From the er—the oat-bin, or whatever it is. But that wasn't what I meant by making a decision. Oscar, if you were swimming in very deep water and found that your water-wings were filled with lead instead of air, what would you do?"

"Me? Toss 'em away and start paddling for dear life."

"Sound advice," Miss Withers told him. "That's what I'm going to do. And now shall we look at the horses?"

"I saw a couple of pals of yours in the beanery," Piper told her as they came out of the grandstand. "Barbara Foley and that cowboy, Latigo Wells. She was giving him the works—big soulful eyes and everything."

Miss Withers looked pleased. "Of course! I suggested it myself—told her that if she wanted to help avenge her sister it would be a good idea for her to play up to the two or three young men who might have had a love motive—and find out."

The inspector was dubious. "You didn't suggest that she go so far as to hold hands with him under the table?" And Miss Withers was forced to admit that she had not.

"I don't suppose you could overhear what they were talking about?" she asked.

The inspector looked at her. "Hildegarde! What do people usually talk about when they hold hands under the table?"

Miss Withers sniffed. "How should I know? Race horses, probably."

She learned in the next few minutes that she was right.

Babs Foley and her tall and rangy admirer were shouldering their way through the crowd in the direction of the paddock. The girl's voice came high and clear. . . .

"Of course it'll be all right, silly! My woman's intuition tells me Santa Claus will win—I've always believed in Santa Claus."

There was an expression in Latigo Wells's face which showed that he was not too firmly convinced in the reality of the old gentleman with the whiskers.

Miss Withers pulled at the inspector's sleeve and they let themselves be carried with the current of the moving crowd. "Fancy meeting you here!" she said as they came up with Latigo and the girl. "Having any luck?"

"Luck!" sang out the girl as if it were spelled in capital letters. "All the luck in the world—but we're saving it for the big race, aren't we, Latigo?"

Her companion seemed faintly embarrassed, ill at ease. He nodded painfully.

"On Santa Claus to show," continued Babs. "Every cent we can beg, borrow or steal!"

"That's just the trouble," Latigo murmured. He scratched at his long upper lip.

Babs drew closer to him, smiling up into his face. "Oh, don't be a wet blanket," she begged. "We will win, I just know we'll win. This is *our* day!" She was breathless, misty-eyed. . . .

Miss Withers saw the expression on her face and hastily blew her nose. "The race track is no place for sentiment, Oscar," she said softly as if to convince herself.

"I wish I had the money in a poker game," Latigo Wells said after a moment. "You can't always tell about horses. . . ."

The quartet was finally thrust against a breast-high railing and held there by the pressure of the gaping crowd behind them. Beyond the railing was a small circle of trodden sand with a plot of green grass in the center.

"Here they come!" cried Barbara excitedly. On the far side of the paddock appeared a stocky young man in a red jacket, astride a fat horse. They plodded into the paddock leading a procession which consisted of a long line of prancing blanketed thoroughbreds, each with a stableboy at his bit. They paraded once around the ring.

Suddenly the green center of the ring was filled with

jockeys—hard, tiny men in brilliant silks. Here and there officials, large and soft, moved pompously and serenely among them.

Off came the blankets. "Jockeys up!"

Miss Withers was a little disappointed. "They look just like other horses to me," she complained. "Only the legs are longer. . . ."

"That's Santa Claus!" interrupted Barbara. "There— number four!" Her voice, too, sounded disappointed. He looked old and sleepy.

"Where's his whiskers?" Latigo drawled, and rolled a cigarette.

The inspector was amused. "They don't show much life as long as they're held by the stableboys," he explained.

Another signal and the nine thoroughbreds moved obediently out of the paddock and along the sandy lane which led to the gate between grandstand and clubhouse. "They're numbered according to rail positions," Piper explained. "Easter Bunny has the choice spot, two is Verminator, then Toy Wagon, Santa Claus, Tom-Tom, Good News, Prince Penguin, Wallaby, and Head Wind."

Miss Withers stared curiously at these blue bloods of the turf. They all looked alike to her, in spite of variations in color and trappings. Head Wind, the pampered beauty king, seemed hardly to differ from the dubious long-shot who ambled along just ahead—Wallaby, that would be, according to the program.

Head Wind was tossing his head high in the air and Wallaby's hung low, as if abashed at the presence of so much superior horse-flesh. One of the horses toward the head of the line jerked away from the handler and started back for the stable, but was immediately recaptured.

"They know what's going to happen!" the inspector explained.

"I wish *I* did!" Miss Withers sighed. The horses were prancing sideways as they neared the entrance to the track and in the distance a bugle rang out sweet and clear. There was something in the sound which made the schoolteacher's blood pound with a strange excitement.

"They all look like winners!" she cried. "I'm going to bet again."

The dark cave beneath the grandstand was a frenzied

madhouse now, with a long line of would-be bettors standing before every bookmaker's table, each desperately anxious to get rid of the money on his person before post-time. The hands of the clock showed twelve minutes to three. Twelve minutes—720 seconds . . .

They took their places in the nearest line and Miss Withers saw Babs Foley put a large roll of bills into the hand of Mr. Latigo Wells. "You make the bet—for luck!" the girl was saying. "We'll sink or swim."

The line moved forward, stopped again. Then the voice of the bookmaker drowned out the other sounds. "Listen, brother, once your money is down on the line you can't change your bet! You've got two hundred bucks on Verminator. . . ."

He was talking to Thwaite, the veterinary, whose habitually waxed mustache drooped sadly. Thwaite plunged one hand into his pocket and brought out a fistful of silver. "One fifty, one sixty-five . . . two dollars, then!" he cried. "On Tom-Tom!"

"Okay, two bucks on Tom-Tom." The bookie wrote the ticket and the veterinary put it deeply away in the folds of his wallet. He departed, avoiding Miss Withers's eye.

"Treason in the ranks," murmured the schoolteacher. "A rebellion on a small scale."

The line moved up again. Suddenly Miss Withers noticed a small, somewhat dingy little man hurrying toward the farther doorway.

On an impulse she told the inspector to hold her place and drew Latigo Wells aside. "Look!" she said. "Ever see him before—that man in the doorway?"

Latigo frowned with consternation. Finally he shook his head. " 'Fraid not, ma'am."

"Nonsense!" Miss Withers snapped as the distant figure of Abe Thomas vanished. "Didn't he come to the stable after Violet Feverel left last Sunday morning and try to rent a saddle horse?"

Latigo grinned widely. "Not on your life, ma'am. It was a different guy altogether."

"You'd swear it wasn't he?"

"On a stack of Bibles. You see, I know who that guy was—the one who wanted to ride horseback without the usual outfit of boots and breeches."

"Well for heaven's sake who?"

"I don't exactly know his name," Latigo explained. "But I've seen his picture."

"In the papers?"

Latigo shook his head. "In the bottom of the birdcage in Miss Barbara's apartment," he concluded. Then he got back into line. Miss Withers watched as he exchanged seven hundred dollars for a tiny slip of paper and shook her head as the girl led him away toward the track, still singing of how Santa Claus couldn't fail them.

"Your turn, Hildegarde," the inspector was saying. But she pushed him forward.

"I—I want to think for a moment," she said. The inspector made his own modest bet on the favorite, Head Wind, and looked around. "You'd better play safe, Hildegarde——" He saw that he was alone.

Mr. Don Gregg, making his lonely way from the paddock to the front of the grandstand, was somewhat surprised to be seized upon from the rear by an excited schoolteacher.

"Young man!" she demanded as soon as she got her breath. "Why were you following Violet Feverel last Sunday morning?"

Don Gregg didn't change expression. "Abe Thomas told you that," he said softly. "I wouldn't believe everything he says if I were you."

Miss Withers stared at him, not unkindly. "You're tearing up your ticket," she informed him.

Hastily, a little ruefully, he rejoined the torn halves. It was a scrap of paper which represented a bet of fifty dollars on Good News to show.

"I still wouldn't believe everything you hear," Gregg told her. He put the torn ticket carefully away in his pocket. "I'm going to need that when Good News comes home four lengths ahead of those other goats," he said. "It's about time I had some good news from somewhere. . . ."

Miss Withers stared after him, shaking her head. Then she hurried to the nearest bookie and put down two dollars—two more——

The frog-faced bookmaker gaped at her. "Listen, lady, is this a system?" But he took her money. Then he leaned closer, pointing at his slate. "What's the matter with this one?" he wanted to know. "I'll give you nice long odds on him, because nobody around here knows the horse and they're not betting on him. Give you fifty to one. . . ."

Miss Withers had exactly eight dollars in her purse.

"Like Babs Foley, I'll sink or swim," she said softly. "Eight dollars on the—er—the nose of the poor little horse that nobody has bet on."

She took the ticket and hid it hastily in her purse as the inspector beckoned to her.

"Come along—if you want to see any of this race!"

"I'm coming along," she told him. "Yes indeed, I'm coming along amazingly." And she followed him meekly through the doors and out onto the terrace and into the bright sunshine.

Unfortunately they had come too late to get grandstand seats. "Nothing for it but a shove to the fence," the inspector decided. By much use of his shoulder and an occasional flash of his badge they finally worked their way to a vantage point exactly at the finish line, in the very shadow of the judges' stand.

Across the far track, beyond the rooftops and the rising green of the trees, Miss Withers could see a flash of sunlight reflected from the turret of the distant Gingerbread House and she wondered idly if old man Gregg was watching through his telescope. She had a very good idea that he was, for if her suspicions were correct the outcome of this race would be very important to him.

Far to the left she could see a line of slowly moving horses, with here and there the bright flash of a jockey's colors. Then a stentorian voice roared from a dozen loudspeakers, *"The horses are nearing the starting gate!"*

Beside her a man with a cap over his eyes was praying devoutly. Miss Withers was not at all surprised to find that it was Highpockets, the colored boy from the Thwaite stable. She was no longer surprised at anything.

He had no eyes or ears for her. "You lucky seven!" he muttered. "Oh, you lucky number seven. Come on, Prince Penguin . . . win this race and I promotes you to a king. . . . The man pays me one hundred dollars does you win, lucky seven. . . ."

"He's betting the post position," Piper said. "Well, Hildegarde, you may as well break down and tell me which nag you're betting on. Did you take my advice and bet the favorite?"

She nodded, realizing that her hands were trembling. "They seem an awfully long time about it!"

The loud-speakers roared again: *"There's a little trouble up at the starting gate—Head Wind is delaying the start!"*

The inspector offered his binoculars, but Miss Withers trembled so that she could hardly focus them. Then she got a glimpse of the gate, a high contraption which was no gate at all, but only a means of dividing the horses. The horse on the extreme outside was standing on his hind legs and kicking methodically at an assistant starter who nimbly dodged for his life.

The crowd was swept by a great groan from the thousands who had put their money on the favorite.

"Just a minute!" came the announcement. *"Ladies and gentlemen, Head Wind is having a fit of temperament and will be started from outside the gate!"*

"They're taking him out in the weeds!" moaned Piper. "Hildegarde, we're done for!"

Miss Withers only sniffed. Piper took the glasses. "They've lined him up outside and they're going to hit him with a strap to make him start with the others," he announced.

Suddenly there was a great gasp from the crowd. After a split second there came the faint sound of the starting bell. . . .

"They're off!"

"And Head Wind is ahead!" cried Miss Withers happily. It was true. The big sorrel was coming down past the grandstand at least two lengths ahead of the field. "Come on, Head Wind!" cried the schoolteacher. "Come on. . . ." She noticed men turned to look at her.

"Quiet, Hildegarde!" ordered the inspector. He spoke to her politely, wearily. "It doesn't count, even if Head Wind stays ahead all the way around. Because he forgot to bring his jockey along."

Miss Withers peered along the fence toward the starting gate, where a small man in bright maroon silks was sadly picking himself up from the track. At the sound of the starting bell the favorite had taken a notion into his head to begin the race on two legs instead of the usual four.

The announcer's voice rang out in the loud-speakers: *"A mishap, ladies and gentlemen. . . . Head Wind has unseated*

*his rider and is disqualified. . . . Now the horses are at the
quarter and it's Good News, Santa Claus and Tom-Tom. . . ."*

From somewhere in the mob behind her Miss Withers
heard a shrill "Yippeeeeeee!" that could have come only from
the throat of Latigo Wells.

"Come on, Good News! Come on, Santa Claus!" screamed
the schoolteacher, fumbling for the binoculars. The horses
flowed in one smooth stream on the far track. . . .

*"On the back-stretch it's Good News, Santa Claus and
Prince Penguin . . . with Easter Bunny closing ground fast
along the rail. . . . Now it's Good News, Santa Claus and
Easter Bunny. . . ."*

"Come on, Easter Bunny!" Miss Withers shrieked.

"They're at the half!" cried the announcer. *"It's Good
News, Easter Bunny and Santa——No! It's Verminator in third
place, by a neck. . . ."*

"Come on, Verminator!" Miss Withers cried. The inspector looked at her. "Hildegarde! Make up your mind!"

The announcer's voice was higher now, tense and breathless. *"At the far turn it's Easter Bunny and Verminator, then
Good News, Toy Wagon, Wallaby and Tom-Tom . . . the rest
trailing. . . . Wallaby and Toy Wagon are fighting it out at
the rail position——"*

"Come on, Wallaby! Come on, you lovely horse!" Miss
Withers had almost no voice left. Beside her she could hear
the monotonous praying of Highpockets as he called over and
over for "lucky seven come home for yo' papa. . . ."

"Wallaby's coming through on the rail!" the announcer
said. *"He's coming up fast. . . . Now it's Easter Bunny and
Verminator with Wallaby forcing out Good News for third—
Good News is dropping back—Toy Wagon is making his
bid. . . ."*

Miss Withers impolitely snatched the glasses from the
inspector. She could see one horse far out in front, a brave
beautiful horse who thought he was winning the race. That
would be Head Wind, running wild.

Then, in a little clump along the rail, she saw four horses
so close together that their riders could have shaken hands.

*"At the three-quarters it's Easter Bunny, Verminator
and Wallaby, with Toy Wagon close behind. . . . Verminator's
rider is calling on him. . . ."*

The little jockey had ridden Verminator to triumph in six

major handicaps and loved him like a brother. "This is it!" he sobbed into the ears of his plunging mount. "This is the big race, boy. Try . . . anyway!"

Verminator plunged forward, wobbled, and closed half a length. *"It's Easter Bunny, Verminator and Toy Wagon——No! Wallaby is coming through on the outside. . . ."*

The roar from the crowd was one great wordless gasp. Miss Withers tried to call out "Come on, Wallaby!" but her voice was only a dismal croak.

Thundering down the homestretch, jockeys humped on the withers and swinging their bats, hoofs thudding in unison. . . .

Wallaby came on. He passed Verminator. He passed Easter Bunny, whose jockey called on her for one last grand effort and who was already giving everything she had.

"Wallaby!" thundered the announcer. *"Wallaby wins! Then Easter Bunny and Toy Wagon. . . . This is not official until you see the red flag. . . ."*

The horses galloped on around the first turn, wheeled and came back. Wallaby wore a flowered horseshoe wreath. The riderless Head Wind trotted to the judges' circle and wondered where was his wreath. Verminator limped off the track, his jockey walking beside him crying unashamed. "He ran the last furlong on his fetlocks!" the boy sobbed. "I couldn't use the whip!" Wallaby's rider dismounted and did a little Irish jig on the track.

Miss Withers sank back against her escort. "What a thrill!" she gasped.

The inspector glared at her. "Hildegarde, what horse were you rooting for?"

"Why—the one in front!"

"But which one did you bet on? Didn't you want your horse to win?"

She nodded weakly. "Oscar—Oscar, I got so many good tips on this race that I—I couldn't resist. . . ." She opened her hand bag and showed him. "I bought a ticket on each horse—to win!"

For a moment Miss Withers thought that her old friend was going to faint. "Hildegarde," he exploded as soon as his powers of speech returned, "you ought to be in a museum, under glass. You ought to be framed. . . ."

"Framed for the murder of Violet Feverel, Oscar? Like some of the suspects in this murder investigation?"

The inspector said he didn't mean it that way.

13

The Pay-Off

"Great sport," said the inspector dryly. "But Hildegarde, are we getting any *foradder?* With the murder, I mean?"

"Murder?" echoed Miss Withers. "Oh, you mean Violet Feverel! Do you know, Oscar, I've had the feeling all along that there was something wrong with that murder. Something accidental, haphazard, even a bit insincere."

"Huh? Well, the commissioner thinks it's a murder. It'll do until one comes along."

"Which may be any moment," Miss Withers pointed out. "Anyway, I haven't wasted my afternoon. At least I picked the winning horse!"

"And *how* you picked it!" the inspector jeered. "You'll never get rich that way." Then he remembered something. "Say, that Wallaby horse was a long-shot, wasn't he? What odds did you get?"

She produced the ticket. "The man said fifty to one," she explained. "Does that mean I get my money back?"

The inspector shook his head wearily. "I bet the favorite on form and he doesn't even get in the money—and you bet every horse in the race and a fifty-to-one shot comes in! Hildegarde, you can collect four hundred dollars for your eight-dollar ticket!"

She nodded brightly. "Even with the other cheaper tickets I bought I'm more than three hundred and sixty dollars ahead, Oscar. You know, this beats teaching school!"

She led the way toward the bookmaker's station. "Really, my conscience bothers me about this," she said as she accepted the fat roll of bills, noting that the frog-faced bookmaker eyed her with a new respect. "Gambling is against my principles—and besides, think of all the people we know who wanted and needed to win so badly! Why should I guess right and they so wrongly?"

"None of 'em bet on Wallaby, then?" Piper asked.

She shook her head. "Only one person concerned in this investigation had a hunch on Wallaby," she said. "That was Violet Feverel, and she couldn't be here to play her hunch."

The inspector digested this. "Say, how did Violet get the tip?"

Miss Withers frowned. "I wish I knew," she said softly. Her elbow jammed into the inspector's ribs and he stopped short. His companion was pointing just ahead, where young Don Gregg was moodily scattering the fragments of his ticket.

"Bad luck?" Miss Withers called out as they drew closer.

Gregg nodded. "Good News was bad news for me. You know, I counted on that name. I thought it was about time I had some good news." He flipped away the scraps of paper carelessly.

"I always knew," he continued with a faint smile, "that horses can sleep standing up. But I never knew until today that a horse can sleep while he's running."

The young man withdrew. "Not a bad loser, at that." Miss Withers gave him credit.

She waited while Piper cashed in the ticket he had bought in behalf of his fellow-officer, Captain Joel Tinker. "Tinker's kids like Easter bunnies," the inspector said cheerily. "He can buy 'em a lot of chocolate rabbits with this fourteen dollars his horse paid for a show bet."

Miss Withers was thinking about something else. "Oscar, did you notice that everybody today seemed to bet on a horse because they liked his name—because like Babs they believed in Santa Claus, or like Don Gregg expected good news, or like Eddie Fry, who once had a toy wagon?"

"Sure," said Piper. "It's as good a way as any other of betting. Is that why you bet on Wallaby?"

Miss Withers stopped. "Oscar, do you know what a wallaby is?"

"Of course I do," he came back. "It's a mythical monster, like the windigo of the north woods, or the side-hill gouger down in the Blue Ridge, whose legs are short on the right side because he always runs on a slope. He travels backwards to keep the sand out of his eyes and . . ."

Miss Withers shook her head. "Wrong, Oscar!"

"Well, then . . . it's out of that Alice in Wonderland book you always talk about!"

"Slithy toves?" Again Miss Withers shook her head. "A wallaby is a miniature kangaroo, a marsupial of the genus Macropus. Although the wallaby is often no larger than a rabbit, the female carries her young in a pouch as do larger kangaroos. . . ."

The inspector hurriedly said that he was sorry he'd asked. The crowd was thinning out a bit now, although two lesser races remained to be run.

Miss Withers saw the Thwaites, calculating over a *Racing Telegraph* furiously as they tried to pick long-shots for the final events. "There's a woman who never gives up," Miss Withers observed.

The inspector looked at his companion quizzically. "I'm getting wise to you, Hildegarde," he said. "I know what you're hanging around this place for. Are you trying to solve the Feverel murder by watching how the suspects act and trying to get a line on their characters?"

"Something like that," Miss Withers admitted. "But I'm floundering in deep water, Oscar—without my water-wings."

"It's a good idea, all the same," said the inspector. "Come on—I see that colored boy over there. Let's put the bee on him."

Miss Withers shook her head. "Oscar, you can't stride up to people and demand that they tell you their thoughts. Walk softly. . . . Let's follow him."

Highpockets was shuffling sadly in the direction of the exit gate, a picture of dejection. Suddenly he caught sight of Latigo Wells and Barbara who were moving in a parallel direction and who seemed to be in much the same mood. Yet they clung very closely together.

"They face adversity by sticking to each other," Miss Withers told the inspector. "I have hopes for them."

So did Highpockets have hopes. He rushed upon the couple with shrill cries.

"Listen, Miss Ba'bara—I been mighty unlucky but I know I can hit this next race. I gotta have five"—he looked thoughtful—"anyway two dollars."

Latigo shrugged his shoulders. "Miss Foley and I are busted," he said. "We need our money."

"Yeah," Highpockets returned. "But Miss Foley still owns a horse. That Siwash horse, he's a mighty fine animal. And you're going to lose him . . . unless you lend me the loan of two dollars."

"Lose him? What do you mean?" Barbara turned to Miss Withers and the inspector, who were coming closer. "Hello—can you people figure out what he's talking about?"

Highpockets was excited, voluble. "Your sister—she didn't pay the board bill for her horse. Over two hundred dollars due already. An' the law says that when an animal's board has run four months, the stable can have the sheriff come and auction it off for the cost of the board bill!"

Highpockets took a deep breath. "Miss Thwaite, she know you don' know about that law. She's fixing to auction off Siwash to herself on the fifteenth of next month. Of course she's gotta send you a notice in the mail, but leave it to her to send it to the wrong address or something, like she's done befo'."

Miss Withers was indignant. "Oscar, can that be done?"

The inspector nodded and Latigo interrupted, "It shore can, ma'am. It's part of the old Herd Laws."

Highpockets bubbled with enthusiasm. "I overheah 'em talking lots of times, and Miss Thwaite she sure wants that Siwash horse. Now do I get my two dollars?"

But still Babs Foley was doubtful. "We've only got our fare back to the city," she admitted. "I don't see any chance of paying that two-hundred-dollar board bill. I don't think the horse is worth more than that—certainly he isn't to me. I'm sick of race horses anyway."

"Let Maude Thwaite have the nag if she wants him so bad," Latigo agreed. "I've seen all the horses I want to see in my life."

Miss Withers protested: "But Siwash shouldn't go into the hands of that woman! Besides, he's worth more than that, he must be. Couldn't you sell your equity in him?"

Latigo said he didn't think there was much demand for retired race horses. "Come on, honey, we got to rush to catch that train!"

The man and the girl hurried away, still arm in arm. So it was Miss Withers, after all, who loaned Highpockets his sadly needed two dollars.

Yet there was still one more entry for the notebook before Miss Withers got out of the place. At the very turn-stile of the west gate she and the inspector came upon the drab and gloomy figure of Abe Thomas in the grip of the loquacious Eddie Fry.

"You're a man who knows horses!" Eddie was saying excitedly. "I tell you it can't lose—I got the tip straight from a jockey's brother-in-law. It's a red-hot three-horse parlay at Tijuana tomorrow—Velociter to Mad Frump to Shining Jewel!"

The young man's spirits were seemingly undampened. "This is a chance in a million," he pleaded.

The inspector saw the look on Miss Withers's face. "Steady, Hildegarde!"

She shook her head. "I wouldn't bet unless I could see the horses run," she said. "And I don't suppose I could get to the Mexican border by two o'clock tomorrow. . . ." The sentence ended a little wistfully.

Eddie Fry turned his barrage on the newcomers. "I tell you I can make a fortune on a parlay like this," he insisted. "Start, say with a ten-dollar bet—if the parlay works we'll win thirty on Velociter, bet it on Mad Frump and make two hundred, bet the two hundred on Shining Jewel and we'd have over two thousand when he comes across the line a winner. . . ."

Miss Withers shook her head slowly and Eddie Fry shrugged his shoulders. "Somebody else will stake me!" he said hopefully. "There's that Gregg—he ought to be willing to take a chance. Hey, Gregg!" Eddie rushed toward the exit gate.

"He's already forgotten about today's losses," Miss Withers observed. "There's a young man who couldn't hold a grudge!"

"There's a young man who's a fool for gambling," Abe Thomas put in. The old family retainer seemed a little more drab and dusty, if possible, than usual. It was as if he had been left out in the sun and wind for a long time. His eyes were avid and his expression would have seemed envious to Miss Withers if she had not heard his principles in regard to gambling.

He seemed anxious to talk. "You made a killing today, didn't you?" he accused Miss Withers.

She looked surprised. "I don't remember confiding in you," she said stiffly. "How did you know——"

"Pardon, ma'am," Thomas apologized, "but I couldn't

help hearing you. I was standing just behind you at the rail and I heard you cheering the winner."

"Naturally I was a little excited," Miss Withers snapped back.

Thomas nodded. "It was quite a horse race, ma'am. When Head Wind left his jockey and threw the race, I knew it was going to be something! And then when Wallaby came through on the rail . . ."

Suddenly he stopped and drew himself up. "I've got to be getting home—Mr. Gregg may need me," he explained. He moved away.

The inspector had an idea. "What's your hurry, man?" he cried. "We're due at the Gregg place this afternoon and if you've got the flivver here you can give us a ride. . . ."

But Abe Thomas was moving nimbly through the crowd, out past the exit gate. "A crusty sort of a guy!" the inspector complained. "Now I suppose we'll have to take a taxi."

There were few taxicabs to be had. Stout Captain Joel Tinker, Cerberus of the gateway, wouldn't have listened to the idea anyway. He accepted his winnings with the heartfelt joy which only an underpaid minion of law and order could have felt. "Say no more," he maintained. "Wait here until I get one of my boys to relieve me and I'll drive you over to the Gregg place."

"That's luck," the inspector said. "Hildegarde, you're batting .300 today."

She nodded. "That's because I threw away my water-wings, Oscar. I've forgotten all about People's Exhibit A, the briar pipe. It was my main clue—but it was an hallucination. Didn't somebody say that when the probable becomes impossible then the improbable is the truth?"

"Sounds like Gertrude Stein to me," the inspector protested. And then Captain Tinker drove up in a battered roadster and flung open the door.

"All aboard for the Gregg homestead!" he sang out cheerily.

"And all aboard for a solution of the Feverel murder," Miss Withers added. "Wasn't that what Pat Gregg promised to give us if we called upon him right after the big race today?"

The inspector was inclined to doubt that possibility. Miss

Withers shook her head. "It stands to reason that *somebody* knows who killed Violet Feverel," she protested.

"Too bad that that certain somebody isn't you—or me!" the inspector said sadly.

"Maybe it is," Miss Withers murmured. There was a very tiny suspicion in the back of her mind. It involved a dozen "ifs," but all the same it intrigued her tremendously. She toyed with the possibility during the five-minute ride to the Gregg homestead.

Captain Tinker sent his little roadster careening along country lanes until they came out at last upon the county highway which led up the hill to the Gregg home. Again the mare and the red colt escorted them to their destination. As always the Gingerbread House stood somnolently among its elms, but in contrast to its usual loneliness three automobiles had been parked in the driveway.

One was a taxi with a driver drowsing at the wheel, his cap pulled over his face to shut out the late afternoon sun. One was the steaming station-wagon with a tattered tire on one badly bent rim, and the other a light roadster which Miss Withers recognized as belonging to Eddie Fry.

"Of all people!" Miss Withers said to herself. "You're coming in with us, Captain?"

Captain Tinker thought he might as well wait in the car. "I'll drive you on over to the village when you get through in there," he promised.

The inspector rang the bell and after an interminable wait Mrs. Mattie Thomas opened the door. Her eyes were red-rimmed with sleep and her shapeless body was sheathed in a bright orange and green coolie coat with woolen slippers beneath.

She looked at them blankly. "I think Mr. Gregg is expecting us," Piper said.

The woman nodded. "Come on in," she said. She managed her sugary smile, but it seemed more strained than usual. She pawed at her hair. "I been having myself a nice nap," she apologized, "That is, I was until this doorbell started ringing. . . ."

The door closed out the sunlight and Miss Withers wrinkled her nose at the mingled, musty odors of the old house. "You may as well go in with the others," said Mrs. Thomas. She pointed toward the living room with its horsehair furniture.

Miss Withers and the inspector came to the doorway and stopped. Within the room was what seemed to be a vast crowd of people. Barbara Foley, Latigo Wells, Eddie Fry—even Don Gregg himself. Latigo and Eddie Fry seemed about to fly at each other's throats.

"It's open house!" said Miss Withers cheerily. "And we're all here to see old Mr. Gregg!" Her voice seemed to calm things.

"We came to try and sell Mr. Gregg my equity in Siwash," Babs hastily announced. "As you suggested. . . . Mr. Gregg always wanted to get that horse back."

"And if we can get some dough from him, we'll still get married!" added Latigo.

"We were here first!" Eddie Fry insisted. He turned to Don Gregg. "Just let me talk to your father, that's all I ask! He'll give you the money to bet that three-horse parlay with me. . . ."

"I rode home with Mr. Fry here," explained Don Gregg, "because Thomas didn't seem to be anywhere around . . . but I tell you all, I doubt if my father has any spare change to put into other people's gambling games——"

"And Thomas isn't here yet?" Miss Withers cut in.

"Yes, he's here," admitted Don Gregg. "He arrived just a moment ago as the four of us were pounding on the door and trying to get Mattie to snap out of her dreams and open up. Thomas is upstairs trying to find out if the old man is up and can see us. . . ."

It didn't take Thomas long to find out. He came running down the stairs, all expression sponged from his face.

He stopped, clutching at the doorway. "Mr. Gregg!" he babbled. "It's Mr. Gregg—I can't wake him up!"

Nothing but the trump of judgment would suffice to waken Mr. Pat Gregg, the inspector discovered. As he led the mad rush up the stairs, down the long hall and into the old man's bedroom, the inspector was trying to remember what he had learned about first aid. But there was no need for first aid.

Pat Gregg sat calmly in the easy chair at his desk in the tiny cupola room beside the telescope which was still trained upon the track at Beaulah Park. He was in his shirt sleeves. One arm was stretched across his littered desk and upon that arm rested the dead man's face.

From the shoulders up Pat Gregg was tinted a reddish purple in color.

"Get the doctor!" Abe Thomas was crying.

"Get the police!" Babs Foley screamed.

The inspector's first thought was to call in Captain Tinker, but that took no time at all. The captain was at the outer door as they flung it open, his face wearing an expression of mild puzzlement.

"Funny thing to find in a flower bed," he observed before they could speak. "I don't see the sense of it."

He was holding a man's blue silk sock. There was sand ground into the sock. . . . Strangely enough, the grains of sand were on the inside rather than the outside where they might have belonged.

The captain looked from his discovery to the strained, tense faces of the people in the doorway.

"Hey, what's up?" he demanded. With one breath they told him.

14

The Pendulum Swings

Dr. Peterson came down the narrow stairs which led from the cupola into the bedroom. "And that's that!" said the young doctor.

A barrage of wary eyes met his. "You'll want an autopsy, Doctor?" That was Captain Tinker, no longer jovial.

Dr. Peterson shrugged. "If the family likes. But it's clear enough. This was the third attack—and Gregg went out like a light. It's a clear case of what we call a cerebral accident—burst blood vessel in the brain. The first attack was three weeks or so ago when he keeled over on the stairs. The second was last Sunday morning—and I told him there'd be a third if he didn't forego all excitement. But he wouldn't follow orders—he must have died as he was looking through his telescope at the finish of the race. . . ."

"Oh, no!" cut in Miss Withers. Her eyes burned with an inner light.

"Oh, yes!" corrected Dr. Peterson. "You can get all the medical experts up here that you like. They'll bear me out."

"Gregg was murdered!" Miss Withers went on. "*This* is the genuine murder—the other was accidental, insincere! Remember my telling you, Oscar?"

"Nonsense," said the doctor. "This is no murder. There's not a mark on the dead man . . . not even a wound that would be made by a BB."

Miss Withers's voice lost a trifle of its jubilance. "Doctor, can you tell me how long this man has been dead?"

Dr. Peterson said it was the easiest thing in the world. "I'll stake my professional reputation that Mr. Gregg died between the hours of three o'clock and three-fifteen this afternoon," he said. "And he died from excitement—apoplexy, or a kindred ailment. His blood pressure was high, always."

The inspector, who had a prisoner, looked puzzled. "That fits," he admitted. "The big race was run at three o'clock. . . ."

"And I was at the track, so you can let go of my arm!" cried Abe Thomas. He wrenched out of Piper's grasp. "I was standing in the crowd right behind you—and as the race ended I saw Miss Withers here when she pulled out tickets on every horse in the race! She looked at you, Inspector, and she said, 'I bought a ticket on each horse—to win!'"

There was a long silence while everyone stared at the schoolteacher.

Miss Withers nodded. "So I did, Oscar."

Piper nodded. "Well, that gives *you* a sort of alibi anyway," he admitted as Thomas drew away in ruffled dignity.

"An excellent one, I should say," Miss Withers put in.

"Nobody needs an alibi!" insisted the doctor with unnecessary heat. "I tell you this is a natural death."

But everyone furnished perfect alibis all the same. "Barbara was with me all the afternoon," Latigo Wells insisted.

Miss Withers nodded. "And she was with Mr. Fry here on the morning of her sister's death, wasn't she? How convenient!"

Eddie Fry said that if anybody thought he'd leave the track when an important race was being run that person needed to be sent to Bellevue for observation. Don Gregg didn't speak very clearly at first—his tongue seemed leaden and thick. Miss Withers noticed that he kept staring toward Abe Thomas. "I was at the track," he finally managed. "We were all at the track—and as the doctor is willing to write a death certificate, I don't see what need there is——"

"You won't order an autopsy, then?" queried Captain Tinker.

"Of course I won't!" young Gregg snapped back.

"Then I will," said the state policeman, after Piper whispered to him.

The inspector said that he knew just the man to perform it. "I'll phone Dr. Bloom," he said.

Miss Withers, trembling with excitement, was questioning the hysterical Mrs. Thomas.

"You didn't leave the house all day?" demanded the schoolteacher.

Mattie Thomas shook her head. "Of course not! I didn't even get up and dress. You see before Abe left he took Mr. Gregg his lunch, so I could stay in bed. I was in bed most of the day—I always sleep when I got nothing to do."

"And nobody came here?" Miss Withers asked.

The woman shook her head. "How could they? Nobody's been to this house since the nurse left last night. If they did come they couldn't get in without ringing for me to open up. . . ."

"And you heard nothing, noticed nothing out of the ordinary?"

The fat woman shook her head miserably.

Captain Tinker was still on the friendliest terms with the inspector, but he made it clear that this case had happened in his own bailiwick.

"They'd better all go," he decided. "I can't see enough evidences of foul play to make it worth while to hold any of these people," he told Piper. "Unless you have objections?"

"If you ask me," said the inspector truculently, "I think we ought to lock up the whole bunch and sweat the truth out of them. But it's your show, Captain."

" 'But we know nothing really; for truth lies deep down,' " quoted Miss Withers softly. "That's from Euripides."

Captain Tinker hesitated. "After all, there's nothing to be done about it until we get an autopsy report," decided that officer finally. "They all got pretty good reasons for coming over here. And they furnish alibis for each other, as long as they were all locked out until old Thomas got home."

"Locked out—unless somebody had the simplest kind of a skeleton key," Miss Withers whispered to the inspector. "Did you notice that front-door lock? I could pick it with a toothpick."

The captain was hastening down the stairs to bring the good word to the six frightened people who waited there. The inspector was about to follow when Miss Withers beckoned to him.

"Look around this bedroom," she said.

The inspector took in the room, with its closed windows and its rumpled bed. "Looks like Mrs. Thomas was a bit slow with her housework today," he said.

Miss Withers nodded. "For a man who died painlessly and instantly in his armchair in the cupola, that bed is in quite some disorder," she suggested. It was true—one sheet looked as if it had been tied into knots.

"Oscar, *this* is the real murder," she kept repeating. "We can only glimpse it vaguely through the smoke screen that a clever killer has thrown everywhere—but this is the real genuine eighteen-carat killing."

"Okay, but where are the clues?" Piper wanted to know. He studied the windows carefully but all were tightly screened. As he walked across the room Miss Withers noticed that his shoes grated. There was a faint film of sand on the floor. On an impulse she opened the closet door, but it was empty except for a few suits of clothes. On a hanger was Pat Gregg's checkered coat and vest which matched the trousers which the body still wore.

Without a qualm she picked the pockets, finding them quite barren of interest. The billfold held little more than an ownership card for the station-wagon, some unpaid bills for horse feed, and a note scribbled on perfumed blue stationery. The note had been folded and unfolded until it seemed about to fall apart at the creases.

It was dated a little more than three weeks previously and signed with a flourish—"Violet Feverel."

"I hereby acknowledge receipt of $900 back alimony," it read. "Paid to me this day by Mr. Patrick Gregg in behalf of Mr. Don Gregg."

The inspector stared at this sad record of a business deal

between the two who now lay dead. "This receipt," said Miss Withers thoughtfully, "secured his freedom for Don Gregg—for a few moments. That Feverel woman must have had a good laugh as she had him clapped back into jail for default of what alimony had piled up while he was locked in behind bars."

"No wonder the old man had a heart attack when he heard she'd crossed him that way," the inspector agreed.

They looked around the room carefully but there was nothing else of interest. The key was not in the door today, nor had it shown up among Gregg's belongings. At least this time Thomas had not had to break down the door.

There was some meaning in all this, Miss Withers was sure. Her mind seemed full of disorganized, uncorrelated material. "Oscar, it's like having the first two and the last two letters of a word in a crossword puzzle. All we need to do is to fill in the blank spaces. . . ."

"Yeah," agreed the inspector. "All we need to do is to figure out how any one of our suspects can be in two places at the same time!" He laughed dryly. Then, "What are you staring at, Hildegarde?"

"Two places at the same time . . ." she repeated thoughtfully. "Oscar, it just struck me that——"

She broke off short. With a sudden rush of ice to the back of her neck she noticed that the doorknob was beginning very softly to turn.

Her first impulse was to scream and her second to duck down behind the bed. Paralyzed, she stood and pointed. Finally the inspector caught on. It was not in him to debate—he flung himself at the door and wrenched it open. "Thomas! what in——"

But it wasn't Abe Thomas. It was young Don Gregg—looking as if his years had come upon him all at once. There was a strange pinched look about his nostrils and his eyes were bloodshot.

"The captain says to come downstairs," he said quickly. "Nobody is supposed to be up here until my father's body is taken away."

He held the door open and they hurried through. At the head of the stairs Miss Withers noticed the tall grandfather's clock. It was not ticking now.

" 'But it stopped short—never to run again, when the

old man died,' " she quoted with a shiver, staring at the inert pendulum.

Don Gregg looked at her curiously. "No, it didn't," he explained. "Thomas just came up and stopped it. Said it didn't seem decent for it to go on ticking now."

Downstairs Captain Tinker had been thinking things out for himself. "I don't see any way that this could tie up with your murder case in the city," he said to the inspector. "Especially on account of what Dr. Peterson says. But if you want to lend us your medical examiner, sort of sub rosa, so to speak . . ."

Miss Withers nudged the inspector and he nodded. "I certainly do," he said.

Tinker nodded. "I'll stay here in charge until he comes," he decided. "He ought to see the body where we found it. I'll have our own coroner here at the same time and then they can collaborate down at the mortuary in the village."

"How very cozy!" Miss Withers remarked. She was suddenly anxious to get out of this house, away from the dull stare of Don Gregg.

"Mrs. Thomas had a fit of the vapors," Tinker went on, "and her husband took her to the kitchen. I let the rest go—after all there's nothing to indicate murder here and we know where to find them."

Miss Withers's sniff was loud enough to make the inspector wheel and face her. "What's up, Hildegarde?"

She stared at him and shook her head. "I'm ready, Oscar," she said, tight-lipped. "Good night, Mr. Gregg." The young man nodded.

Captain Tinker said they could take his car and he would have one of his own men pick it up at the village. "I'll stay here and keep the death watch," he said with an attempt at lightness. "It's not the first time."

Miss Withers said politely that she hoped it was not the last and followed Piper down to the car.

"I telephoned Dr. Bloom," the inspector told her. "He made quite a fuss but I finally got him to promise that he'd come up here. I'd feel more certain of this cerebral accident stuff if Bloom said so."

Miss Withers sniffed again. "He won't," she said. "And Oscar, we're not going to New York tonight . . . not if you happen to know a good dependable burglar."

"A what?"

"A burglar," the schoolteacher continued calmly. "Do you know of a dependable crook who can break into my apartment, take Dempsey for a walk, and feed him as per instructions?"

The inspector thought it might be possible. "Sergeant Swarthout is handy with burglar tools," he said. "But why do you want to stay up here tonight?"

"It's time this whole mystery was solved," she snapped back. "And it won't be solved by absent treatment either. I intend to stay in the front-line trenches. . . ."

"Until Dr. Bloom finds that Gregg died a natural death?" Piper suggested with a grin. He guided the roadster out onto the main highway.

"Which he won't!" Miss Withers stoutly retorted.

They managed to get dinner of a sort in Beaulah's one hotel—a little country inn temporarily overflowing with race-track followers. Miss Withers even noticed one or two of the jockeys picking daintily at dishes of lettuce and spinach, and she realized how they kept that slightness of figure and why they wore that pinched and hungry look.

Miss Withers ordered lavishly and barely touched her food. When the inspector chided her she shook her head impatiently. "I'm putting two and two together," she explained. "Right now they add up to something in five figures plus decimal points, but I'm still trying."

"It's a shame we can't get rooms," the inspector complained. "A good night's sleep would do wonders. . . ."

" 'To sleep: perchance to dream'!" Miss Withers returned. "Oscar, I couldn't sleep until I hear what Dr. Bloom reports." Suddenly she dropped the spoon in her coffee. "Oscar! Did you hear me? 'To sleep: perchance to dream: ay, there's the rub; For in that sleep of death what dreams may come . . .' "

"You're tired, Hildegarde," said the inspector kindly. "You're overwrought. I'll see if I can't find a place for you to lie down. . . ."

"Oscar!" she exploded. "Don't be any more stupid than you have to be! I'm quoting Shakespeare for a reason!"

"Yeah? What reason?"

Miss Withers leaned toward him, her plain and somewhat equine visage tense with excitement. "Pat Gregg dreamed strange dreams during his other attack," she explained breathlessly. "He dreamed of being the pendulum of a clock and then of being a red Barbary ape swinging in a tree. . . ."

"So what? He had nightmares! I don't make anything of that," growled the inspector.

"No," said Miss Withers, "you wouldn't. But perhaps Dr. Bloom will. You wouldn't make anything of the bullet that struck Violet Feverel's horse, nor the horseshoe fastened to a hoe! You wouldn't see any meaning in the dreams of a man at death's door, nor significance of a few notes scribbled on the back of a race-track program! You wouldn't understand . . ."

"About the briar pipe?" Piper grinned. "I always smoke cigars myself."

"Forget the briar pipe, will you?" demanded Miss Withers. "Throw it overboard, it's a Jonah."

"And all those apples you wasted trying to find a man with false teeth!" the inspector jibed.

"Wasted?" said Miss Withers calmly. "Perhaps." She looked at her watch and saw it was after ten. "Don't you think Dr. Bloom has arrived at the Gregg place by now?"

"I'll find out," Piper promised. "Anything for peace in the family."

He got up and made a telephone call. "Bloom's at the house," he announced as he came back to Miss Withers's table. "He says the young man tried to keep him from examining the body until Tinker threatened to send him to the local hoosegow."

"But what did he find?" demanded Miss Withers.

Piper shrugged. "Nothing as yet," he admitted. "The old boy is mighty cautious. But he says he isn't satisfied that the death is natural and they're going to send for an ambulance to bring the body down to the local undertaking parlors."

"We might be able to meet them on their way!" Miss Withers said, rising from the table.

"But Hildegarde, you've seen the body," protested the inspector. "You're not going to tell Bloom how to do his job, are you?"

She looked at him. "I'm perfectly capable of making a suggestion or two," she said.

She took up her position outside the Marble Hills Mortuary and when Dr. Bloom and the local officials arrived with their grim subject she cornered the medical examiner.

"Doctor, I want to know just what is a cerebral accident," she demanded.

"But this is no time for a medical lecture——" he began testily. "If a man has hypertension or high blood pressure he is likely to be subject to thrombosis or cerebral embolism or some other form of what we call cerebral hemorrhage—the result of too much pressure of blood on the brain."

"And an attack in the form of a cerebral accident could not be artificially induced?" she went on.

Dr. Bloom frowned and then smiled faintly. "Certainly. You could get the victim to run up twenty flights of stairs. . . ."

"I was thinking of another method," Miss Withers said. She told the doctor what it was.

"Good God!" he exploded. "I never heard of such a thing. But still——" The doctor's face lit up with an innocent childlike excitement. His fine white teeth clicked nervously and he clawed at his beard with his stained dark fingers. "The marks on the ankles—yes, it could be! Anyway," he decided, "I'll go and see!" He hurried away into the mortuary after the others, but Miss Withers had all the confirmation she needed.

She rushed back to the hotel where she had left the inspector peacefully drowsing upon a settee. It was getting on toward midnight now and the hotel lobby was deserted.

"Wake up, Oscar!" she cried. "I know who killed Pat Gregg!"

"Eh? What's that?"

"Snap out of it, Oscar. I need you to drive the captain's car." Her excitement finally communicated itself to the drowsy inspector.

"Okay, okay," said he. Halfway to the door he stopped. "Where are we going?"

She pushed him forward. "We're going to ring doorbells," she said.

"Yeah—but whose?"

Miss Hildegarde Withers stared him full in the face. "Dead men's doorbells!" she said.

15

Ordeal by Fire

"Hadn't you better switch off your lights?" suggested Miss Withers.

"But how can I see to drive?" protested Oscar Piper. "I don't know these roads nor this car. After all, Hildegarde . . . !"

"If we can't see, we can't be seen," the schoolteacher told him. There was moonlight enough so that after the inspector's eyes became accustomed to the dimness he could steer the borrowed roadster along an approximation of the middle of the winding country highway.

"I don't see why we couldn't do all this in the morning," Piper was complaining.

"Nonsense, Oscar!" she said. "We'll trap our key witness. Drag a man out of bed when he's heavy with sleep and you'll get the truth out of him. He won't have his mind keyed up to lying—it's an old dodge, but I'm staking everything on the chance that it will work."

"Just to smash an alibi?" Piper asked.

She nodded. "The best alibi in the world," she said softly. They rode on up the hill, with a stone wall on the right. Miss Withers knew that beyond the stone wall was a green pasture, a pasture with a Yellow Transparent apple tree in the middle of it. But there was no sign tonight of the mare and the red foal—both were undoubtedly safe within their sadly mortgaged stable.

Suddenly the inspector jammed on the brakes. "Look!" he cried. "Tinker must have left some men on guard, after all!"

He stopped the car and both of them stared up the hill toward the Gingerbread House which loomed darkly against the stars. There was a faint flicker of flame. . . .

"The captain would have stationed policemen, not Camp Fire Girls," she pointed out acidly. Suddenly she found it

173

difficult to breathe. "We seem to be just in time, Oscar, there's something very wrong going on here."

He nodded. "You stay here in the car and I'll go see," he said. He fumbled in the door pocket of the car.

"O-o-oh no, you won't," Miss Withers retorted. "I'm staying right next to you, Oscar Piper."

They got out of the car and went swiftly up the hill. The light still flickered, tiny yet clear.

"It's awfully close to the rear wing of the house!" Miss Withers whispered.

So it was. Indeed, the fire flared against the very wall of the house. As they came closer they could see that now and again a dark figure moved between them and the light.

The inspector took his hand out of his pocket and there was a police automatic in his fist. "Tinker's," he explained in a low whisper. "I hope he keeps it well oiled."

They crept closer, still in the shadow of the stone wall. But the dark figure which moved about the feeble fire took no note of them.

"Wait, Oscar!" Miss Withers begged with trembling voice. "Wait and see what he's doing."

They were within fifty yards of the house. "I know what he's doing—he's setting fire to the place!" Piper returned hoarsely. "It's arson, Hildegarde."

Miss Withers whispered that there were worse crimes than arson. "Wait—wait and watch!"

They wormed their way closer, slipping from shrub to shrub in the garden. Still the dark figure remained dim and mysterious. At times it seemed to be performing a sort of weird dance around the growing flames.

"Pouring on kerosene!" explained Piper, barely moving his lips. "Good Lord, he's trying to burn down the place and everybody in it."

The red light grew higher, red flames licking along the wooden siding, rising above a window frame. . . . The window was open and inside a flaring curtain was licked up in an instant.

"I'm going . . ." said the inspector. But Miss Withers gripped him with all her strength.

"No, Oscar! Not yet!"

The shadowy figure reappeared. It was a man with something in his hand.

"He's got an ax!" gasped Piper. "Must be mad as a hoot-owl!"

But the mysterious figure was crouching beneath the window, crying out in a high-pitched, hysterical voice, "Fire! Fire! Fire!"

Inside the house a woman screamed horribly. The inspector rose to his feet and went forward on tiptoe, Miss Withers still close at his heels. They were out in the open now, but the man who cried "Fire!" had no eyes for them.

He stood near a side doorway which opened out into the garden by a stone step and the ax was upraised. Suddenly a woman, still screaming, burst from the house. It was Mattie Thomas, in spite of her fat body sprinting like a deer. She missed the step, landed sprawling in the grass and scuttled, still howling, into the shrubbery.

The man with the ax never moved. There was light enough from the burning house so that Miss Withers could see a man inside the bedroom, a man who struggled into his trousers and clutched frantically at household treasures on bureau and wall. It was Abe Thomas.

"Now!" cried the schoolteacher and let go the inspector. He made one magnificent plunge and caught the shadowy figure in a flying tackle. The two men went down in a heap together, the ax flying harmlessly to one side.

To Miss Withers's relief she saw that only the inspector got up. He was holding his antagonist helpless with a neat arm-lock.

Miss Withers was not too surprised to see that it was young Don Gregg who writhed beneath the inspector's grasp.

It was at this moment that Abe Thomas, his arms full of miscellaneous objects, burst out of the doorway. He stopped short, dropping boxes and clothes. "What—what——" That was all he could say. His mouth opened and stayed open.

Don Gregg was sobbing, great dry gasping sobs. "Let me up!" he begged. "Let me go!" His face was horrible in the red glare.

"Get the bracelets out of my hip pocket, will you, Hildegarde?" said the inspector. "I've got my hands full."

She came closer but she did not follow out her instructions to the letter. She looked down at Don Gregg sympathetically. "You wanted to kill him, didn't you?"

Gregg nodded wildly. "I was going to kill him and then throw the body inside the house and let it burn. . . ."

Miss Withers found the handcuffs. "On his wrists, Hildegarde!" cried the inspector.

But she still hesitated. Abe Thomas was making ineffectual efforts at beating down the flames, but she called him. "Help me, will you?" she said.

Thomas came toward her, still too dazed by sleep and terror to speak articulately. "Wha——" he began. "Wha——"

"Hold his wrists so I can slip these handcuffs on," suggested Miss Withers. Thomas grasped Don Gregg's hands, held them up. . . .

Then Thomas squealed shrilly as the schoolteacher quietly snapped the cuffs across his own wrists and stepped back.

"You can let your prisoner up, Oscar," she said calmly. "Relax," she told the young man. "He murdered your father, but the law will take care of him for you in due time."

Abe Thomas chose that moment to strike down at the inspector's head with the heavy manacles, but it was a dodge that Oscar Piper had met too many times during the course of his twenty-six years on the force. He dropped the surprised Don Gregg, ducked neatly to one side and drove his knee into his assailant's groin with disastrous results for the old family retainer. Abe Thomas lay down on the grass and moaned. It was all over.

Young Gregg looked wistfully toward the ax. "Ah-ah!" said Miss Withers. "Let him stay there—it's more important to put out the fire."

As a matter of fact, the blaze was subdued more easily than the schoolteacher had feared—far more easily than Mattie Thomas, as it happened. The fat cook came out of the bushes to fling herself upon her manacled and helpless husband with moist protestations of eternal devotion. When the writhing captive succeeded in kicking her off she attempted valiantly to assail the inspector. But finally she too was put under control.

A very chastened Don Gregg knelt on the grass. "I must have gone crazy," he said slowly. "But it seemed the only way. I didn't dare come to you—I was afraid I'd go back behind the bars if I admitted what I'd have to admit."

"So you thought of this gentle method of righting the scales of justice?" Miss Withers asked.

He nodded. "I only had the kerosene from a couple of old lamps," he admitted. "It wasn't much of a bonfire."

The inspector rubbed his burnt and blackened palms. "It was enough!" he decided. Then he turned upon Miss Withers, who looked in the pale moonlight more like a scarecrow than the figure of avenging righteousness that she felt. "Hildegarde, don't you think that the time has come when you could safely take an old friend into your confidence and tell him what in the merry hell all this is about?"

The schoolteacher pointed down toward Abe Thomas, whose face was a pale mask of reptilian hatred. "You've got your murderer in handcuffs," she said calmly. "What more do you want?"

"Sometime—at your convenience—I'd like to know just how *we* solved this mystery," the inspector said wistfully.

16
The Case for the People

Inspector Oscar Piper came out of the Duke County Jail and took a deep breath of the moist air of early morning. It was Sunday again, and just a week since at this same hour a doomed girl had gone galloping through Central Park to her appointment. Seven days from murder to arrest—that wasn't so bad, thought the inspector. Nor was he dissatisfied with the result of his long and amicable argument with Captain Tinker.

He walked down the stone steps of the jail and along the sidewalk toward where an angular spinster awaited him in the front seat of a borrowed roadster. He stopped and his feeling of warm satisfaction left him.

Before he could speak Miss Hildegarde Withers greeted him. "At last, Oscar! What was the matter, couldn't the sheriff find his keys?"

Piper said that he was sorry about the delay. "We were

deciding who'd have him," he explained. "Abe Thomas, I mean. I finally convinced the captain that our murder came first, so we decided that he could keep the prisoner for a couple of days and have his chance at the publicity, and then we'll extradite the rat and try him in New York for the Feverel job."

The inspector leaned into the roadster, then moved as if to look into the rumble seat. "Hildegarde, I must be getting absent-minded! I could swear that I left another prisoner in your charge because you said you wanted to question him. . . ." His tone was sarcastic.

"I let young Gregg go home," Miss Withers cut him off. "He told me what he knew. All of a sudden he realized why he had been left behind at the track—and he guessed the significance of his boyhood air gun being planted where he hadn't seen it in years! He went mad—but he's sane enough now. And there are chickens and livestock on that place of his, including the mare and the red colt. Somebody has to feed them this morning."

"Yeah? What about arson charges that I could bring?"

She shook her head. "It isn't arson to make a pretense of burning your own house, Oscar. Besides, he was desperate. That young man suddenly realized that he had been unintentionally shielding the murderer of his ex-wife and of his father. He had no hope of convincing the police of that fact, particularly since his own alibi for the first murder depended only upon Thomas's word. So he tried to execute rough justice with his own hand."

Piper shrugged. "All right, you win. Regarding Mrs. Thomas you win, too—because we're all satisfied that she didn't know what was going on. So she's being sent to some relatives upstate. But never mind them, Hildegarde. What about Thomas?"

She smiled at him. "Thomas? I told you, he was the murderer!"

"Yeah, I know, I know. But how did he pull it off? Don't hold out on me, Hildegarde. The reporters will be swarming up on the first train and it wouldn't look well for me to stall when they ask me how I did it."

Miss Withers climbed wearily out of the car. "It's been a long time since I wandered around in the courthouse square of a country town," she said. "Come along, let's stroll in the park where the reporters won't be able to find you until you know all. . . ."

Because of their fatigue and nervous reaction everything in the fresh and dewy morning seemed intensely clear to the two oddly assorted collaborators, clear as a landscape seen after weeks in a darkened sickroom. The inspector, like most city-dwellers inclined to avoid walking as the plague, found a park bench beneath a spreading elm and lit his last cigar. "Well, Hildegarde?"

"It was a murder among murders," she said thoughtfully after a moment. "Getting at the killer was like peeling an onion—there was always another layer. Yet it *was* Thomas, Oscar, who killed Violet Feverel!"

Piper nodded impatiently. "I know that—the guy even brags about it now. But how did you figure it out? He didn't even have a ghost of a motive. Family servants don't kill because somebody did a bad turn to the old master or his son. . . ."

"He had a motive," Miss Withers said. "But let's go back for a moment. We know Thomas came from Australia twenty years ago, got a job with Gregg when he was a wealthy breeder of race horses and stayed. He watched over the son of the household, watched him ride his bicycle and shoot his air gun. He attended horses; while his employer was away at the tracks he ran the place. And he saved his money.

"But life holds more than working and saving, Oscar. Even for a dried-up, dingy little man. There was a cook in the Gregg household, the fair fat Mattie. Proximity will work wonders—but it took twenty years for Mattie to win Abe Thomas. They were married last year—and it would be my own guess that Mr. Thomas at once decided that he had—er—come a cropper is the term, I believe. That large and sentimental woman would make any man desire to throw it all away and go back to his native homeland. Without the wife of his bosom, naturally—yet he couldn't go back without his 'pile.' So——

"Meanwhile Don Gregg left home and married a professional model about the time the two old family servants underwent matrimony. Nor did that marriage turn out too well. The young couple were divorced, but the bride kept her wedding present from her father-in-law, that big red race horse. She kept him out of vanity and perhaps out of spite. . . ."

Miss Withers shrugged. "Anyway she kept the horse and tried to have him schooled into a lady's saddle mount. She also managed to get the court to award her a big alimony from Don Gregg, who couldn't pay it. Neither could his father, for the old man had been guessing more wrongly on the races than he liked to admit.

"And then, Oscar, Abe Thomas saw his great chance. In an announcement of the season's big race at Beaulah Park, only a mile from home, he saw that one of the horses—a nag so dubious that bookmakers were even then offering almost thirty-to-one on him—was entered under the name of 'Wallaby'!"

"So what?" demanded Piper.

"Wallabies come from Australia," Miss Withers explained. "Like the koala or honey-bear, the animal carries a certain sentimental meaning for the native of that far continent. I noticed today that almost every better risked his money because of some hunch, some sentimental association connected with the name. Wouldn't it seem reasonable that when Abe Thomas finally broke his lifelong rule against gambling on the races, he would plunge on the horse which symbolized the continent 'Down Under' which he longed to revisit?"

"Okay—so he bet on Wallaby," said the inspector impatiently. "But where's the murder motive . . . ?"

"Not so fast," she told him. "Remember the notations made by Pat Gregg on the back of the race-track announcement? I found out through Eddie Fry that the old man had been sounding out bookmakers on where to get the best odds for a large sum of money on a long-shot in this race—and we know now that Pat Gregg didn't have a large sum of money of his own! He was placing the money as a favor to his old employee, Oscar." She sniffed. "Only—he *didn't* place it."

The inspector was waking up. "You mean—he gave it to Violet Feverel to bail his boy out of jail?"

She nodded. "He wanted the money desperately—and he was positive that there wasn't one chance in a million of Wallaby winning. If Wallaby lost, Thomas would never know. Pat Gregg went down to the city and called on the beautiful estranged wife of his son—he paid her the nine hundred dollars which wasn't his own and took a receipt——"

"How do you know he went down there? Maybe she came up to the farm?"

"Nonsense! He wouldn't want Thomas to get wind of it. Besides, that blue notepaper on which the receipt was written could have come from a desk in Violet's apartment, but never from the Gregg home. Anyway, don't blame the old man too much. The boy was in jail without ever having broken any law and Violet Feverel had played with him like a cat with a mouse. As a climax she had the boy rearrested because he hadn't paid alimony while in alimony jail—with the nine hundred dollars safe in her bank!"

"A nice girl!" the inspector observed.

Miss Withers shrugged. "Even though money isn't worth much any more, people seem to want it just as badly. Anyway, the girl didn't deserve to be murdered. . . ."

"Yeah, why was she murdered?" Piper pressed. "Was Thomas sore because she got his dough?"

"Wait, Oscar. I thought so at first, but it was far deeper than that. Thomas had to kill Violet Feverel—in order to kill the old man!" She held up her hand. "Why did he want to kill the old man? Because he knew he was being double-crossed!"

"How could he know it—unless he was a crystal-gazer?" Piper objected.

"Worse than that, Abe Thomas was a snoop," said Miss Withers. "Remember, Gregg collapsed on the stair when he heard that his son was back in jail. He was put to bed, unconscious, by his faithful servant—who, if I am not mistaken, calmly went through his master's pockets!

"There was proof enough in the billfold—the receipt. Too bad we only looked through the trousers last Sunday—it might have helped us. Anyway, Thomas's first impulse must have been to confront his employer. But he had no chance to get his money back, no chance of legal redress. He knew that it was impossible that the old man could have got hold of nine hundred dollars anywhere else, so Thomas took a tremendous plunge. He went to see Violet!"

"Listen," complained the inspector. "Are you making all this up out of your head?"

"He went to see Violet, begging for the return of his money," Miss Withers continued. "That was how she got the hunch to bet on Wallaby—for though she sent him away with a merry sneer, he did succeed in convincing her that the horse would win. There's nothing easier than to let oneself be inveigled into betting on a horse. . . . Even I . . ." She sighed reminiscently.

"Violet told Eddie Fry, as a joke, that somebody had tried to borrow back money that had been paid to her, saying he wanted to bet it on Wallaby. How like her to see the essential humor in playing the little man's horse—with his money! She would have done it, if she had lived.

"But she couldn't live. She'd sealed her own death warrant when she sent Abe Thomas away empty-handed. Not that he blamed her for that. No—but she was the one person in the world who knew that he had a grievance against his employer. Thomas killed her to cover up the murder of his employer!"

"Oh—but Violet was killed first!"

"In most cases of double murder, Oscar, the second murder is to cover up the first, but here it was vice versa. Violet Feverel's tongue had to be quieted at the same time or before the murderer could attack his real victim!"

"Say!" the inspector muttered. "*That* could be . . . !"

"It was, Oscar," the schoolteacher said firmly. "Abe Thomas was no fool. He planned both murders to look like natural death. In the case of Violet he realized that a scapegoat might come in handy in case murder was suspected. Don Gregg had a real motive—so Thomas with the innocent connivance of his employer and his wife worked out a pleasant little plot to get Don Gregg out of jail by a fake writ on the eve of the murder!

"He planned to free the young man in order to give himself an excuse to spend the night in town, knowing that his wife would lie in his defense and that even if the truth did come out about his part in the jail-break, no one would blame him except as a very minor accessory.

"He left home that Saturday night very early—before sunset because the chickens had not yet gone to bed—and came down to the city. He parked the station-wagon on an all-night parking lot, leaving hidden there an efficient but supposedly harmless little air pistol in addition to the weapon which he had artfully concocted out of a hoe and a horseshoe. The shoe had to fit Siwash—but that was easy, for the horse had been stabled up here at the farm during many winter seasons and presumably there were old shoes about.

"Oh, it was tight, Oscar, tight as a drum. The man was touched with pure genius and for a while he had the luck of the devil. He got Don Gregg out of alimony jail without a hitch. Perhaps he suggested the Turkish bath, knowing how difficult it would be to check an alibi there. Anyway, he took the young man there in a taxi and after the steam and the rubdowns and whatever they have in such places both men lay down on their cots.

"But imagine his amazement, Oscar! Thomas lay there pretending slumber until such time as the young man was asleep, and suddenly he heard his companion get up, take his clothes from the locker and stealthily creep out of the place!"

"That must have been a shock," agreed the inspector.

"Thomas soon saw how he could turn it to account," Miss Withers continued. "It was raining and the boy had calmly appropriated Thomas's blue coat. That showed he intended to return before morning."

"Hey, where did he go?" demanded Piper.

"He had one idea, that young Don Gregg," Miss Withers explained. "He wanted to confront the woman who had been persecuting him. Most of that night he stood in the rain watching the lighted windows of the apartment that had once been his. He admitted as much to me a little while ago, after I explained that we knew he had been seen trying to follow Violet that morning. . . ."

"Did we?" Piper asked doubtfully.

"Certainly, Oscar. He followed Violet to the stable and after her very noisy friends had departed toward Harlem, he tried to rent a horse and follow her into the park. Perhaps he meant murder, Oscar. Perhaps he hoped to catch her in a meeting with a man which would give him grounds for going back into court. . . ."

Piper brightened. "You know, I figured she must be covering up something. . . ."

"So did everybody else in the case," Miss Withers admitted. "They all figured that Violet must have had a secret, passionate side to her nature. She was actually as cold as a new Frigidaire, and as empty. Anyway, Don Gregg tried to follow her. . . ."

"And he was the guy who stole the bicycle from the Western Union boy?" the inspector burst in.

She nodded. "And took a spill on it too. Tore his clothes—because I saw Barbara mending them with stocking thread. The bicycle was wrecked and he changed his mind. He left it in the park and walked back to the Turkish bath—if he had continued on half a mile he would have come upon his wife's dead body. Back at the baths he found Thomas gone—and began to worry. Had the man gone out searching for him? He went back to bed, being naturally tired after a night outside in the rain, and slept through the long hours of the morning."

"That covers him," Piper said quickly. "But hurry, Hildegarde, those newspaper boys will be here in twenty minutes."

"We'll go back to Thomas," said Miss Withers calmly. "While Don Gregg was staring up at the windows of Violet's apartment Thomas was speeding northward in the station-wagon. There was nobody at the parking lot between the hours of one and six—and the drive at that time would not take an hour. He was hurrying to the farm; he had work to do there.

"Already, remember, Thomas had done away with Pat Gregg's faithful police dog, Rex, who always slept in the old man's room. He did it by means of the powdered glass he so brashly mentioned to us as being used on dingoes in Australia. That left Gregg unprotected. And Thomas knew that the worst risk he ran would be of being discovered as helping a minor jailbreak, and that public sympathy is with the prisoners of alimony jail.

"Anyway, Thomas must have parked the car a distance from the house, crept up to the old man's room and opened it with a key which he had prepared for this moment. Opening the door, he slipped quickly to the bed in the darkness and deftly knocked Mr. Gregg unconscious with a blow on the neck under the ear. Remember that pale bruise—it wasn't a hard blow, for he just wanted to stun him. My guess would be that he used a sock filled with sand. . . ."

"I've heard of it being done," said the inspector stiffly.

"Heard of it—you probably invented it!" Miss Withers accused. "Anyway, with Gregg unconscious the murderer worked swiftly on a plot which was far and away the most clever, I might say over-clever, that I have ever heard of. He had wanted a safe and sane murder, without a trace. So he hit upon the idea of stringing the old man up by the heels and leaving him there to die from the pressure of blood on his brain!"

The inspector's mouth opened. "Upside *down?*"

She nodded. "He knew that Gregg had had one collapse and was subject to high blood pressure. It struck him that apoplexy might be brought on artificially. He was strong enough to lift the old man, for he had done it on the stairs only a short time before. Anyway he left Gregg hanging by his suspenders. I presume they were knotted and caught in the trap door which led to the cupola. That was the only place in the room where he could have been tied up, for there was no chandelier and besides, the stairs offered an easy way to carry the victim up in the air.

"Leaving Gregg, as he thought, to die a slow and horrible death, Thomas hurried out of the room, locked the door, and got back to the city. He replaced the station-wagon on the parking lot where it was to be serviced by the attendants when they came on duty at six. From it he took his parcel of weapons and calmly walked down the street and appropriated the first taxicab he found empty!"

"But why a hack when he had a car?" the inspector protested.

She smiled. "Oscar, I'm afraid you're going to flunk this course. Naturally he didn't dare risk having his car identified. Taxi drivers often leave the keys in their cars, for who would steal a taxi anyway? So—Thomas stole a taxicab from outside a restaurant and drove calmly to the most convenient place where he could overlook the bridle path on which he knew Violet must ride if she rode at all. His plan was perfect—a BB shot must sting the horse into a frenzy and throw the rider. Before she could get up Thomas would give her a fatal blow with the horseshoe club he had designed, thus placing all blame on the big thoroughbred she was riding. The wounds would appear to be made by a horse's hoof!

"So far he had played in remarkable luck, but here he struck his first obstacle. Abe Thomas was a poor shot, Oscar. He didn't realize how poor a shot. True enough, as Violet Feverel cantered into range he managed to hit the big red horse. But Siwash didn't throw his rider—perhaps he was gentler than anyone thought. So the murderer, desperate, tried again—and this time he missed the horse completely!

"Already a park attendant was coming in sight and Thomas had to decamp with his job unfinished. He had no more use for the air pistol and the horseshoe club, so he tossed them into the first pond he saw. He had no fear of there being traces, for as far as he knew he had not harmed a hair of Violet Feverel's head!"

"Then who in blazes——" began the inspector.

"Oscar, he showed genuine surprise when he heard the girl was dead—for he had come to her apartment as soon as he got rid of the taxi and regained his own car with the natural purpose of killing Violet then and there, perhaps with his bare hands. He had to kill her—for it was necessary to cover his other murder! He might have thought of pushing her from the window, another excellent way of faking an 'accident.' If we hadn't been there he might have killed Barbara by mistake. But when he saw us he instantly thought of a very plausible lie—and a lie which would cover him on the murder which he thought he had committed up at the farm.

"His amazement at Violet's death was genuine, for he did not dream that his wild shot at the horse had struck her throat and cut the jugular. But he accepted the news as an evidence that fate was on his side and took us up to the farm to show us a dead man. He ran a fearful risk, he knew, that he would not have time to cut down the body before we found it. But he covered that neatly by rushing into the house and letting the door blow shut in our faces—by accident!

"It took him only a few seconds to get up the stairs, and here was the third trick of fate. For he found that the suspenders had broken or slipped out of the trap door, letting the victim fall to the floor where he got off with nothing worse than terrific bruises and a coma.

"Desperately the murderer tried to cover up his traces as we rang and rang at the bell downstairs. He got the sick man into the bed, placed the suspenders on the trousers and threw whatever gags and bindings he had used out of the unscreened window of the tower. By the way, he left the cupola window open, which gave us a faint hint, or should have done so. To cap it all, he locked the door—and broke it down from the outside! Sounds like a lot—but we waited outside for at least ten minutes.

"When we were coming up the stairs he rushed down crying for a doctor—and I imagine that he was much relieved when he learned that Gregg's only memory of the whole thing was the dream of being the pendulum of a clock. You see, of course, the significance?"

"You mean, the old man got an inkling of what was going on while he was tied up feet topmost?"

Miss Withers nodded. "Just as we dream of being afloat on an iceberg when the covers slide off the bed. The mind fictionizes and elaborates. That nightmare was an important clue, Oscar. But to go on. . . .

"Thomas was temporarily unable to continue with his real murder, mainly because there was a Gibraltar-like nurse watching over the old man. So he bided his time, letting suspicion fall on those of Violet's friends and relatives who might have had a real reason to kill her. Who would suspect him, the humble employee of her ex-father-in-law?"

"I would have, only there wasn't any motive!" Piper protested.

"Exactly! The motive hadn't come into being yet! Anyway, Thomas bided his time. Perhaps he was afraid to trust his luck too far. Perhaps he decided to wait until the big race and see which horse won. If Wallaby lost then he had no kick coming.

"But he laid his plans, Oscar. When he failed to raise any money at the bank, a last desperate effort to follow his hunch on the race horse with the Australian name, he got ready for the big moment. There would be dramatic justice about killing his enemy at the moment of the race's climax. Besides, the race-track event gave him a chance for an alibi unique among alibis. . . ."

"But Thomas was at the track, Hildegarde!"

She nodded. "For a little while before the race. But I timed our trip from the track to the farm with Captain Tinker and it took less than five minutes. Thomas knew his wife would be in bed most of the day; he had nothing to fear from her. Oscar, that man scurried away from the track, leaped into the station-wagon and got home while the race was being run!"

"But, Hildegarde. . . ."

"But me no buts. When he knew that Wallaby had won—perhaps he read the news in the face of the old man at the telescope—Thomas struck. Again he used the sock filled with sand and this time a twisted sheet instead of a rope to hang the old man with. Oscar, he repeated his performance of the previous Sunday morning and then hurried back to the track in time to be seen supposedly leaving!"

The inspector was bubbling with suppressed excitement. "I've got you!" he said. "I've found a hole in your case big as a house. Hildegarde—maybe a man could see through a telescope the finish of a race almost a mile away. I'll even concede that with his telescope trained on the finish line he could see you and me leaning over the rail yelling at the horses. Still"—this was the inspector's moment of triumph—"still he couldn't *hear* what we were saying! And Thomas quoted word for word your remark when you showed me the fistful of tickets—something about how you bought a ticket on each horse to win!"

Miss Withers didn't say anything. "Now who's flunked the course, Hildegarde?"

She smiled. "Well, Oscar, since you ask for it——Do you remember our meeting with Thomas last Monday when we stopped him by the pasture fence and I amused you so much by tossing him an apple?"

The inspector nodded blankly. "Well, perhaps you didn't notice, but his motor made so much noise nobody could hear anything. You told him to shut it off, that you wanted to talk to him. And he nodded and obeyed, staring at your lips. . . ."

"What? You mean to tell me there's parlor magic hocus pocus mixed up in this?"

"Parlor magic nothing. Lots of people can read lips without realizing it. That was one of the amusing things about the old silent films; every once in a while you would catch the hero saying something incongruous while kissing Theda Bara or chasing Lillian Gish through the foliage.

"I'll admit," she continued, "that I nearly went crazy trying to answer that question myself, Oscar, until I remembered what Thomas had unintentionally demonstrated previously. And that telescope is powerful enough so that the man at the other end could almost read the program I was holding.

"I myself, when looking through the telescope, noticed

that I could see the clods of earth flying from the race track when it was being prepared for the race. That optical instrument brought the finish line—and we who stood at the fence at that exact spot—within a few feet of Abe Thomas's eyes!

"He was undoubtedly searching for some gesture, something that he could mention which would prove that he was near us all the time. And then fate tossed in his lap that flash—perhaps half guesswork—of what I was saying to you. That completed his plot—gave it the little extra fillip that made it perfect. And remember, mind you, he was confident that Gregg's death would be set down as a natural attack of apoplexy!"

There was the mournful scream of a train whistle in the distance. "Hurry, Hildegarde. . . ."

"There's not much more. Thomas had a shock when he learned from you that we wanted to ride over to the farm from the track. He had thought——"

"Wait a minute! Why did the old man want us to come and see him today after the race? Do you think he was getting wise?"

Miss Withers shook her head. "Oscar, he had just realized what might happen if by a miracle Wallaby won! He would then owe Thomas some twenty-five thousand dollars or more. We can only guess—but if worse came to the worst and the horse won, it is my firm belief that the old man was going to try his best to pin the Feverel murder on Abe Thomas.

"It would have been so neat—removing at one time a menace to himself and a menace to his son. For the old man, Oscar, believed that his son had killed Violet Feverel. He was sure of it, which accounts for his unwillingness to see the young man. If the improbable happened and Wallaby should win, I think Gregg intended to kill two birds with one stone and try to frame Abe Thomas to save himself and his boy!

"But to return to the old house. Thomas had a flat tire on the way home and drove straight on without stopping to change it. That did not fit in with his usually careful nature. He arrived only just in time, for the others were already on the steps ringing at the door.

"He made them wait in the living room and rushed upstairs. His victim was dead—indeed, had died within a few minutes of being hung up so horribly. Thomas must have got a start when he saw that the bonds made dull marks on the dead flesh and that the upper half of the body was so livid with distended blood vessels. But that was as it may be. He hoisted the dead man up into his chair, hoping it might still appear as a natural death from excitement of watching the race.

"Again he got rid of his aids by tossing them out the window, where he could easily pick them up on the garden path. It would not take ten minutes, Oscar—even remembering that he replaced the sheet on the bed. The four who waited downstairs did not notice the passing of time, for they were watching the quarrel between Mr. Fry and Latigo Wells. (Over Barbara, I presume—though when Eddie Fry ran away at the bridle path, I think she crossed him off the list.)

"Thomas came down the stairs shouting the alarm, as he did before. And we were fooled, Oscar—fooled first by his very real surprise on finding that Violet was dead! Then fooled by his drab exterior, his sober habits—fooled by the perfect alibi of the telescope!"

Miss Withers shook her head sadly. "There were clues enough, if I hadn't been wasting my time worrying over briar pipes and on trying to solve the murder through an attempt at applied psychology."

"That was what we were doing at the races?"

She nodded. "I was looking for a person who would be capable of betting everything he owned in the world on a long-shot—for that's what murder is, Oscar. I didn't find such an impulse among our suspects. Most of them bet moderately on middle-class horses chosen on name alone. Barbara and Latigo plunged with the money which had been in Violet Feverel's bank account and which I presume came originally from poor Thomas. But they plunged on a *show* bet—not risking the whole breathless leap. Our murderer had more daring than that, Oscar. He would have bet to win!

"Oh, I was right—only our murderer couldn't bet because he didn't have anything to bet with. Getting his tip third or fourth hand I won a pocketful of money which I don't know that I have any right to keep. Anyway, that line of approach petered out. . . ."

"We got him, which is all that matters," said the inspector complacently. He leaned back on the bench, relit his cigar. "You know," he admitted, "I wasn't so badly fooled as I might have been. I thought all along that Thomas must have had something to do with that attack on Barbara Foley last Monday when her saddle was tampered with on the bridle path. . . ."

Miss Withers smiled at him. "*Such* a report card you're going to take home this month, Oscar! Because that 'attack' on little Babs was the only thing in this whole affair of which Thomas was perfectly innocent!"

"What? Then who in blazes——"

"Not Thomas, anyway," Miss Withers told him. "He had no way of knowing that Barbara would try riding the horse because I did not put the idea in her mind until Sunday afternoon. And ten minutes after the girl fell off I phoned the farm and found him there where he belonged! No, Oscar—it was not Thomas. But knowing how badly Maude Thwaite wanted the ownership of that striking-looking beast, it is my opinion that she thought up a neat little idea for discouraging Barbara in any plans of keeping him. All the woman meant to do was to cause a fall, and not one fall from a horse in a thousand is fatal."

"All the same—— Say, there must be some way of getting her for that! Malicious assault, anyway. . . ." The inspector was chivalrously irate.

"I've thought of a possibility," Miss Withers said dreamily. She might have said more, but there was the sound of honking horns in the village street. Flashlight powder went off in a brilliant explosion just outside the jail, where Captain Tinker was posing. . . .

"The reporters!" said Piper. "Say, I've got to get over there and keep Tinker from telling how he solved the case. . . ."

"Here's a last tip for you, Oscar," Miss Withers called after him. "Tell the gentlemen of the press that you broke the case through a mistake that the killer made. You see," she hastily explained, "he thought it would be a very clever idea to dig up Don Gregg's childhood air rifle and plant it in his bedroom closet in case anybody ever noticed the BB shot in this mystery. Of course we realized at once that no young man of thirty would keep such a toy in his bedroom all those years. . . ."

"We sure did!" agreed the inspector happily, and sprinted for the jailhouse steps.

17

Going . . . Going . . . Gone!

The headlines of THE RACETRACK MURDER flared and were almost instantly forgotten. Inspector Oscar Piper received gratifying commendations from his superiors and then slowly found himself sliding into that state of uneasy apprehension which is the lot of a Tammany cop in a non-Tammany administration. Miss Withers's life returned to its usual calm, broken only when the little wire-haired terrier, Dempsey, distinguished himself by giving battle to a massive Great Dane on the street, who with one bite very nearly put an end to the career of the rash little gladiator.

It was on Dempsey's first long walk after he came home from the pet hospital that Miss Withers invited—perhaps the word should be "wheedled"—the inspector to join them.

"It's true there's nothing much doing down at Centre Street in this hot weather," he admitted. "But what in the world have you got to show me that you're so excited about?"

She refused to enlighten him. " 'Yours not to reason why, yours but to do or die . . .' " she told him. They walked several blocks southward and then down Sixty-fifth Street.

"Say, I've been here before!" protested the inspector. Then he saw the Thwaite stables and the auctioneer's flag which hung outside. There was a white and official notice on the door— "Sheriff's Sale—County of New York" . . .

"I thought it might be amusing to see some of our suspects of last month in a different light," Miss Withers said. "There's still an untied clue or two. . . ." She led the way inside while Dempsey wriggled joyously at the strange alien odors of horse, and the inspector followed a little gingerly.

It was like no other auction that Miss Withers had ever seen. No more than a dozen wooden chairs had been placed, in rows of four, across the central runway between the stalls. At the rear was a table. A man in a soiled white linen suit was standing by the table talking to Mrs. Thwaite.

Five or six idlers had wandered in and were sprawled in the chairs waiting for something to happen. Miss Withers motioned the inspector to a seat in the last row. It was nearly ten o'clock in the morning.

On either side of them horses moved restlessly in their stalls. Miss Withers recognized Salt, the little gray mare on whom Latigo had ridden after Barbara Foley. Now she held her head low and her ribs stood out like a washboard.

Dr. Thwaite came in, stared hard at the inspector and Miss Withers and took a seat on one side. His wife carried a silver-capped crop and with it she kept slapping at her high leather boots as if annoyed at her own legs. She stalked up and down in front of the first row.

The auctioneer put out his cigarette. "All right," he said suddenly in a hoarse and tired voice. "Let's get going." He knocked on the table. "Quiet, everybody. . . ."

The only sound was made by the colored boy, High-pockets, as he opened the door of a stall at the end of the line. He led out a big red thoroughbred, brought him almost to the auctioneer's table.

Siwash tossed his head, rolled brown eyes at the unaccustomed sight of so many humans in his stable. For some reason or other he had not been curried that morning and his hocks, mane and tail were at a stage halfway between close-clipped and flowing. Still he looked like a lot of horse.

The man from the sheriff's office made hurried sing-song announcements. Here was the horse. Anybody could look at him. He was a thoroughbred, although papers would not be given with him unless transfer charges were paid. There was a lien of $225 against the horse, at which figure bids could start. . . .

Miss Withers was the only person who got up to inspect Siwash, leaving the inspector to hold Dempsey's leash. She fancied that the red horse recognized her, for he did brighten as she stroked his nose. He even made a friendly grab for her hat, which bore a bunch of imitation grapes. As she went back to her seat he whinnied faintly. That cinched it as far as Miss Withers was concerned.

"Do I hear a bid?" demanded the auctioneer.

Miss Withers said, in a quavery voice, that she would offer two hundred and thirty dollars. The inspector stared at her in blank wonder.

"Well, it's my own money!" she told him. "I won it at Beaulah Park. . . ."

Maude Thwaite, with a hard look at the unexpected intruder, said, "Two-fifty!"

"Two hundred and fifty dollars once!" began the auctioneer hastily. And then the outer doors opened and Barbara Foley came in, followed by Latigo Wells. He wore a new suit, Miss Withers noticed, and carried a guitar case.

"Two hundred and sixty!" snapped Miss Withers. She motioned to Barbara. "You're just in time to rescue your horse," said the schoolteacher. "Sit down. . . ."

Barbara smiled. "We can't sit down. But it was nice of you to think of telling me about this. After all, we get everything bid above the amount of the lien. If I had any use for a race horse, I'd try to do something about it. But we haven't, have we, Latigo?"

The rangy young man shook his head. "No use for hosses at all."

"We've got to get down to the broadcasting station now," Babs went on gaily.

"Then you're not going to bid on your own horse?" Miss Withers said blankly. The auctioneer was shouting that the horse was going, going, gone to Mrs. Thwaite for two hundred and eighty-five, so Miss Withers blurted out a hasty "Two-ninety."

"Of course not!" Babs said. "Artists don't need horses. You must listen in on us some Monday morning. . . ."

"Listen in?" Miss Withers gasped.

Babs nodded proudly. "We—just us—are the Drygulch Duetizers—every Monday over WOOF. We'll be at WJZ as soon as we pick just the right sponsor. Listen in. Our theme song is 'Red River Valley.'"

"You know it," Latigo reminded her. "It goes—'Come an' sit by my side if you love me, do not hasten to bid me adoooo . . .'"

"I know it——" began Miss Withers. Then, "Three hundred and ten dollars!" she shouted. "Good-bye, you two, and good luck!" she called after Latigo and Barbara.

"We got good luck!" Barbara sang back merrily, displaying her ring finger. There were two rings on it, one bearing a diamond chip as big as a minute, and the other a plain platinum band.

"It happens even to radio artists!" Miss Withers whispered complacently to the inspector. "At last I have my happy ending—at least," she corrected, "I have a happy ending if you can advance me fifty dollars." She pawed hastily in her purse. "I seem to be over my head already, Oscar."

The inspector started so unexpectedly that Dempsey barked and tried to jump up on his lap.

"Good Lord," Piper said, "I've only got ten dollars with me."

"Give!" said Miss Withers desperately. Mrs. Thwaite, in accents bitter as gall, was bidding three hundred and twenty-five from her seat in the front row.

"Three twenty-six!" cried Miss Withers. She leaned toward her partner. "Oscar, do something! We can't let that big beautiful horse go into the hands of that woman! She'll make a hack of him—break his spirit and his heart. She'll rent him out to every heavy-handed newcomer, bring out saddle sores on his back and ribs on his sleek sides! Oscar, we can't let him go to her!"

The inspector shook his head. "Hildegarde, you're plain nuts. But——" He hesitated and was lost. "Stall!" he counseled. "Raise her a dollar a crack while I promote something." He dashed away.

Mrs. Thwaite was a little desperate. She raised the ante to the tune of three hundred and seventy and scowled as Miss Withers gave a plaintive "Three seventy-one!"

The inspector was on the telephone in the deserted office. "Spring 7-3100," he called—the most famous telephone number in the world. "Gimme the top floor and hurry!" he rasped as Centre Street answered.

One minute and four seconds later the short waves went out over Manhattan Island. . . . "Calling car 69 . . . calling car 69. . . . Go to Thwaite Academy—West 65th Street—see officer in charge about a *Code 300.* . . . That is all!"

"That's us!" yelped Officer Shay. He kicked at the starter while the sergeant took out his notebook. "Say, what's a *Code 300?*"

"Riot call," said Sergeant Greeley. The little flivver raced away from the curb. Two minutes later it screeched to a stop before the door of the Thwaite stables.

"I don't see no riot!" complained Shay.

"Come on in anyway," ordered the sergeant. The inspector was in the doorway gnawing at the wreckage of a cigar.

"How much money you boys got on you?" he demanded. "Gimme!"

They produced fourteen dollars and fifty-six cents. "Not enough," Piper said sadly. "I should have sent for the Wall Street detail."

"What's the trouble?" Greeley wanted to know. The inspector told him.

"Hey!" said Shay. "That's the dame who wouldn't stand for us being bounced out to Brooklyn!"

"Yeah! That's the dame that spoke a good word for us after we pinched her sorta unnecessarily!" agreed Greeley. He rubbed his jaw. "There ought to be something we could do. . . ."

"Three hundred and ninety-five dollars!" cried Miss Withers desperately. She had just four hundred in her purse. "How much did you raise, Oscar?" He gave it to her.

"If that woman goes on——" said Miss Withers. Maude Thwaite was going on. She bid four hundred. She made it clear she'd bid double that for Siwash, if pressed.

"Four hundred and one!" Miss Withers offered. By this time the auctioneer suspected that something was up. He knew it for certain when two very large and husky officers in uniform came down and sat in the front row, one on either side of Mrs. Maude Thwaite.

"Four hundred and five!" cried Maude Thwaite, slashing at her boots for all she was worth.

Miss Withers bid four hundred and ten in a faint voice. It was almost every cent she had, counting contributions.

Everybody waited for Maude Thwaite to say four hundred and twenty-five, but she hesitated. In spite of herself she was listening to the conversation which Officers Shay and Greeley were exchanging over her head. She listened and suddenly froze.

"A lerzy stable!" Greeley was saying.

"It sure is. We got to get hold of the Board of Health! Just *smell* the place!" agreed Shay.

"And look at the hay around here! Boy, what a fire hazard! Violation of Ordinances Five, Seventy-six and Five ninety-nine of section four!" Greeley announced.

"In a residential district, too," Shay said. "And how they

treat their horses. . . . Boy, what a case the S.P.C.A. boys have got here!"

"Four——" began Mrs. Thwaite. Her voice died away to a low croak.

"Four hundred and ten dollars I'm bid—four-ten once, four-ten twice . . ." The auctioneer looked at Mrs. Thwaite, hesitating. . . .

"If she bids four twenty-five I'm frozen out," Miss Withers gasped.

"It's a cinch there's traces of hoof and mouth disease in this place," Sergeant Greeley suddenly said in an unnecessarily loud voice. If Maude Thwaite meant to bid anything she changed her mind.

"Sold! To the lady in the funny—I mean, in the green hat, for four hundred ten dollars!"

The two radio officers got up. "Nice place, eh?" observed Sergeant Greeley pleasantly. Maude Thwaite said nothing at all, but she quietly and calmly broke her silver-mounted riding crop over one knee.

"You could eat offen the floor," agreed Officer Shay. "Shall we scram?" Greeley offered his arm and Shay took it with a bow.

They gave a wide salute to Miss Withers and hurried toward the door before she could find the proper words to thank them.

"The nag is yours," said Inspector Oscar Piper. "And now would you mind telling me what in the world you're going to do with a big red pet of a race horse? You can't race him, and you don't want to ride him, do you?"

"Heaven forbid!" said Miss Hildegarde Withers. "I've got a better idea than that." She told the inspector what it was. At first he said it was impossible, and then he said he'd never heard of anybody giving the department a gift like that, but perhaps——

Anyway, before the first red and yellow leaves came tumbling down that autumn, Miss Hildegarde Withers let a bouncing little wire-haired terrier lead her into the stretches of Central Park where she stopped for a while to watch Officer Casey posting to the swift and even trot of a new mount.

Faster than any saddle horse on the bridle path, doomed to a life filled with blood-stirring workouts, pleasant comradeship with men in uniform, and much-proffered sugar and carrots from kind old ladies, Siwash had settled well into the pleasant routine of a happier world. Already as a result of much good departmental oats his stomach had lost something of its extreme leanness, but he still bent his neck to leave a wet mark on the boot of the mounted officer who bestrode him and ran sideways at the breakaway.

Officer Casey saluted as he went rocketing past the angular schoolteacher and the small barking dog. There was a tiny brass plate on the cantle of his saddle bearing the inscription "*Siwash*, presented to the department by Miss Hildegarde Martha Withers, Honorary Life Member, Patrolmen's Benefit Association."

Miss Withers couldn't read the inscription, but she knew it by heart. "After all," she said to the inspector as she dropped into his office at Centre Street later that afternoon, "what better use could I have made of money that wasn't, strictly speaking, my own?"

Inspector Oscar Piper was busily rearranging the grim murder exhibits which filled the cabinets of his office. He pushed a sash-weight farther toward the wall, moved aside a garnet hat-pin which had once been Miss Withers's own property.

There was just room enough for an odd weapon, rusty but unstained with blood, which had been contrived out of a horseshoe and a hoe. Beside it was a man's sock and a toy air pistol.

The inspector nodded absent-mindedly. From a drawer of his desk he took an envelope containing a briar pipe. "Wish I knew what to do with this," he observed to Miss Withers. "And I thought it was going to be Exhibit Number One!" He dropped it on the table.

Miss Withers shook her head sadly. "Anyway, the case seems to be successfully closed without that clue," she observed. "I received this in the mail today. . . ."

She showed the inspector a square official envelope. It contained a blue ticket and a terse invitation under a date line of "Ossining, New York."

At the request of Warden Lewis E. Lawes you are hereby invited to officiate as one of the twelve

legally required witnesses at the execution of Abraham Thomas, at midnight, October thirty-first.
—Please acknowledge.

"I got one too," said the inspector. "Guess the warden thought we might be interested in seeing the end of a case we'd worked on. . . ."

Just then the door opened and Dr. Charles Bloom, medical examiner for Manhattan, looked in.

"Busy, Inspector? Oh hello, Miss Withers. I just wanted to ask Piper if he's got any use for this invitation I just received from Sing Sing."

The doctor produced a square envelope. "I could never stand to sit through an electrocution," announced the veteran of nearly a thousand post-mortems. "So I thought . . ."

Suddenly the doctor's voice died away and his white teeth clicked noisily. "Say—where did you find my pipe?" he shouted joyously and hurled himself upon what was to have been People's Exhibit A. "I haven't seen it since—since——"

"Oh, for goodness' sake!" gasped Miss Withers. She sat down suddenly. "Since you examined the body of Violet Feverel in Central Park!" She drew back and stared at the medical examiner. "Yes—oh, yes, of course. You're middle-aged . . . traveled abroad . . . excellent tastes with money to spend . . . thoughtful and careless by turns . . . and you deal with chemicals. What else was there? Oh, yes—— Doctor, do you really mind telling me if you have—if you wear a denture?"

Dr. Charles Bloom stiffened a little. "What's that? Why—why yes, my dear lady. But nobody except you has ever guessed it!"

The inspector, his head behind his desk, was making faint cackling sounds. "There's nothing funny about false teeth," snapped the doctor as he lovingly filled his lost pipe with fine aromatic tobacco. "Wait till you have to wear the damn things!" And he stalked out of the office.

"Oscar," said Miss Withers after a moment of silence had elapsed, "if ever I grow pedantic on one of our little adventures will you please remind me of that briar pipe?"

The inspector was still cackling as she turned and flounced out of his office, the square envelope from Ossining still gripped in her hand.

As soon as she reached home she sat down at her writing desk, lifted a plumed pen from a tiny glass full of colored stones, dipped it into a well of clear blue ink, and began:

"Mr. Lewis E. Lawes, Ossining, New York. . . ." She dipped the pen again.

"Miss Withers regrets . . ."